AN INCIDENT IN AFRICA

A NOVEL

WALTER SOELLNER

Gossip Park Books
San Jose, CA

An Incident in Africa

To order copies in bulk or hardcover editions, contact gossipparkbooks@gmail.com.

978-0-9966760-0-7 paperback
978-0-9966760-1-4 eBook
978-0-9966760-2-1 hardcover

Cover by Edward C. Rooks
Cover images provided by Walter Soellner

Gossip Park Books
Visit the author's website at www.waltersoellner.com

אֲנִי לְדוֹדִי
וְדוֹדִי לִי

"I AM MY BELOVED'S AND MY BELOVED IS MINE."
SONG OF SOLOMON 6:3

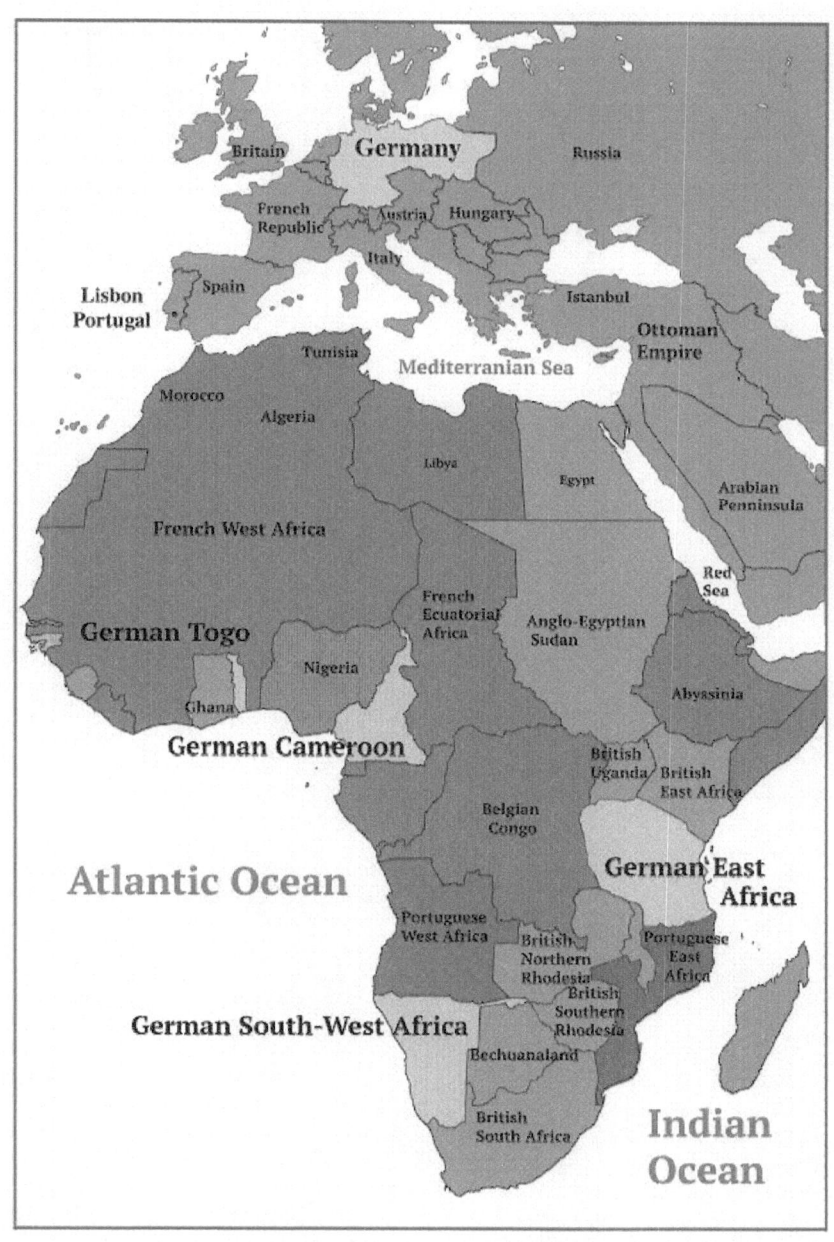

Africa and Europe, 1920

Dedication

To Sandra York Soellner, my lovely and loving wife:
charming, kind, patient, forgiving, and smart.
She who senses the rightness of things:
words, sentences, stories, people.

Books by Walter Soellner

The Perilous Journey
1900-1909

The Storm That Shook the World
1909-1919

An Incident in Africa
1919-1924

ACKNOWLEDGEMENTS

Thank you, my family, friends and booklovers who, from 2007 to 2017, have assisted, consulted, researched, proofread and edited, and bought this third in my family saga series of five books.

First and foremost I must especially thank my wife Sandra for endless hours assisting with concepts and ideas, proofreading the text and helping with the computer knowledge necessary to bring An Incident In Africa to completion.

George and Gilda Forrester: who patiently read iterations of the manuscript, dotting i's and crossing t's at every stage. Thank you, dear friends.

Eve and Kenneth Reid: Thank you so much for consistent, detailed scrutiny of my novel, your helpful marginalia throughout, and for allowing me the use of your Lake Michigan cottage, still my favorite writing abode.

Anna Soellner: For your ever-present positive attitude toward my writing, and encouragement over the long writing process, I thank you.

Edward Rooks: a most talented artist and designer, creator of maps and images, who transforms photos and drawings into true works of art for publication, many thanks.

Jack Ewbank: publicist and whirlwind tech support guru, your lightning fast solutions and measured suggestions continue to be of immense value. Thank you.

I have, for the last four years, attended the annual San Francisco Writer's Conference under the direction of Michael Larsen and found it to be most helpful.

And lastly, but not last in my thoughts and gratitude: Ron Hagen, David Gunther, Greg Winslow, Dr. Stephen Eckstone and Bill Jacobs.

Table of Contents

German South West Africa

Prologue

It is 1919 and Solomon Levi, called Levi, is back home at Kalvarianhof, the grand family estate near Munich, Germany, after four and a half years of fighting WWI in German East Africa with his childhood friend Markus Mathais. Levi and his wife, Katherina, resume raising a family at his father's estate in Bavaria, while confronting the German Revolution following the Great War (1914-1918), the turmoil of the Weimar Republic and the rise of Fascism.

Meanwhile, in far off Africa, Levi's lifelong friend, Markus Mathais, returns to his wife Helena and family in German South West Africa, now occupied by the British South Africans, after fighting alongside his friend in East Africa in the Great War.

He and his wife, Helena, and her family, the Conrads, resume their ranch life only to be confronted with a calamitous crime, a secret with grave consequences, and deadly misfortune. The two families support each other across two continents from Germany to Africa through their tumultuous, heartbreaking ordeals, including murder, deceit and deception. Their enduring friendship, love and loyalty to each other is, ultimately, the essence of the story.

CHAPTER I

Violence and Silence in Africa: February 1919

The Conrad ranch, northeast of the capital, Windhoek, was unusually quiet that day in February, 1919. The Armistice had been signed a few short months ago between Germany and her allies and France, Britain, Belgium, Italy, and America. Markus had lived in the African colony since 1909, where he had married Helena Conrad, and had a son, Rupert, who waited for him at their isolated ranch.

Two weeks before Markus' ship was to dock, his father-in-law, Tomas Conrad, was in town with two of his sons, Wolfgang and Norbert and their houseman, Petre. His other son and daughter, Michael and Christina, were on horseback out in the bush at the ranch, looking for stray cattle.

Helena, still startlingly lovely with her long, light brown hair, was home alone except for their boy, Rupert, now almost six. Their stable boy, Sambolo, was in the barn. Helena stepped back into the kitchen having just placed flowers on the graves of the her mother-in-law, Frau Conrad, dead many years, and the graves of Arnold, killed in the war, and Humboldt, taken by influenza a year ago.

She heard the horse ride up to the house and knew it was Captain Llewellyn. The war was over, but the occupation by the victors continued, particularly with the presence of one South African officer still billeted in her home. They had all tolerated him for over three years, he with his prying eyes and arrogant way.

He strolled into the ranch house, his riding boots loud on the wooden floor.

"Good afternoon, Helena. You look as lovely as ever today in that lavender blouse. Is there any gin left in that bottle?" He gestured toward the buffet.

"Help yourself, as you always do," she said coldly.

"I want you to pour one for me this time," he said. "I have something very important to tell...to offer you. Sit down."

She was startled by his bluntness but complied, sitting in one of the overstuffed chairs in the front parlor. He took a long draft from his gin glass and looked at her.

"I've been assigned the task of recommending as to which German individuals and families are to be deported from this District, that is, repatriated back to Germany." A cold chill crept over Helena.

"We're looking for troublemakers and those who don't cooperate with the new order in this new South African Protectorate. Those who do cooperate, who are 'friendly', will be given every consideration. Do you understand, Helena?"

She despised his stare.

"Will you cooperate?"

"But we have," she began. "We took into our home four of your soldiers. We fed and cleaned and housed you and the three others. What more could we do?" She paused to collect her thoughts. "We accepted the results of the war here in South West Africa. I lost my brother Arnold to this terrible war."

She raised from the chair, her voice strained. "What more could we have done?"

He closed the distance between them. She pulled back slightly.

"It's not what your family did, it's what you can do now for them." He smiled at her as his eyes roamed across her like caressing hands. He stepped closer. She crossed her arms tightly in front of her.

"You could...no, you should be more friendly to someone who holds the fate of this ranch and your family in his hands." He reached out as if to brush some unseen object off her shoulder. His hand lingered on her upper arm, stroking it gently.

"We should be friendlier with each other," he whispered, gazing at her intently. "After all, I've lived here with you for quite some time...in your home, just down the hall from your bedroom."

She looked away saying, "Please, we've done all you've asked. I have a husband and my child is sleeping in the..." He cut her off.

"And I have a wife back in Johannesburg who I haven't seen in months. And you, Frau Mathais...Helena," he emphasized Helena, "You haven't seen your husband in, what, four years? That's a long time for a married woman to be alone." He paused, "a long time to be...well, alone."

He took a short step closer to her and his hand went around her arm. He pulled her in closer. She could smell him.

"I can help your family, and all this." His eyes darted away from her as his arm swept the air. "I can save this, but I need you, your cooperation...because I have needs too." His face was close to hers. He could smell her hair. It inflamed him.

"Please!" she said. His lips brushed her cheek. His other hand touched her chin and turned her head toward him. He kissed her, first most gently, then with greater passion. She tried to pull back but she was in his grip.

His hands slid around her back and pressed her to him. He could feel her stomach and breasts against him. She squirmed loose and turned her back to him.

"No! I have a husband and child," she repeated. He came up behind her, his hands swept around her sides and cupped her breasts drawing her to him.

"I have the papers right here," he groaned in a low voice, "I can sign them right now. I just need you to..." He spun her around and kissed her as his hands pulled her blouse out of her skirt. His hands plunged inside the back of her skirt. He could feel her warm smooth skin. She let out a plaintive sound and, breaking away, she hissed, "No!"

He let her go. "All right, have it your way. I'll just turn your names in to headquarters, but, I'll give you a little while to think about it before I do." He walked to the center of the room, straightened his uniform and ran his hands through his hair. He looked at her as she stared away from him.

"I've to put my horse in the stable. I'll be back. Think about it." With that he strolled out, his boots again pounding on the wooden floor.

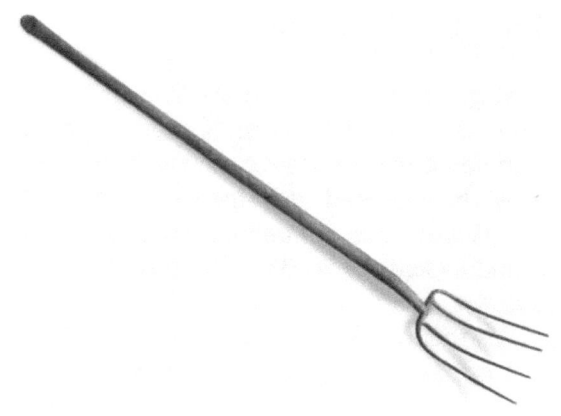

CHAPTER II

The Incident: February 1919

Helena stood there alone, thoughts racing through her mind. *I knew he would try something like this...but to threaten the ranch...and our very right to live here, God in heaven! Can he really throw us out, deport us, to Germany or where else? I've never even lived in Germany, just one short visit. We're Africans!*

She exclaimed in a trembling voice, "Mother of God, what shall I do?"

Pacing back and forth, she clutched the small gold cross on her chest. She stopped and looked in to see young Rupert sound asleep.

I've got to do something. I'll go talk to that brute, maybe he'll be reasonable. He knows I'm not interested in him. I'll talk to Papa, maybe we can bribe him, even if money is so tight now. That's what I'll do. She closed the door to Rupert's room and headed for the stables.

"Well, look who's here." The South African said to his horse, as he fed a handful of grain to the beast. "Now, what do you think she wants?" Helena stepped into the stone barn she had known since childhood. It saw use as both a stable with a dozen stalls, and storage for farm wagons. The tack room and a thick pile of hay were across from the stalls.

"Captain Llewellyn, I wanted to talk to you," she began.

The Captain, one eyebrow raised, said, "I thought you might reconsider my proposal." He smirked at his little joke. She ignored his crassness.

"I'm sure we can reach an honorable settlement with you...I mean, my father and brothers, we could quietly arrange some financial agreement. I'm sure you're anxious to return home and to your wife in Johannesburg. You could go there with...that is, better off financially, and we could stay here at the family ranch." She hesitated. "What do you think?"

He was watching her, eyeing her up and down with a grin on his face. The afternoon sun was behind her and he could vaguely see her legs silhouetted through her long skirt. He casually walked over to her.

"Do you really think I need your meager 'finances'? This so-called ranch barely gets by, and your German currency is worthless." He shook his head smiling and looked away. When he turned back toward her, his face had stiffened.

"My family owns thousands of acres of good land. Not this...this semi-desert you call home. I don't want your money, lovely Helena, I want you!"

With that he grabbed her, kissed her forcefully, and pulled down her skirt from the back.

"No! Stop!" she screamed. She was strong for her size, but he was a soldier in prime shape. They struggled. Her skirt was down around her knees. She slapped him, hit him in the face, he returned her blow with a punch that sent her tripping backward. He gave her a mighty shove toward the hay pile where she sprawled on her back, stunned. He followed her, unbuckling his belt and practically ripped open his trousers.

She moaned half-conscious as he jerked her undergarment off. On his knees now, he reached down, spread her knees, reached up and tore open her blouse exposing her breasts.

"No! Don't! Get off me you swine!" she shouted. "No!"

It was her last word as a full swing crashed into the side of her face. He was on her, pleasuring himself as he had often dreamed of doing. It was the last pleasurable act Captain Llewellyn of the South African Occupation Army would ever experience.

With a terrifying screech, he arched his back and tried to reach around as four steel prongs of Sambolo's pitchfork drove in deep just below the rapist's ribs. He rolled onto his side screaming in pain, struggling, with the pitchfork handle swaying back and forth with his every move. Helena, still naked and sprawled on the hay pile, looked on in a stunned stupor.

No one heard the two riders pull their horses to an abrupt halt and quickly slide out of their saddles. They had heard Helena's screams and knew it was her. Both ran through the barn door, first seeing Sambolo pushing the pitchfork deeper into his victim and simultaneously seeing the naked body of their sister in the hay.

"Oh, my God, oh Helena, Helena!" Christina cried out, already in tears.

Michael, also shouting incoherently, grabbed the dung shovel and began beating the naked man writhing on the floor. In an uncontrollable fury he swung the steel shovel again and again, yelling, "You bastard, you bastard!" Llewellyn had stopped moving and still the blows came. Blood spattered all over the floor and walls.

Finally, in near exhaustion, Michael stopped. Christina had pulled close Helena's blouse and, between sobs, retrieved her skirt. She laid the skirt on top of Helena's bloody abdomen. Sambolo had run to the house to grab a light blanket off the parlor couch and was back in moments.

"We've got to take her to the house," Michael said.

"Yes, yes," Christina said between sobs. Helena was semi-conscious now, in a daze, moaning with each movement.

"I'm sorry, sister, I'm sorry, but we have to take you to the house." The three of them managed to carry her into her bedroom, with Christina laying towels down under her sister to absorb the blood.

"Sambolo, can you ride into town and get the doctor? Do you know where the doctor's house is?" Michael asked the teenager.

"Yes, yes, Michael sir, I know doctor's house. I go quick."

"Good! Go now. Take the best horse."

Michael turned back toward the bed to see Christina dabbing a wet cloth on Helena's rapidly swelling face.

"Michael, Michael, she's still bleeding...there." She lifted the sheet revealing a growing crimson circle under Helena's hips.

"You have to do something!" he blurted out. "You have to, to stop it!"

"Yes, but I..."

"Just do it, you're a woman, just do it!"

Christina, braced by the seriousness of the situation and her brother's sense of helplessness, firmed her resolve.

"Yes. Get me those small hand towels in the linen chest, in my room." He was back in seconds and handed her a stack of delicately embroidered white towels.

"Michael, you have to help me. Michael! Listen! We have to move her knees apart."

He was sweating and blanched, but said, "*Ja*, just tell me what to do."

Helena was slipping in and out of consciousness as Christina told her brother, "First, we have to bring her knees up and then we have to move them apart. It going to hurt her, but..." Christina muffled a cry. Michael reached out and patted his sister on the shoulder. "You're doing fine. I'll help you." She looked up at her brother with a weak smile and brushed away a tear.

"She's going to want to close her knees, Michael, so you have to be prepared to hold them apart. Even if she cries out...she will cry out, brother." She turned to her sister lying still on the soggy bed.

"Helena. Helena. We have to move you a bit. I have to touch you, to stop the bleeding." There was no response.

"Are you ready Michael...you don't have to watch, just be ready to help." He nodded yes. She pulled away the sheet. Helena's skirt was still laying across her. Christina looked at her brother as each put a hand behind Helena's knees. Slowly the two of them brought the knees up. There was no response from Helena.

"Good. Very Good." Christina moved some of the white towels in close to where she would need them.

"Now, let's ease her knees apart. Groans began almost immediately.

"Wider. Wider Michael! I need more room. Bring her knees up more. Hold them, hold them!" Helena's head moved back and forth with soft, plaintive, terrible sounds.

Christina and Helena had seen each other nude on numerous occasions but only fleetingly and in passing. For Christina, this was disconcerting and caused beads of sweat on her forehead. She moved quickly to her task, trying to stop the bleeding as only she knew how. Helena cried out in pain and rose her head off the pillow and, as expected, tried to close her knees. Michael pushed hard against the opposite knee from his side and wanted to say, hurry up, but bit his tongue in silence.

"There, that should help—at least till the doctor gets here. Let her legs down now, Michael." The two siblings leaned back, emotionally exhausted, as Christina placed a wet cloth on Helena's forehead. There was complete silence in the room.

CHAPTER III

The Vigil: February 1919

Out on the little-used road from the ranch to town, Tomas Conrad, his sons Wolfgang and Norbert, along with their houseman Petre, pulled up their horses abruptly as they peered up the road at a dust trail.

"Someone's riding hard this way," Petre said. "Can you tell who it is?"

"It's Sam!" Wolfgang shouted. They spurred their horses toward the oncoming rider.

They all pulled up together, Tomas asking Sambolo in an agitated voice, "What's going on?"

"I have to get the doctor! Frau Helena hurt bad, that..."

"What? How? How bad?" Several asked at once.

"That bad man Lu-ella, he attacked Frau Helena in the barn, tore her clothes, she hurt bad." Sambolo had tears running down his face. "I kill him, I kill him! Tomas, sir!"

"What?"

"I stab him with pitchfork...Michael and Christina take her in house. She bleeding bad. I gotta get the doctor!"

He was about to pull his horse away toward town when Petre spoke up. "Tomas, sir, I'll go to town and get the doctor. My horse is fresh."

"Yes, right you are. So go, man. Quick as you can." With that, Tomas and the others spurred their horses into a cantor and then a full gallop, knowing that the horses would just about make it to the ranch at that speed.

Their horses were lathered in dusty sweat as the five riders pulled up to the ranch house. The three Conrads and Sam were off their horses in a flash and raced to the front door. Tomas, not so nimble, followed behind. All of them pushed through the door into Helena's room. Michael and

Christina were on either side of the bed. A woman's form lay still beneath a single white sheet. Spatters of dried blood were visible on the sheet and floor. A porcelain pan, also white, was overflowing with blood soaked towels. To the recently arrived, the scene was appalling. Norbert, the youngest, let out a gasp, his hand covering his mouth. Tomas spoke first.

"What happened? We heard, but..."

"That bastard attacked Helena...we got there just...and well, Sam he...stabbed him with the pitchfork." Michael couldn't say more as he relived the terrible event, wiping his cheek.

Tomas crowded in close, only now realizing...seeing the battered face of his eldest daughter.

"My God, daughter, look what he's done to you." Tears streamed down his face. Christina put her arm around her father.

"How is she? How is she?" he asked.

"I think we stopped the bleeding, I'm not sure...I did my best Papa, I did my best." Christina was shuddering with sobs. Wolfgang came to her and half lifted her out of the chair.

"Come sister, come away for a few minutes." The brothers took turns holding Helena's hands, whispering sweet words to her. Norbert was on his knees at the foot of her bed praying, "Please God, make her better."

"Is there anything we can do until the doctor gets here?" Someone questioned.

"Cold towels to her face, it should help keep the swelling down. Is she...still bleeding? Can we...should we...should Christina check?"

Helena lay there, with her swollen lips, gurgling in uneven breaths. They tried to give her water, but she just gagged on it. She seemed asleep, and the family thought this was good. It took hours and was late evening when the doctor finally arrived in his two horse carriage, the faster to travel out to surrounding patients. Petre guided him through the starlit darkness.

"Thank God you're here, Doctor." Tomas Conrad said. "This way, this way. She's been asleep since...for hours."

Several kerosene lamps gave off their oily glow in Helena's room. "I need better light. Bring candles if you would." The doctor set to work immediately.

"Gentlemen, please leave the room. Christina, please stay and give me assistance." After a cursory exam, he said, "Let's check her bleeding." It was pretty much the same process that Christina and Michael had performed earlier.

"Yes, good. You did well, young lady. You probably saved your sister's life. The bleeding has stopped for now." The qualified statement startled Christina.

"For now?' You mean it could...she could start bleeding again?" The doctor turned to her:

"Your sister may have suffered some internal injuries. It's hard to tell just now. We'll have to just wait and see. She mustn't be moved unnecessarily. I brought a bedpan for her evacuations. I suggest you hire a nurse for a few days. I know a good one in town. Shall I send her out?" With that he continued his examination.

"Bring that candle closer." He took it from her and with one hand, propped open Helena's right eye. He brought the candle in close and moved it back and forth. A slight frown crossed his lips. Christina picked up on it.

"What? What's the matter, Doctor?" He turned to her.

"Those blows to your sister's head have given her, I believe, a mild concussion. Helena is in a deep sleep. I don't know how long she will be like this. Again, we will have to wait and see."

While the doctor examined Helena, Tomas, his sons, and Petre and Sambolo went to the barn to see Llewellyn's body. He lay on his side where he had rolled, the pitchfork still in his back, and the bloody dung shovel nearby. They stood there silently for a few moments, taking in the scene of the crime. Dried blood was everywhere, including a large smear on the hay pile. Sambolo stood off to one side holding a lantern.

Tomas turned to him and said in a low and emotional voice, "You've done good here, Sam. You probably saved my daughter's life. I thank you...we all thank you. You're a brave young man, taking on this disgusting, evil person. From the bottom of my heart, I thank you, Sam." They all gathered around Sam, agreeing with their father's words and shaking the young black teenager's hand.

Finally, Wolfgang, pointing to the body, asked, "What are we going to do now?"

"Get that pitchfork out of him, wrap him in a canvas and we'll deal with him in the morning. And leave the bastard where he is." Tomas said turning away.

They all went back inside to check on Helena. She was still motionless, but her breathing seemed back to normal.

"We'll take turns sitting with her. I don't want her to wake up and not find a familiar face." The entire family retired to the parlor except Norbert, who volunteered to stay.

CHAPTER IV

The Plan: February 1919

Wolfgang was the first to say it. "We've got a big problem on our hands, don't we Papa?" His father was slumped in the same overstuffed chair Helena had sat in earlier that day.

"Yes, a very serious problem. We've killed a South African Army Officer. Yes, he committed a terrible crime, but they won't see it as we do. We're at their mercy, and that's a hell of a place to be." Tomas seldom swore so it caught everyone's attention. They were interrupted by Petre, the houseman.

"Sambolo and I wrapped up the body, sir. I found these papers in his coat. They look important. I saw your name on them." He handed the papers to Tomas. In bold typeface across the top of the first page read:

Recommendations For Repatriation And Deportation

The Conrad patriarch skimmed the title and mostly empty page. "Llewellyn was going to deport us, that bastard!" Tomas handed the paper around.

"So his job was to recommend who got deported?" Humboldt asked.

"They're going to think we killed him because of that!"

"He's right Papa." Christina injected, "We'll look guilty...Helena's injuries, her face, will heal in a week or two and it will just be your word...our word, against a dead army officer. And they still see us as the enemy." Everyone sat quietly for a long time. Several of the men lit cigarettes, Papa his pipe.

"Go easy on that, son, it clouds the mind." Tomas directed his comment at Wolfgang, who was pouring himself a third brandy. Wolfgang wheeled around, brandy in hand.

"I've got an idea." He was excited with his scheme and spoke rapidly.

"Now hear me out. We don't report Captain Llewellyn's death. We haven't seen him in days, we say. Everything's normal here at the ranch. Llewellyn often doesn't return to the ranch for days, sometimes a week or more. We act like nothing has happened!" He looked around the room. Everyone was staring at him. "But everybody has to agree to this, everybody! Including Helena." He stopped for a moment.

"Do you think she can do it?" He first looked at Christina, then Tomas and then around to everyone.

"It's hard to say, in her condition." Christina said.

"She's tough," offered Tomas, "and a lot is at stake. She'll manage it, I'm sure of it, if she has to."

Michael was next: "But when they see the body...How are we going to explain that?"

"We're not!" Wolfgang said. "And they won't! That's part of my plan. We hide the body, bury it out, far out on the Savannah, or someplace. I haven't figured that out, yet."

Michael again: "But what about his horse? It's in the stables. Do we just turn it loose out there, or what?" Silence again.

Tomas started slowly. "Wolfgang. It's a good idea, but it has to be done completely. We have to kill the horse and bury it with Llewellyn. All his gear and this damned paper, too. It's our only chance to avoid being charged with murder and probably hanged!"

Everyone was overwhelmed by the audaciousness of the idea. Christina, with a worried look on her face, asked, "Can we really get away with this, Papa? I mean, they'll be looking for him when he doesn't report in to Windhoek."

"Of course they will, my dear, and they'll search this ranch, every corner of it, probably several times, looking for anything out of the ordinary, because we will be the first suspects, the first people they'll want to blame. We're going to have to get our stories straight, and stick to them. They're going to question us, probably individually, looking for discrepancies."

Michael had an idea, or more like a question.

"How can we divert attention away from us to somebody else? I mean, maybe he had an enemy, or big debts, or a lady friend he jilted, or something like that? What do you think?"

"I never realized I had so many clever sons. Michael, you've given us something to think about." Christina brought up something else everyone had thought about, but no one had mentioned this tragic day.

"Markus is due home in two or three weeks. What will we tell him...how shall we tell him about this horrible thing that happened to Helena...and what happened after that?"

The secret plan devised by the Conrad family including Petre and Sam, began the next day. The entire group crowded into Helena's room after first noting her rapid improvement. She was awake, taking liquids. It pained her to chew and talk to Papa and Christina and the boys.

The side of her face showed severe swelling with large patches of black and blue bruises, but the doctor was pleased after his examination. He also heard of the plan, but the group decided not to employ a nurse, to keep the number down as to who knew what.

After explaining their solution as how to protect the family, Helena agreed. They agreed to explain her facial bruising by claiming Helena fell off her horse. It was a common occurrence in ranch country and would be readily accepted. She was clear headed enough the next day to suggest that someone check Llewellyn's room for what he would have taken or left, if he had decided to vanish. It was probably highly unlikely that he would do such a thing, but the group agreed to take every precaution.

A lengthy discussion was held as to where the burial should take place. Way up beyond the old cabin there was a steep deep gully. In nature's way, during a rare cloud burst, a new gully was cut, leaving this one dry year round.

"Yes, it's probably the best place," Tomas said. "Be sure to make a drag to cover your tracks. Don't take a wagon, too hard to cover the trail. Throw him over his saddle, let him ride his horse to his grave."

Christina and Papa stayed home with Helena the next day. The rest of the men headed out with shovels for the uplands. Gone all day, they returned after dark, dusty and dirty. The task was done. Now, it was time to wait and prepare mentally, as surely the South Africans would come.

A South African enlisted man did arrive at the ranch several days after the burial, inquiring about Captain Llewellyn's whereabouts. The family greeted him cordially and sent him on his way with the story that no one at the ranch had seen the captain for over a week, but that that was not uncommon.

In the meantime, Helena was making rapid improvement. She was up and about the ranch house and garden and having an important decision to announce to everyone concerned. She asked for a family meeting including the doctor, Petre and Sambolo. All gathered in the parlor as requested.

"As you know from the ship wireless message I received, my husband's boat will pull into Swakopmund Harbor in about ten days. I want his homecoming to be a joyous one after these long, terrible four years away."

She stopped for a moment and looked at the faces of her loved ones. "Several of you have not had a chance to read the wireless Markus sent me, and I do want to share one part of it with you. He says, in part, that I, and we..." she hesitated, "must be prepared to see a much battered man, than the one who left four years ago." He says, "I tangled with a leopard and several hyenas and they scratched me up pretty good." He says, she continued, smiling, "They were worse than any of the British!" Everyone smiled or laughed lightly as they saw a tear run down Helena's face.

"So, what I wanted to say to you all was, what happened last week, is in the past, and I want it to stay there. I fell off my horse and was injured. That's how I got these bruises on my face and why I walk a little slowly. I hurt my hip."

She stopped, feeling a bit embarrassed, and looked intently at everyone.

"Do you understand, dear Sam, my savior?" She smiled at him.

"Yes, Frau Helena." She looked at Petre.

"Of course, of course, Frau Helena." Her eyes traveled rapidly around the room to a chorus of, "Yes, of course, not a word."

CHAPTER V

Scars Old And New: February 1919

Captain Mathais, one of the few German Army officers from German South West Africa to have fought in German East Africa, was among the few returning soldiers to the British occupied former German colony. Striding down the gangplank, he fell into the arms of his wife and family. The cheers and shouts and laughter abounded as the entire Conrad clan jostled around Markus as he hugged and kissed his little boy, Rupert and his wife, Helena.

"Oh, my love, God has sent you back to me," she whispered in his ear holding him close. "I prayed for this moment for four long years."

"My boy, my boy, you look splendid! Welcome home!" Tomas Conrad gushed, avoiding the true appearance of his son-in-law. Tomas' sons and daughter chimed in with warm greetings and questions.

"You sure gave those Brits and South Africans a good drubbing." blurted Michael.

"Quiet, quiet! They'll hear you." Wolfgang admonished as he looked around the crowded dock.

"Oh, that's alright, the war is over," Markus said. Several of the Conrads looked at each other, but said nothing.

"I have so much to tell you, my dearest, so very much," Helena said as she clung tightly to her husband's arm. Two carriages were hired to accommodate the family for the ride to the train station.

"We'll have you home by dusk." Norbert offered.

The train pulled into Windhoek on a blustery afternoon, with Petre and Sambolo having arrived earlier with the ranch wagons. As they rode through town on the way to the ranch, the wagons passed the destroyed wireless station Markus had labored to create five years earlier.

"A lot has happened since I worked there. So much..." his voice trailed off.

16

"Yes, my dear, and the South Africans have taken over most everything. We even had to billet four of their soldiers at the ranch for several years."

Markus turned to his wife in surprise. "At the ranch...for several years?"

Back at the ranch after a long, hearty, happy dinner prepared by Petre and Christina, the entire family retired for the night.

"Oh, my dear, those must have been terribly painful." Helena and Markus were lying nude under a thin sheet after making gentle love. She ran her fingers over the deep scars that crossed his face.

"My prayers have been answered and God brought you back to me," she whispered. "I will thank him for the rest of my life." She leaned over and kissed his wounds.

To feel her warm soft body against his brought on a rush of passion again to him. He was erect in seconds, and he pulled her up, so she lay on top of him.

"Oh you," she whispered as she reached down and guided him. She raised her arms, arching her back as his hands slid around the backside of her hips. "God has given me heaven on earth," she whispered while smiling.

Two weeks after Markus returned home, ranch life resumed a normal pace. The secret remained just that, and the horrible incident faded bit by bit in most minds that knew. Several South African officers rode out to the ranch one day and again made inquiries about their missing officer. Markus had been informed, in a matter of fact way, that a certain Captain Llewellyn, who was the last of the soldiers billeted at the Conrad's, simply never returned to the ranch one day.

He sat casually in the front parlor as the Conrad women served tea to the two South Africans.

"That was quite a bloody show you and von Vorbeck put up in East Africa, I'll say that for you," one of the officers said to Markus.

"*Ja*, well, we knew the country. It gave us an advantage."

"Right you are, but we got you in the end." The man had a twinkle in his eye. Markus just made a noncommittal 'that's the way it goes' gesture.

"Now let's get down to the purpose of our visit. You say you got back three weeks after Captain Llewellyn disappeared?"

"That's right, three weeks...back on the troop ship from East Africa."

"And no one here at the ranch had seen him during those three weeks?"

Christina and Helena tried to answer at the same time. "No, we..."

Helena answered. "No, it was common for Captain Llewellyn to be gone for a week or ten days, but he always eventually returned."

"And you," he looked at the two women, "don't know where he went during these...absences?"

"Of course not. It was not our place to question one of your...a South African officer."

"Quite right, quite right." He looked at his companion, who spoke up.

"May we see his room?"

"Yes of course. This way." Helena led the way to the hall of bedroom doors.

"It's just as he left it." The two officers entered, examined what there was to see.

"Would you kindly bundle up these things. We'll take them with us. As the two officers turned to go, "One last thing. Did the Captain ever bring a friend...a guest, to visit? A lady friend?"

Later: "You seemed a bit apprehensive while those officers were here. Are you all right, my dear." Markus came up to Helena and held her gently.

"It's nothing. It's just that we've had to put up with those...soldiers for years, right here in our house." Helena made every effort to not get emotional, but could not stop a tear from trickling down her cheek.

"Oh, I'm so sorry dearest. Did they ever treat you badly?"

A tremendous crash caused the pair to jump. Christina had heard Markus' question and dropped the silver tray with the tea cups.

"I'm so sorry...I tripped...just look what I've done." She began to cry.

Helena immediately went over to her and in a low voice said, "It's all right, it's all right, dear sister...we can manage anything." Markus, at first startled by the accident, and seeing Christina upset, assumed she felt badly about breaking the tea service.

"Don't worry, Christina," he put his hand on her shoulder, "it's only broken china, we can go into town and you can pick out the prettiest set you like." Christina continued to sob quietly.

CHAPTER VI

Kindness And Harshness: March 1919

Markus rested several weeks at the ranch, fawned over by his brothers and sister-in-law while Tomas enjoyed it all. Finally Markus rode into town to find work.

The telephone and wireless system always needs skilled workers, maybe I can get my old job back, he thought.

The town was crowded with "foreigners", South Africans looking for opportunities in their newly conquered land. He made inquiries and went from place to place looking for agents in his field. He finally was directed to the director of telephone and telegraph service for Windhoek.

Richard Thomas, the director, ushered him into his office.

"Sit down, sit down. Mathais, is it? What can I do for you today?" The South African man sitting informally in a wooden chair behind the big wooden desk seemed a very likable sort to Markus. Several new telephones sat on the director's desk, the likes of which Markus had never seen before.

Progress, he thought.

"I'm looking for a job. I used to work on the big wireless transmitter here before the war." Markus wasn't sure if he should say any more about that, and surely not the fact that he blew it up so the South Africans couldn't get it.

Thomas's eyes lit up.

"You're not that fellow...what's his name...from the Conrad ranch, who built that beautiful transmitter and then blew it up, are you?" A big smile on his face. Markus was taken aback and couldn't help smiling back sheepishly.

"Yes, I'm afraid I am that man." Thomas got up and out from behind his desk, came around as Markus stood up. Thomas reached out and shook his hand vigorously.

"We listened to those crystal clear broadcasts from your wireless station and were amazed at the technology. You Germans had the finest equipment in the world back before the war." He stopped a moment, "Well, there was Marconi of course.

"So you're looking for work, huh? It's kind of tough for you Germans now. There's a lot of fellas up from Johannesburg looking for work seeing's how they just announced that Repatriation and Deportation Order."

"What?"

Markus left the office of Richard Thomas of the Windhoek Telephone and Telegraph Company in a daze. He was feeling good; Thomas was going to see what could be done for him because of his unique skills. His mind wandered back to the other startling news.

A Repatriation and Deportation Order? Does that mean what I think it does?

Back at the ranch that evening, during dinner, he brought up the subject of the Order with everyone at the table.

"This is certainly something we should be concerned about." There were subtle looks around the table. Markus picked up on them. "What? What have you heard?"

Helena took the lead to avoid "complications" in answering her husband. "Of course, you remember Captain Llewellyn, who roomed here and has gone missing."

"Yes, of course."

"Well, he mentioned some deportation order and told us it meant changes for us. That's all we know of it."

Markus shrugged, "Well, it was good of this Llewellyn fellow to let us know something like that was being planned." This time Markus missed the darting eyes around the table.

"I'll look into it tomorrow. I hope none of our friends will be affected. By the way, I had an interview with a Herr Richard Thomas at the Telegraph Company. He thought I might get a job there."

Several days later, he was offered a job at the Telephone and Telegraph Company. Each morning he rode the family's best horse into Windhoek. Rebuilding the wireless station was his main task, and he relished the challenge. He and Richard Thomas worked well together and became friends, letting all the memories of the war fall into the past.

Riding back home one late afternoon, he was surprised to see a dozen South African military horses tied up in front of the ranch house. Sambolo was near the barn. Markus pulled up, dismounted and asked, "What's going on?"

"The soldiers, they searching everywhere for something. I don't know."

Markus handed the reins to Sambolo and hurried to the house. He walked into the front parlor to find the entire family gathered together, with several South African officers present.

"What's going on here?" he asked sharply. Before he got an answer from the officers, Tomas Conrad got up, stepped quickly over to him and said, "These gentlemen are conducting an investigation into the disappearance of Captain Llewellyn. They seem to think we may have information that could help them in their search."

"Please sit down Mr. Conrad," one of the officers ordered. "And who are you, sir?"

"I'm Markus Mathais. My wife, Helena, you apparently have already met."

"Yes, we have already questioned her...and the others." The officer's eyes swept the family. "It seems you were the last people who saw Captain Llewellyn before his disappearance," he said in a gruff voice.

"Why did you not report Llewellyn missing? He was billeted here, yet you did nothing for weeks after his disappearance. Why is that?"

Helena stood up and offered, "We told you earlier, the Captain often did not return for a week or more. It was not our..." She was cut off by the investigator.

"I did not ask you. Please sit down, madam. I was talking to the men." He eyed Markus for a moment: "Aren't you the German that gave us so much trouble in East Africa?"

Markus was taken aback by the rudeness of the South African, but replied in a calm steady tone.

"I was an officer in German East Africa during the war, yes."

"Yes, well, it isn't German anymore," the officer sneered. "How you must have resented losing. You must still resent us South Africans being here in what used to be German South West Africa. Tell me, Herr Mathais, do you still resent us?"

The eyes of the entire Conrad clan were on Markus, but he was not going to fall into the verbal trap the investigator set. "The war is over. I'm just a civilian now, I work hard, and I just want to live in peace and raise my family."

"And take jobs away from South Africans? You Germans are very clever. But let's get back to what we are here for. We want to know what happened to one of our distinguished officers and we think some of you may know something about that...and we are going to get to the bottom of this!"

With that, the lead officer turned, and without saying another word, led his contingent out of the house. Markus and Tomas followed them to their horses. In a conciliatory tone, Tomas offered:

"We will cooperate in every way, officer."

"You're damned right you will!" The South African spit out, wheeling his horse and spurring his mount away.

"Why are they so suspicious of us, do you think?" Markus wondered aloud. Helena heard him.

"They are vexed because Captain Llewellyn is an embarrassment to them, I suppose. After all, he has a..." she hesitated a moment, "a colorful reputation in town."

"You don't say."

German South West Africa

CHAPTER VII

Wilhelmina Oldendorf: April 1919

M arkus continued his routine in Windhoek and was enjoying the work-a-day anonymity. On his lunch breaks and after work, he discreetly asked around about Llewellyn, visiting the local beer garden and newly formed pub. No one knew much about the elusive captain, so Markus decided to visit what he found out to be a brothel on the edge of town.

He was greeted at the side door of a nondescript two story wooden building by a shockingly young woman in the flimsiest of a prewar white cotton dress. "Do come in, sir." she purred. She was thin with hardly a shape to her, and Markus felt immediate pity.

"May I speak with the owner or..." he felt embarrassed asking probably a seventeen year old girl, "or the madam, or...manager?"

"Just this way." It was almost dark in the overly perfumed room into which he was led. The young girl pulled a cord and Markus could faintly hear a distant bell.

An older woman, probably in her late forties, entered. She wore a sweeping gown that at one time must have been very beautiful.

"Good afternoon, sir. What would you like today? We have three lovely ladies available. You've already met Heidi, and also, a very lovely black, very voluptuous, very clean, and, of course, at a much lower price than our other girls." She hesitated, looking at Markus' face.

"Or would you like several, together? We can give you a very good price?"

Markus cleared his throat.

"Thank you. What I would like is some information...about a person I think visited here. It will..." Her face hardened.

"We don't discuss our customers. Now, if that is all you wanted, you'll excuse me."

"I'll pay, for a few minutes of your time, just a few minutes." She looked at him.

"How much is...what would it...what would I pay for one of your ladies...for Heidi here?"

"She's more expensive. As you can see, she's young, very young, almost virginal."

"*Ja*, so what would that be? I have the new South African money?"

"I'll take the old German money if it's in coin."

"*Ja?*"

"Ten minutes of my time for ten marks."

"I have that in South African." He dug down into his pocket.

"Heidi, go upstairs." she ordered. "Now, who is so important that you would trade ten marks for talk instead of for Heidi?"

"There's a South African officer who disappeared. He has a colorful reputation around town and I'm looking for him. If you have any information, I would very much appreciate your telling me. Of course, I will not mention anything about this visit to anyone."

"Of course you won't. I see a wedding ring on your finger. Your wife would not approve of your visit here." She grinned nonthreateningly, in a way that was almost kind. "So, what is this officer's name?"

"His name is Captain Llewellyn, of the South..."

"Him?" The madam stood up. "That, that nasty evil prick! He beat one of my girls near to death! She couldn't work for a month, poor thing." She sniffled then continued: "Disappeared, huh? I hope somebody killed him! I know his type. They're all a bunch of bastards!"

She looked intently at Markus. "Why are you interested in him?" Markus looked back at the sad and angry face in front of him. In a second he made the decision to tell this woman the story that brought him to her door.

"I want to help the South Africans find this man because they think my family knows something about his disappearance. To complicate things, this Llewellyn fellow was billeted at my family's ranch for a couple of years while I fought in East Africa. They don't like German veterans." She softened and listened intently.

"And the government here has the Repatriation and Deportation Order. If these South Africans don't like somebody, they can force them out of the country. Our own country!"

They both sat on the couch silently for a moment.

"He used to come in here pretty regularly 'til he beat up Liesel. I threatened to tell his commander if he ever came back, so he stopped coming."

"Are there any other houses...businesses, like this in town?"

"You mean whore houses?" She laughed and he joined in. "No, no other houses. I know about a few women, but they're more like upper class 'ladies' bored with their husbands. He might have hired one of them, but I doubt it. He wasn't interested in the really cultured girls. He probably couldn't control them like he could one of mine."

"Do you think he could have run off with a woman? He did disappear."

"Anything's possible, but I haven't heard about any women disappearing. This is still a pretty small town. I think I would have heard. I wish I could help you more, Herr...oh, never mind. Better I don't know your name."

Markus looked at the woman sitting next to him again.

"I would like to know your name. Your real name." She looked up at him and smiled. She put her hand gently on his arm.

"It's Wilhelmina Oldendorf. It's kind of you to ask. If you need any more help, let me know."

Back at the ranch that evening, Markus found an opportunity to be alone with Helena. He told her what he was doing and where he went that day. He told her what Madam Oldendorf said about Captain Llewellyn beating up one of her "girls". "She said she hoped someone would kill him!" He didn't notice Helena's hand tighten to clutch the edge of the chair. "I just hope he turns up and puts an end to this."

Helena strained to answer. "Yes, yes of course."

"Are you feeling all right, dear?"

"Too much dinner," was all she managed to say.

"I just can't figure how he could just disappear and no one knows a thing about it." Markus sat there in his own intense thoughts. "Did you know they even questioned the railroad people, Helena?"

"I'm going to bed."

CHAPTER VIII
Escalation: May 1919

E vents did not get any better over the next few days. The authorities in Windhoek sent word out to the ranch that Sambolo and Petre, the two black ranch workers employed by Tomas Conrad, were to report for further questioning at military headquarters within 48 hours.

This new threat to the family secret, still hidden from Markus, caused apprehension among the family members.

"Do you think Sambolo can hold up under isolated questioning, especially with white officers in military uniform?" Norbert asked Wolfgang with Christina listening.

"That would be scary for any of us, and we're white."

"Not so loud! We don't want Markus to hear."

The two black men were held overnight and released the next morning. With Markus at work, Wolfgang, Michael and Norbert took the carriage in to town to pick them up. They arrived at the military headquarters and reported in.

"Sir, we're here to pick up Sambolo and Petre."

"Sign this, and go around back. They'll be released to you there." They pulled the carriage around to the side of the building and waited.

"Should we go knock on the door?" Michael asked.

"Let's wait a few minutes." Wolfgang replied. Finally the door opened and the two black men walked out. The Conrads got down to greet them.

"Jesus, Petre, what happened to your lip?" The left side of Petre's upper lip was so swollen it was three times its usual size. Scrapes were on the side of his face.

"Those bastards beat you!" They turned to Sambolo and discovered a shut eye and swelling.

"You too, Sam! I'm so sorry. Let me help you." Sambolo was limping.

Norbert exclaimed: "I'm going in there and tell them what lousy bums they are!"

"No you're not, Norbert! They'd just love to get you in there. You'd come out of there beat up or worse, if you came out at all. Let's get home and tell Papa."

"Maybe we should stop at the doc's and have him look at you fellas."

Petre mumbled through his swollen face, "No, no, we just want to get back to the ranch."

"We didn't tell 'um anything, I mean, nothing about..." Sambolo began.

"We were together the whole time," Petre promised softly. "Sam didn't breath a word. One of them was real mean. He did the hitting until another one finally stopped him. After that they just pushed us around." He paused. "They got it in for us...for everyone at the Conrad ranch."

Back at the ranch Petre and Sambolo chose to rest and recuperate after sharing their story with Helena, Christina and Tomas. Later, when Markus arrived home and heard the story, he visited the two men in their cottage near the barn. Returning, he found the entire Conrad clan gathered in the front parlor. There was a subdued tension in the room as the sun slowly settled onto the western horizon.

The dark secret hung like a stormcloud over the heads of those who knew.

"They really think we know something about Llewellyn's disappearance," Markus began. "Of all the possible explanations for his absence, they seem convinced we did something to him. It's confounding." He looked to Helena and then Tomas.

"What do you think we should do?"

"Sit tight." Tomas said.

"But surely there is something...some way to prove we know nothing of this disappearance. The fact is soldiers disappear all the time...desertions, accidents, sickness, sometimes they get lost, or just run home." Markus scratched the side of his head. *I wonder what Levi would do?* The thought brought back memories of old times. "I'm going to talk with the local commander, we shouldn't be harassed like this."

"I don't think that's a good idea." injected Tomas. "It'll just remind him we're here."

CHAPTER IX
A Shot Through The Roof: May 1919

It was a quiet Saturday at the ranch. Helena, Christina and Petre were preparing the noonday meal. Sambolo came to the open veranda windows and knocked on the wood frame. He could see Tomas and Markus lounging in the parlor.

"Mr. Tomas, sir, I see plenty of riders coming, big cloud of dust."

"Oh?" Tomas and Markus got up and peered out the window facing the road to town.

"That's a military unit coming," Markus said. Just as the two men stepped through the front door, they were met by Norbert, freshly in from a hunt.

"No luck. That big cat got away again, I was going down toward..." he was interrupted by the sound and then the sight of a company of South African Mounted Rifles. They were brought to a halt close by the house and ordered to dismount.

"You have your orders, Sergeant. Begin the search."

"What's going on here?" Tomas insisted, as he approached two officers.

"Don't interfere or you'll be arrested. Stand clear!" demanded Captain Perkins, the mean spirited officer from the previous visit. "We're going to get to the bottom of this, once and for all."

"But what's the meaning of this? We haven't done..." Tomas started to say, only for Markus to interrupt his father-in-law.

"Stand back, Tomas, stand back. Let them do what they want."

Helena and Christina came out of the house onto the front porch to see squads of soldiers fanning out on their way to the out buildings.

"A thorough search of the house this time!" commanded Perkins as he approached the house. "You there! What are you doing with a gun! You God damned Germans!" The commander pointed to Norbert.

"I was just out hunting a big cat that was after our cattle." Norbert cradled an old 1898 Mauser rifle in his arms. Captain Perkins pulled his revolver from his holster. On seeing this, several other soldiers brought their weapons to the ready.

"Drop that gun!" ordered the South African officer.

"It's just my hunting rifle." Norbert raised the muzzle of the rifle up slowly to show the officer the weapon.

"Sergeant! Disarm that man and confiscate that rifle!"

"Yes, sir." Several enlisted men and the sergeant approached Norbert and took hold of his rifle.

"You're not taking my gun, it's my Papa's." Norbert was a strong, well-built nineteen year old and he managed to keep hold of his gun in the struggle. Still on his feet, he wrestled with the three soldiers for control of the firearm.

A deafening shot rang out and a flash of fire from the muzzle, as the skyward aimed rifle discharged, blasting a hole into the ceiling of the porch. A wooden shingle flipped end-over-end as the heavy hunting bullet ripped through the roof. Screams from the women were heard as nearby soldiers ducked instinctively. Captain Perkins charged toward Norbert as the three South African soldiers struggled for the rifle. The four men were flailing and stumbling on the porch as Perkins himself lunged for the rifle, cursing.

"Release that rifle you dirty..."

At that instant, one of the enlisted men tripped, fell against the Captain's revolver causing it to discharge. More shrieks as Norbert was flung against the wall on the front porch by the force of the almost point blank shot into his stomach.

"No!" Markus shouted as he ran to his young brother-in-law. Norbert's sisters dashed down the porch to him as blood poured from the wound.

"Jesus Christ! Look what you've done, you oaf!" yelled Captain Perkins impulsively to the soldier that bumped him.

Pandemonium broke out as the Conrads ran to assist Norbert, pushing away the shocked South African soldiers.

"Oh dear God," Helena said as she and Christina knelt beside their fallen brother. Tomas came close.

"Norbert, my boy, Norbert!" He turned, and in a rage flung himself at Perkins.

"You did this...with your hatred. Why couldn't you just leave us alone!" He stumbled while he lurched, trying to beat the Captain with his fists. Perkins stepped back and Tomas fell to the ground at the Captain's feet, moaning in agony. Perkins went pale as he backed away from the old man before him.

Surveying the disastrous scene he muttered, "Christ! Sergeant, see what you can do for the boy, and call off the search for now. I'll leave a squad with you. Clean this up as best you can, I'm going back to base."

As Perkins turned to mount up, the Sergeant asked, "Captain, sir, shouldn't we send a doctor out from town?"

Perkins, back on his horse and having regained his composure, said, "With that wound?" He paused. "Right Sergeant, we'll send someone out."

As he rode off he said to himself, "Damn it, this muddies the water!"

CHAPTER X

The Void That Can't Be Filled: May 1919

That night Norbert lay in his bed, his father's arms around him, as his life slipped away. The golden glow of a half dozen candles flickered from an evening breeze through the window. A military doctor was there. He wiped blood off his hands with a towel before turning to look at Markus. He shook his head silently.

The entire Conrad clan gathered in Norbert's room: Tomas, Helena, Christina, Michael, and Wolfgang. Sambolo and Petre also edged into the dreadful scene. Moans and muffled weeping hung in the heavy air.

Everyone was stunned by this forth grievous calamity to befall the Conrads. First Arnold, dead of his war wounds, then Humboldt of influenza, next Helena's assault and finally this newest tragedy. Even Markus, still without knowledge of Helena's terrible secret, could hardly believe the scope of the family's misfortune.

Five days later Norbert was buried next to his brothers Arnold and Humboldt, and their mother who had died years before. Grief permeated the ranch house for weeks, and Tomas in particular was inconsolable.

Captain Perkins never resumed searching the ranch for clues into Captain Llewellyn's disappearance, but he persisted in his grudge and suspicions against the entire Conrad family. Even after Wilhelmina Oldendorf wrote a letter to Captain Perkin's commanding officer, outlining the physical abuses Llewellyn had perpetrated upon some of her girls, Perkins maintained his hostility toward the Conrads.

Several times after Captain Perkins recklessly killed Norbert, Markus and Helena and others discussed what to do about the man's appalling behavior. "Should we go to the authorities? Do we just have to accept this injustice?" they asked each other.

"Could Perkins retaliate? Yes he would! But we should do it anyway!" Markus pushed for justice.

Others, including Helena, demurred. Finally he relented. "At the least I must say something to the military command. This can't go unpunished."

Tomas silently listened to these discussions. Finally he said, "We can't win this. They defeated Germany on the battlefield...as far as they're concerned, we're the enemy, and we are at their mercy. They will not embarrass themselves with a court martial of Perkins. Let it end. I don't want to risk any more of my children."

Markus went back to work in Windhoek and tried to put the outrage out of his mind. Life resumed at the ranch at a mechanical pace: what needed to get done got done, but little else. It seemed everyone lived in a depressed melancholia.

"I just can't shake off this terrible feeling," Christina sniffled to Helena as they sat together on the sofa in the middle parlor. "I stay up all night wanting to sleep and come the morning I don't want to get up." The two sisters leaned in to each other.

"Yes, I know." Helena said. "This is a terrible time for the Conrads. But I know one thing, sister." She almost whispered to her younger sibling. "I know that no matter how low the light gets, no matter how bad things may seem, they always get better. God is just, you'll see." She squeezed Christina's hand.

"The dreadful war is finally over. We spent four long years not knowing whether Markus was dead or alive, and he came back to us. We're going to get through this as a family because we have to, and because life does get better, even from the lowest lows. I pray for that every day." She wiped a tear from Christina's cheek. "You're a lovely young woman with your whole life ahead of you. I know it will be a happy life. Things will get better for all of us, you'll see."

Kalvarianhof, February 1919

CHAPTER XI

Bavaria, Winter: February 1919

Kalvarianhof, the grand manor house and farm of the Levi family in the forests near Munich, in Bavaria, Germany was a white wonderland to the eye in February 1919. Foot thick snow, untouched in its purity, blanketed the house, the out buildings and the surrounding landscape. The only tracks in the icy white powder led from the barn to the woods where timber harvesting continued through the winter. The horse drawn sled dragged the cut logs easily to the clearing where they would lay, stacked for drying for a year. Wood smoke rose from two Kalvarianhof chimneys creating a blue haze in the cold air.

In earlier years, before the Great War, the Levis burned mostly coal. But now, with the country bled dry of resources by the carnage of the war, inflation and the miner's strikes for higher wages, even coal had become a luxury. Otto Levi, always wise where his Imperial Marks were concerned, switched to the unlimited supply of free wood fuel on the estate.

They had weathered the war better than most, with the rich resources of the farm and forest. Paper money was less valuable by the day, so Otto and Friedl had taken to bartering, like so many other

Germans. Otto, early on, sensing the economic dangers of the war, gathered a considerable amount of Imperial gold coin and had hidden it away in the undercroft of the old manor house, before the Kaiser converted gold marks to paper money. Otto made it a point not to reveal his precious secret, feeling secure in the knowledge that it was there when needed. Raising their own food, gathering their own fuel, and bartering for other necessities had worked well enough.

Now they waited for word from their son Levi, away for over five years serving as an officer in Kaiser Wilhelm II's East African Colonial Forces. Five long years had passed and the world had changed forever. Rebecca, Levi's daughter was now five years old and while Katherina, his wife, spoke constantly of Levi, he remained an unknown stranger to the little girl.

For months the newspapers had articles about homeward bound soldiers, lists of names of those returning and those who were never to be seen again. The telegram only stated that Levi was safe and would be arriving by ship from Africa sometime in early 1919.

One snowy afternoon, the telephone rang in the front parlor at Kalvarianhof and was picked up by Freidl, Levi's mother.

"*Ja*, good day...what operator? I can't hear you...Long distance? Where?" Her heart beat faster as little Rebecca ran up to her grandmamma.

"I want to talk too!" She shouted. "Who is it...is it for me?"

"Berlin? Oh my! Otto, Otto! It's a call from Berlin! Hurry dear, hurry!"

Otto came scurrying in, favoring a sprained ankle.

"Who is it, Friedl? From Berlin?" Rebecca, sensing the excitement, started jumping up and down. "Me too!" she shouted.

"Oh, my God!" Friedl burst into tears.

"Levi, Levi, it's really you! Oh, my son, my son...your voice," she couldn't talk through her sobs. Otto grabbed the receiver but Friedl was reluctant to let go. "Go get Kathi, quick, quick!" her husband urged. He put the receiver to his ear and heard a storm of static.

"Hello? Hello? Operator I can't hear a thing." Through the crackle of the copper wires swaying in winter storms between Berlin and the family estate in Bavaria, Otto finally heard his son's voice for the first time in five years.

"Papa, Papa,!" Levi blurted out, "It's so good to hear your voice."

"Levi, my boy, you're safe again in Germany, thank God! Where are you and when are you coming home? Should we come up to Berlin?"

"No, no, Papa, I'm still in the army. I have to be processed, and there's a big welcoming ceremony for General von Vorbeck, a parade up Unter der Linden and through the Brandenburg Gate. All of us from East Africa will participate...but is Katherina there?"

"Yes, yes, here she is." Katherina rushed down the front stairs almost tripping on the last step and ran into the parlor. Otto held out the telephone earpiece as far as the black cord would stretch. She took it, came closer, and almost touching the boxed wooden telephone speaker on the wall with her lips.

"Levi, darling, is it really you at last? I've missed you so, darling."

"Yes, yes, I love you, too."

"I'm so sorry, I can't stop crying. Oh, darling, I've waited so long for you, to hear your voice, for your safe return. What? Yes, I understand...how soon my darling? Several days then...Yes, I understand."

The operator interrupted the conversation: "Your time is up. Each soldier gets three minutes. You have fifteen seconds."

"My dearest Kathi, I love you so...I'll call again and let you know when the troop train leaves Berlin. I love you."

"Yes, yes, me too. *Auf Wiedersehen* my love." Everyone had tears streaming down their faces and were hugging each other.

"Why is everybody crying?" pouted little Rebecca, starting to sniffle herself.

Friedl, wiping tears with a soggy handkerchief, said, "We have to call Ilsa and her husband, she'll be thrilled to hear her brother is coming home soon. And the Obermaiers. I'm sure Levi will call them, of course, but we must call as well, and Frau Mathais and Anji... Oh, we have to get the house ready, and my baking! Isn't it wonderful Papa, Levi's coming home at last!"

CHAPTER XII

Soldiers All and Fighting Too: February-April 1919

The troop train finally pulled out of the snowbound Berlin station near the end of February, 1919, crammed with soldiers, sailors, sea marines and assorted other men, mostly from Germany's African colonies. Most were able-bodied but some were still on stretchers, and others had missing limbs. Levi thought the saddest of all were the blind, and the ones with terrible, disfiguring face wounds.

"God, I'm lucky," he mumbled to himself as he shifted his thin frame on the wooden railcar bench.

"There you are, Captain Levi. We've got a compartment. Come on, before it fills up." It was Captain Kohl, who fought in German Cameroon. He reached up and got Levi's carrying bag down from the net shelf.

"And we've got schnapps to smooth the rails!" Both men smiled broadly.

As Levi and Captain Kohl settled into the soft cushioned seating in the eight-man compartment, someone exclaimed, "We seem to be slowing down." Several soldiers looked out the window as the southern suburbs of Berlin slipped by. With a screech of steel brakes on steel rails, the train came to a jerking stop.

"Now what?" someone said. Moments later, the conductor came hurrying down the narrow passage. Levi slid open the windowed compartment door and caught the train man's arm.

"Why are we stopping?"

"It's the Communists, the Socialists and the Monarchists, fighting it out right across our tracks! Can't you hear the gun fire?" He pulled away and hurried on.

"What? Who's fighting?" He turned back to see several men hanging out the window and looking toward the engine.

"Did you hear that...what the conductor said?"

"*Ja*, well, they don't like the present government. All those soldiers of different stripes, that is, different ideas of what the government should be. They're all against the Weimar Republic." Captain Kohl turned to smile at Levi. "You really are out of it, aren't you? At least I got to read British newspapers while in the prisoner-of-war camp in Cameroon." He shook his head in exasperation and looked at his companion.

"It's like this. The Monarchists want the Kaiser's son, August Wilhelm, to assume the throne, to be king of Germany. The Communists, that is, the Spartacus Bolsheviks want a revolution like the Russian revolution, where they killed the Tsar and his whole royal family. The Socialists want a strong labor government where they control big industry. Now, the Weimar government is just trying to create a working, duly elected democratic state. But it seems these other groups don't want to cooperate with Weimar, so we've got all these veterans fighting in the streets!"

Levi slumped into the cushions and stared at the floor. "More fighting? I've just spent four and a half years fighting in Africa. Now I come home to find fighting in the streets! Damn, will it never end?"

The train did move on eventually, and the sounds of civil unrest moved on with it. The schnapps helped Levi slip into a dreamless sleep as rousing army drinking songs rolled down the aisles of the train. Beer and liquor were easy to come by for these men, held together by bonds of comradeship from the war. They, who saw slaughter and mayhem for four long years...they knew they were the lucky ones, still in one piece or near enough so. They were heading home, if to an uncertain future.

None of these soldiers were the same men who had left their civilian lives in what seemed a lifetime ago. Fear, pain, and deprivation had altered them and had altered the people they left behind. Wives, lovers, mothers, fathers all were affected by the World War, as the Germans already called it.

The troop train stopped north of Munich in the town of Nuremberg. Levi had just enough time to jump off and hurry to the line forming at the telephone booth.

"Kathi, my love, it's me. I'm in Nuremberg. We stopped just to let off some of the men. You have no idea what it means to me to be back in Germany, to see the landscape and the towns...but there is so much fighting up in Berlin...you can't imagine what's going on up there."

"Yes, yes, my darling, it's like that here in Munich as well. Will you be on the next scheduled train from Nuremberg, or..."

"No. They're letting the troop train go straight on through."

"Levi darling, be careful in Munich, at the station, when you transfer. They're still fighting here too. The Soldiers and Workers Council is trying to set up a communist government in Bavaria...but it's quiet in the village, thank God. We'll meet you at the train station in Munich."

"No, my love, as you said, it's too dangerous. I'll go straight through and see you at the village depot...in a few hours, my love."

And so after almost five years apart, Levi and Katherina were in each other's arms at last. Of course, everyone came to the village train station. They hugged and kissed and laughed and cried and touched him to believe their eyes. Otto drove the seven year old Mercedes through the snow and Willie, the farm hand, brought the one horse carriage to accommodate the rest of the family.

As they passed familiar landmarks Levi heard the 'clink, clink' he knew from his earliest childhood. The blacksmith's shop and stables were lit with several bare bulbs and from the glow of the coal forge fire. Two men were busy shoeing a farm horse. The sweet smell of coal smoke was like a warm greeting to him. The two vehicles passed the last of the village houses and entered the dark forested lane to Kalvarianhof.

Finally at home and in the kitchen alcove, the Levi family enjoyed coffee and cake while little Rebecca asked one question after another.

"You look different from your picture." She stared at her father, a familiar man she did not know, for a long moment. "You're so brown. Does everyone turn brown when they go to Africa?" The innocent gaze and the innocent question brought laughs.

Later, in their own bed in their old bedroom and in a private emotional meeting of their bodies and minds, the years of separation slipped away in the rhythm of their lovemaking. Katherina held her husband's lean hardened body in a tight embrace until the power of sleep loosened her firm hold. The young family, with Rebecca asleep nearby, finally commenced their new life together.

"By the way my dearest," Katherina began soon after Levi's return, "I have the most exciting development to share with you. Professor Adelmann has secured a lectureship for me at the University in Munich. I've been teaching in the Archeology Department for the last four sessions. I'm so thrilled...imagine, me teaching at the University of Munich!"

She was bubbling with delight in telling how her hard work in the dig in Palestine before the war had paid off, when so many men were called away to duty. "It was genuinely shocking and saddening to hear how many of our finest young professors died in the war. It left holes in the teaching staff and I was offered a job. I love what I'm doing. And now I couldn't be happier, with you home safe and Rebecca taking to you so. Thank you, my dear husband." She kissed him then.

When she pulled away he said quietly, "But I didn't do anything."

"You survived," she whispered.

Days passed into weeks, as Levi walked the woods and fields of the snowbound estate, clearing his mind and planning his future. He also reflected on how everyone had aged...how the war had imposed pain and suffering on everyone, soldier and civilian alike. Even the buildings at Kalvarianhof needed serious maintenance. He made a note to himself that when spring came he would return the estate to the beauty he remembered from before the war.

The Iron Cross

CHAPTER XIII

Tales Of Beauty and Valor: April 1919

In the evenings around the wooden table in the alcove, Levi regaled everyone with stories of the grandeur of the former German East African colony. "To see the tens of thousands of wild animals in endless savannahs, and the deserts and jungles, with strange exotic tribes of people...it's magnificent, a whole other world. The endless vistas of the Serengeti plains stretching to the horizon...we crossed that vastness time and time again, Markus and I and all our comrades."

He paused, reflecting on some inner vision, and then continued. "Swamps and mountain ranges...*ja*, we have the Alps, but those are different from the mountains in Africa, steeper and higher with so much snow." He stopped for a moment and then laughed.

"And Queen Victoria's gift! Did you know she 'gave' Kaiser Wilhelm Kilimanjaro? Can you imagine, giving the Kaiser a mountain! It's a lone mountain with a snowcapped peak, rising out of the landscape. That's something I'll never forget."

He was interrupted by his mother, Friedl. "Here we are, your favorite: potato soup with Maggi. You always loved Maggi in your soup."

"He loved Maggi in everything, Mama," Ilsa said smiling.

"And I still do! We didn't have it in Africa after the first few months."

"Oh, my rye bread is still in the oven!" Friedl exclaimed as she scurried to open the wood fired oven door. "Here, pass this to Levi, and the butter too." she commanded. Bread dumplings and a slab of goose breast followed, floating in a golden brown.

"Mama, you're spoiling me!" He looked across to Kathi, and winked. "How will my wife ever keep up with your cooking!"

The stories continued after the meal was done. "Do you want to hear about our friend Markus in Africa?" he asked, knowing the answer. "Well, first I must tell you about the brilliant leadership of my commanding officer, Colonel von Vorbeck. He led us in pursuing and being pursued by the British, Belgians, Portuguese and South Africans for the entire four and a half years of war."

Colonel von Vorbeck, Commander
of the Imperial German Army in East Africa

It was twenty minutes of near disaster, brilliant victories and clever escapes. Otto brought a pitcher of beer and refilled the glasses.

"A toast to the brave men who served: Prost!" It was bittersweet for Levi, reflecting back to the many, many comrades, white and black, buried out in the vastness of Africa, too many in unmarked graves. Only a pile of rocks marked their resting places, just enough to keep the animals from digging them up.

"*Ja*, so that leads me to the exploits of Markus Mathais. Can you believe he was awarded another Iron Cross!" Levi enjoyed this telling. "He flew from German South West Africa and nearly made it all the way to German East Africa on some secret mission before he crashed in a rain storm. I've forgotten the name of the tribe of those natives who found him and took him in. They were kind, caring and gentle folk, that's for sure. They saved his life, and for almost two months they nursed him back to health with their folk medicine. I won't even begin to tell you what some of that medicine was made from...another time maybe." They laughed as he took a long draft of his beer, but quietly as his daughter, Rebecca, slept on the wooden bench.

"And Markus had all sorts of encounters with leopards and hyenas and other wild animals..." Levi stopped and shook his head, "He got himself pretty scratched up, I can tell you!"

His little family audience, spellbound, asked: "And you, Levi?"

"*Ja*, well, I didn't do much. I was with headquarters company." he demurred.

CHAPTER XIV

Shock, Peace And A November Surprise: April 1919

With a bit of luck and Otto's village contacts, Levi got a temporary job helping to finish the large Aerodrome started during the war. It was at the same grassy air field where his friend Markus had made his first solo flight. It was also the airfield where old Bavarian King Leopold III started the first Royale Bavarian Military Air Corp. in 1913.

This is a lucky break for me, he thought as he trudged the mile or so back through the snowbound woods to Kalvarianhof. Most days I can walk to work!

Kalvarianhof, with its isolated location in a clearing, in the former hunting grounds of royalty, seemed far away from the turmoil in the cities. Of course, the newspapers were full of the clashes of the opposing political groups, but the visceral effects of an unstable society didn't reach to their forest home.

Civil unrest continued in most German cities, including Munich, with gangs of soldiers of one faction or another fighting each other. Surprisingly, civilian life seemed to go on as usual with city dwellers flowing around and through the armed skirmishes.

Finally, on a Spring day, April 5th, 1919 the Congress of Soldiers' and Workers' Councils proclaimed a Communist Republic in Bavaria to great protests. Sporadic fighting still continued even as most citizens waited to see what exactly this new form of governing would be like.

Katherina took the train into the city several days a week for her lectures at the university, and one day, Levi accompanied her. His intent was to meet a former colleague from the Berlin to Bagdad Railroad Company that he had worked with before the war. The construction and architectural firm was located near the main train station.

"I take a street car to the university or I walk on nice days if there are no troubles in the area," Katherina said as the two stepped down from the train.

"So, I go this way and you that," she pointed. "I can get away for lunch; shall we meet at Dolmaiers?"

"Yes, noon would be fine, but be careful. Who knows what lurks around the next corner."

"I'll be ever alert, dearest. Don't worry." They came together for a hug just as gun shots reported off in the distance. They both turned their heads toward the sound. He squeezed her hand as she slipped away.

Levi knew well the city of his youth, but the address was new to him. It was located in a poorer neighborhood near the converging rail lines. As he moved along the crowded sidewalks bustling with peddler carts selling roasted chestnuts, vegetables, pots and pans, and all manner of household goods, he also saw a disturbing sight.

Soldiers and civilians with guns, milling around casually. Obviously the military men had no officer in charge and no apparent leadership. And there on the street were his other comrades, soldiers of the Great War, veterans all, sitting on the pavement, alone or in groups of two or three, selling pencils or cigarettes from tin cups. Most wore their dress uniforms with military decorations on their chests, proving their valor.

Most disturbing of all to Levi were the missing limbs: stumps of legs, empty sleeves folded up and pinned neatly, vacant stares from damaged eyes, face wounds that repelled, and soldiers that appeared to be shivering, shaking at times, cowering against dark memories of the war. *I've seen all this on the battlefield*, he thought, *but in Munich, on the streets?*

He was appalled and embarrassed. How could the government abandon these brave men...and the others, what are they waiting for? His mind was reeling. *Why are they reduced to begging, for God sake!* He dug into his pocket and pulled out what he had in paper and coin. He gave it all to the men along the street.

"Thank you my friend, for serving...for your sacrifice," he said to each of them. *My God, it's the least I can do*. Something's got to be done.

He finally arrived at a coal-dust-covered building, the result of being near the rail lines. The construction and architectural company was on the second floor, and to his surprise, his old boss Herr Gustoff Liebermann met him at the door.

"Greetings, old friend, I see you survived the war!" They exchanged a hearty handshake as Liebermann ushered Levi into a small suite of offices. Piles of blueprints and hand drawn plans for buildings, bridges, factories and other assorted projects littered the desks and tables.

Looking around, Levi commented, "You seem to be busy enough, Herr Liebermann."

"*Ja*, it looks so, but most projects are on hold because of politics...and please, enough with the 'Herr Liebermann'. It's Gustoff to you."

A half empty Schnapps bottle drained into two glasses as the men settled into cracked leather chairs. As talk about the war ended, Gustoff asked, "What have you been doing since you got home, my friend?"

"Working on the big aerodrome at the village air field. I was lucky to get the job. Now it's done, and I'm looking for a new opportunity. I was hoping you'd have something I could do with my skills."

Gustoff swung his arm in an arc. Only a one-armed draftsman was working, head down, at a draftsmen's table across the room. "My nephew. He does good work, but I pay him very little. He's also missing half a leg." They stared a few moments at the veteran.

"There just isn't any business for an additional man, at least not full time." Both men looked at each other.

"Tell you what. I can hire you with half time pay, and the other half time you spend looking for business for this company. You bring in business, you go full-time salary. What do you think?" Levi was silent a moment, so Gustoff added, "With your contacts and reputation, I'll bet you can find us a contract or two."

He was grinning broadly. "You've got a deal, Gustoff."

Lunch at Dolmaier's with Katherina became a celebration when Levi explained about his new position. Levi became even more animated as he told his wife about a large new estate planned beyond the woods near Kalvarianhof.

"It's for a big industrialist...one of those men who made a fortune during the war." He saw Katherina's reaction. "I know, I know. I don't like it either, but it's work." Over the next few weeks, Levi beat the pavement in Munich, approaching companies and corporations he felt might need architectural work. No one seemed to be expanding their facilities.

"Try the government agencies," Gustoff suggested, "They're the only ones with real money...*Ja*, them and the war profiteers!"

The Brandenburg Gate, Berlin 1919

CHAPTER XV

The Coldest Hearts Of The Vastly Unjust:

January 1920

O n January 10th, 1920 The Versailles Peace Treaty was ratified in Paris officially ending the most dreadful and bloody war in recorded history. News came by telephone from Levi, who was in Berlin exploring a possible government contract to repair several bridges across the Rhine damaged during the war.

"*Ja, ja*, that's right Papa, the war is finally, officially over." Otto got to the phone first and listened intently as Levi continued, "The Reichstag has just voted on the treaty and it passed, though many denounced it as vastly unjust and a betrayal...it puts all the blame for the war on us. We lose our colonies, all of them, and must pay reparations!" Otto could hear the anguish in his son's voice.

"It's going to bankrupt the country, Papa. It's going to create inflation and injure almost everybody...I think there's going to be trouble, big trouble over this." He continued in a dejected voice after a moment of reflection.

"Well, at least it ends the Armistice and the war is officially over. Now maybe we can get on with our lives."

Otto added, "*Ja*, but we expected Germany would get a reasonable treaty like what American President Wilson proposed...even the British supported most of Wilson's ideas. But the French want revenge."

"Those reparations, yes!" Levi exclaimed. "How can Germany recover if it's giving up everything to France and Belgium and England and America? You're right, the French have ensured this treaty will cause a lot of trouble." Silence on the line, until finally, "*Ja*, well, I'll be home on the train tomorrow. 'til then goodbye Papa."

Levi did secure a contract to repair two bridges, with, surprisingly, help from the French. They wanted the bridges over the Rhine repaired for their trade, not as a gesture of friendship after the Great War. Nevertheless, it meant work for Levi's skills and good news for the family and for Gustoff.

Political unrest in Bavaria and greater Germany continued with the Prussian Monarchists seizing power in Berlin through a coup in March. It lasted a short week, with fighting in the streets of many cities, until the national Weimar government regained control of the old Imperial capital, and drove off the communists who had controlled half of Berlin. In April, the rightwing extremist German Workers Party changed its name to the National Socialist Workers Party, and continued their nationalistic rightist agitation. All this turmoil stressed the greater portion of the German people, but at Kalvarianhof the mood was good.

Katherina had a special surprise. "We're going to have an addition to the family in November, darling."

Levi laughed ecstatically. "With my bridge work on the Rhine, and a new baby!" he laughed, "Life is good again at Kalvarianhof!" He swept Kathi off her feet, and both smiled gaily as they swirled around in pure joy.

Power plant turbines, Windhoek

CHAPTER XVI

Fire: April 1920

One of the turbines is smoking pretty badly, we've got to shut it down!" Markus shouted over the whining machine. He was in the powerhouse that supplied the wireless transmitter, telephones and electricity to the Windhoek Telephone and Telegraph Company and the Military Headquarters nearby.

"*Ja, ja*, but the batteries are not charged enough yet, five more minutes."

"No! Now! It'll burn up!"

"But we'll be in the dark! A few minutes, just a few minutes more!"

"For God's sake, can't you see, you're destroying the turbine!" Markus reached for the bright red hand lever when Henderson grabbed his arm.

"I'm the foreman, and I say we leave it on for a bit longer. This has happened before. We'll turn it off shortly, and it'll cool down like always. Then we just..."

A deafening blast filled the generator house as acidic smoke rolled through like an evil storm cloud. Coughing and gasping, Markus and Henderson grabbed each other and headed toward the door as sparks and sizzling electrical wires danced and zapped anything they touched.

"Sound the alarm! Is everyone out?" A high pitched bell began ringing as the wood timbers of the roof caught fire.

Richard Thomas, Markus's boss, came running out of their office with others. "What happened?"

"The turbine overheated and blew." Markus yelled. "I told him, I told him!" Moments later the fire brigade pulled up and went into action.

"What a mess! There goes our power." sighed Thomas. Fortunately the fire was extinguished rapidly and the building itself was saved.

A crowd of civilians and several military men had formed. Wilhelmina Oldendorf was there with Heidi and several of her other girls. Of the people Markus did not want to see, Captain Perkins was in the crowd accompanying his commanding officer, Commander Northrop.

"What happened?" the commander asked. Thomas, Markus and the powerhouse foreman were in a little group watching the firemen. The foreman stepped forward and explained that the turbine overheated and blew up.

"I tried to turn it off, but that German, Markus, told me to let it run to charge the batteries. He stopped me from pulling the emergency stop lever just before the explosion." Markus overheard the foreman.

"What? That is patently false!" He turned to confront his accuser.

"That is exactly the opposite of what happened! I told you to turn off the turbine because it was overheating. It was smoking, for God's sake. You wouldn't let me pull the lever. You said you were the foreman and you made the decisions. That's what happened." Markus looked at the commander and then at Thomas.

"No, no, he did it. He did it," yelled the foremen.

"You liar, you..." Markus began.

"That will be enough." the Northrop ordered. "There will be an investigation into this accident. You both can make a written statement."

Captain Perkins had been intently watching the heated exchange and leaned into the commander and said, "That's the German I told you about, concerning Captain Llewellyn's disappearance."

Markus could not contain himself. He spat out, "You killed my brother-in-law, you bastard!"

"That was an accident," Perkins shot back, "caused by that Conrad fellow menacing us with a rifle."

"Liar. You reckless..."

"Silence! That will be enough from both of you," the commander ordered.

"The investigation will determine what happened here. That will be all."

Later, back in their wireless office, Thomas said, "That powerhouse foreman is a cussed man, hard to get along with and always with a chip on his shoulder. I believe you, Markus."

"Thanks, Richard. Now, I just have to convince the investigators." They looked at each other.

"Right, convince the investigators."

German South West Africa

CHAPTER XVII

The Inquiry: April 1920

Markus told the Conrads of the events at the powerhouse, about Captain Perkins being there, and the accusation leveled that he, Markus, was responsible for the explosion.

"This is precisely what we don't need right now," he said with deep frustration.

"Surely they will see it was the foreman's responsibility." Helena offered.

"I hope so."

Commander Northrop opened the investigation by ordering Captain Perkins to take statements and interview the witnesses. Markus and the foreman gave their sworn statements in writing. Richard Thomas offered to be a character witness for Markus and also submitted a signed statement. Soon after he did he received a visit from Captain Perkins. Later that day the two friends met in the wireless office.

"That scoundrel Perkins came by and demanded I withdraw the testimony I wrote for you. He threatened my job! Said if I didn't rescind, he'd see to it that I got fired."

"That sounds like Perkins, alright." Markus said. "I don't know why he has it in for me...for all of us at the ranch, but he does have a grudge. And he's dangerous."

The inquiry convened, with most of the Conrad family present. Perkins lined up several anti-German workers from the Telephone and Telegraph Company, and also two workers from the powerhouse. He crafted an unflattering picture of Markus with circumstantial evidence, and between the men's stories and the anti-German bias of the time, implied the destruction of the turbine was an act of sabotage without actually saying the word.

Richard Thomas jumped to his feet when the accusations were read aloud. "This is outrageous. These are lies by people who still hate Germans, and Captain Perkins threatened my job if I spoke up for Mr. Mathais. Can't you see..."

"Silence! We will have order in this inquiry," the commander demanded.

"Mr. Thomas, you have not been given permission to speak." He paused. "I understand your sentiments concerning Markus Mathais, and I also have been informed of certain questionable actions by Captain Perkins. That will be dealt with at a later date." Perkins stiffened noticeably and raised his eyebrow.

"All the facts have been taken into consideration in my decision, and that decision is as follows." Everyone in the crowded room sat up and leaned to hear the commander.

"First, as regards the operation of the turbine, that responsibility lays with the powerhouse foreman. A turbine did not just explode. It overheated first, producing over a period of time, a distinct sound and smoke. The foreman should have closed down the turbine long before it had a chance to explode, and long before any interference by Mr. Mathais could have affected the turbine. Therefore, this inquiry orders the foreman be relieved of his position." There was consternation among part of the crowd.

"What? He did it, I tell you, it was his fault!" The foreman fumed.

"Sit down and be silent, or I'll have you arrested for interfering with this inquiry." The Sergeant in charge of security moved several of his men to either side of the commander's desk. The Conrads and their friends couldn't hide their smiles on hearing the decision, but sat quietly. The commander shuffled his papers and looked sternly around the room.

"Silence, we will have order here!" Everyone quieted down. "Second, as regards the alleged interference by Mr. Markus Mathais in the operation of the turbine, there are conflicting accounts of this allegation and no proof either way. Therefore there is no charge against Mr. Mathais related to the explosion of the turbine." Again, angry murmurs from part of the crowd and clapping hands and elation by the Conrads.

"Quiet down now, quiet. We have not concluded. Third." No one expected there to be a third item needing a decision. "Third," the commander repeated. "As regards the allegation of a threat of sabotage of the turbine by Herr Mathais, that charge has also been dismissed for lack of evidence. However, certain facts raise questions of the loyalty Herr

Mathais feels to the new government of South West Africa."

Markus burst out, "What? That's absurd! No!"

"Sergeant, if there is another outburst like that, clear the room." He continued: "Consider the strange disappearance of Captain Llewellyn, who was billeted at the Conrad ranch for several years. That incident leaves a dark cloud over the Conrad family, especially given the fact that Captain Llewellyn was in charge of preparing a Deportation and Repatriation Order that may have included the Conrads." Helena gripped Markus arm tightly.

"Next, there is Mr. Markus Mathais' loyal military service in the Imperial German Army in East Africa and his family's strong support of the German war effort here in South West Africa as evidenced by two Conrad men serving in the Imperial German South West African Army." Silence.

"All these present at least a circumstantial set of facts that suggest there could be lingering loyalties to a German cause here. Given these facts, this inquiry recommends that Mr. Markus Mathais be dismissed from the strategically important military installation at the Windhoek Telephone and Telegraph Company wireless station. He is otherwise free to go. That concludes this inquiry. Sergeant, clear the room."

"What? This is so unfair. He has done nothing wrong, nothing!" Helena blurted out and was seconded with other such comments by her family. Markus sat in silence with slumped shoulders.

"Please, let's just go home," he said.

Richard Thomas came over and said, "We'll appeal this Markus. I'll go to the commander and tell him how valuable you've been around the station. He has to listen to reason." Looking around, he saw Captain Perkins laughing with several others. "Perkins did this, that bastard."

CHAPTER XVIII

The Court Martial of Captain Perkins: July 1920

This court martial is convened this 15th day of July, 1920 in the Windhoek Military Base, South West Africa. Commander Northrop presiding."

After the military court clerk finished, the commander spoke. "Read the charges to the defendant," he instructed.

"The defendant, Captain Roger Perkins, South African Occupation Force, is charged with the following violations of the Military Code Of Conduct: First: The Ill-conceived impetuous action leading immediately to the death of a civilian, Mr. Norbert Conrad.

"Second: The brutal savaging of a Miss Lisel (no family name given), an employee of an entertainment establishment in Windhoek, requiring two weeks in hospital.

"Third: Intimidation of a witness, Mr. Richard Thomas, in a military inquiry into the turbine explosion incident. Threatening said witness with job loss if he testified as a character witness for Mr. Markus Mathais.

"Fourth: Conduct unbecoming an officer of the South African Army, in that the defendant, on numerous occasions, performed unseemly acts in public involving ladies and alcohol."

In the court room sat the entire Conrad family, including Sambolo and Petre, and also Richard Thomas, Wilhelmina Oldendorf, Lisel and Heidi. The trial proceeded swiftly with witnesses called, cross examinations, rebuttals and finally on the second day, the verdict.

"This court is now in session," intoned the Commander. "The court has reached a verdict on all counts. On the first count, regarding the accidental death of Mr. Norbert Conrad: Guilty. Judgment for this count: Loss of officer rank and six months in the brig.

"On the second count, regarding the brutalizing of Miss Lisel: Guilty.

Judgment for this count: A fine of one hundred pounds paid to Miss Lisel, and thirty days in the brig.

"On the third count, intimidation of witness Mr. Richard Thomas: Guilty. Judgment for this count: Reduction to lowest enlisted rank and six months in the brig, to run concurrently with the other sentences.

"On the forth count, conduct unbecoming of a South African Officer: Guilty. Judgment for this count: Dishonorable discharge from the South African Army.

"This concludes the court martial of Captain Perkins. Take the prisoner away. Sergeant, clear the courtroom."

The gallery of court attendees watched Perkins as he was led out. He sneered contemptuously at the audience. The door closed and the room burst into applause, hoots of laughter, and everyone speaking at once.

"Finally, some semblance of justice, but still...Norbert is gone. Our dear Norbert." Helena voiced the sentiments of the family, as Christina dabbed at tears with a handkerchief.

Richard Thomas came over to give his regards to the Conrads, and share their relief that finally Captain Perkins was judged and convicted for his terrible crimes.

"I'm glad to see justice done, but I am so sorry your brother Norbert passed away." He was looking at Christina but meant the comment for all the Conrads.

"Thank you," she said. "It's heartening to see justice done in a South African court where South West African Germans are involved." She smiled up at him as several other Conrads joined in with thanks.

CHAPTER XIX

The Interlude and Catastrophe: November 1920

Finally, it had ended. The stress and strain of Norbert's death, the accusations against Markus involving the turbine explosion, and Perkin's threats, all seemed to pass away with the conclusion of the trials. Richard Thomas became a very close friend of Markus and was invited out to the ranch on frequent occasions. He finally convinced Commander Northrop to rehire Markus with the understanding that he, Richard, would be responsible for him.

September rolled into November, Helena, plump with the expected delivery, on schedule to arrive within a few weeks, sat with her husband on the parlor couch. "I'm so happy to have you, my love." Markus said, stroking the back of Helena's neck.

"I feel the same, husband dearest. Truly God must have blessed me that I have such a wonderful family." They smiled at each other.

"Is Christina out riding with Richard?"

"I suppose so. They've been seeing a lot of each other lately; dinner here, the band concert in the park, lunch at the hotel. It looks pretty serious."

"How is Tomas handling the idea of a South African calling on his daughter?"

"I actually think he doesn't mind, after Richard helped with your job and the trial."

"Did I hear my name mentioned?" Tomas stepped into the parlor.

"We were just discussing Christina and Richard, Papa. How do you feel about a South African calling on your daughter?" The two stared intently.

"*Ja*, I've noticed their friendship. He seems like an honest, hardworking man. He's gentlemanly and well educated, as you've told us, Markus." There was a long pause as Tomas collected his thoughts.

"Times have changed. Maybe not to our liking, but they have. The colony is now a protectorate of South Africa. We have to move forward. Those who were once our enemies are now potentially our neighbors and potentially our friends. Wouldn't you say?"

"Of course, Tomas." Markus said. "Richard gave me a job and saw me reinstated after the court martial. He didn't have to do either of those things. He could have hired one of his countrymen."

"That's true," Helena acknowledged.

Tomas continued, "Christina is a young woman of age to engage in social activities with men. We all will keep a close eye on her, of course, and let things unfold as they will."

Four weeks later, on November 22, 1920, Helena delivered a bright baby girl the family christened Charlotte. The Conrad family, after years of uncertainty, finally could celebrate untroubled by the outside world. Tomas was completely taken by the little baby, and if he spoiled her as a way to make up for losing Arnold, Norbert, and his wife Fanny, none of the family could begrudge him.

1920's Christmas celebration and the New Year celebration that immediately followed, were the most splendid holidays ever celebrated at the ranch and all Windhoek. The Great War was over and people were well on their way to recovering from the tragedies and hardships of the past five years. There had been fewer deportations and demanded repatriations than expected, so that fear was also lifted.

After his holiday vacation, Markus returned to work at the Telephone and Telegraph Company. He and Richard were having lunch and a beer in their shared office one day in February when their lives changed forever.

A tremendous explosion occurred in Windhoek, half-demolishing abuilding and blowing out windows for blocks. The two men were hurled out of their chairs and showered with glass.

"Jesus Christ! What was that!" Markus choked as he struggled to get up. "Richard! Richard! Are you all right?" He stumbled over to his boss, not noticing blood streaming down his upper arm from a jagged piece of window glass. Richard had been facing the window and received the full force and shards of glass. Only his glasses saved him from certain blindness. His face was pockmarked with bits of the glass shining from multiple wounds. "Good God, I've gotta get you to the doctor."

"What...what was that?" Richard coughed and spat blood from cut lips.

Markus managed to get them both over to what used to be the windows. "It's the powerhouse! Half the building is gone! Jesus, how did that happen?"

Other casualties were appearing from buildings near the explosion, some lying down in the street. Markus and Richard joined a growing crowd as, again, the fire brigade arrived and medics from the nearby army base began treating people in the street.

Burning embers from the explosion drifted onto the rooftops of adjoining buildings setting secondary fires.

"You two, get a ladder up and get those fires out," shouted the fire chief to his men. The body of Henderson, the electrical foreman, smoldered grotesquely nearby, his clothes burned off.

Commander Northrop came running, followed by a dozen men from headquarters company.

"Another explosion at the powerhouse? How could that happen?" he said in utter consternation as he assessed the site. "Lieutenant, get our medical staff out here, and start sorting the casualties."

Just that moment at the Conrad ranch the newly installed telephone jangled to life. Wolfgang took the receiver from the hook on the wall.

"Conrad ranch....*Ja*, what? When? Are you hurt? How bad? What about Richard? *How* bad? Have you taken him to..." Christina, nearby and hearing fragments of the conversation, interrupted Wolfgang.

"What's happened? Is Richard hurt? Let me talk...who is it?" Helena and Tomas also caught the tail end of the alarming conversation.

"Markus, is that you? What happened...is Richard...Yes, yes, we'll come right away." Christina promised. Cupping one hand over the receiver, she turned to look at her family. "There's been another explosion at the powerhouse. Richard's hurt."

Helena took the phone. "Markus, are you hurt? How bad? Thank God. We'll come right away, should we...*ja*." She replaced the phone. "He had to hang up, there are others needing to use the telephone. He's not badly hurt, just some cuts and bruises. We must go."

Christina cried softly in the arms of Wolfgang. Tomas, stunned, pulled his thoughts together to wonder, "The powerhouse, again? The turbine blew up, again? Were they in the building?"

"I'll bring the truck around." Petre said.

"We're all going. Michael, put some blankets and pillows in the back."

The 1915 Studebaker truck, with its open flatbed on the back, was purchased used, as war surplus, by Tomas from the South African Army. It rumbled as Petre drove it to the front of the ranch house. Michael threw blankets, pillows and their first-aid kit into the bed while the family gathered.

"Sambolo and I put on the side rails." Petre said. "He's staying here."

It was a jarring and dusty ride with Tomas driving and Christina and Helena, Rupert and Charlotte in the cab. Before they came to the outskirts of town, a gray plume of smoke could be seen towering into the afternoon sky. The truck pulled up close to the small hospital, already crowded with relatives and friends of the wounded. Michael, and Wolfgang hopped down from the back of the truck.

"We'll go find Markus and Richard, you stay here. We'll be back in minutes." No one waited. They all headed for the double doors, but the town constable stopped them.

"This door is for incoming patients. If you're looking for someone, go around to the side, they'll let you know if your person is in the hospital. Keep clear, please, keep clear."

Surprisingly, Markus was at the side entrance, his upper right arm bandaged. Everyone rushed to him with questions as Helena gently hugged him.

"I knew you'd come. There are so many injured, mostly from when the windows blew out. Richard is in the emergency clinic." He glanced through the door. "They're removing glass fragments from his face. It looks terrible but the doctor said it was all superficial. We'll have to wait, the hospital is packed."

"When can I see him?" Christina asked as she strained to see over the heads of the crowd.

"The doctor said Richard will have to spend a few days in hospital, to avoid infections and so his wounds can be dressed, but we can see him later this evening. His spirits are high, and although he's cut up some, he'll be all right." Markus said reassuringly.

Everyone had questions: "How could this happen? Didn't they just get a new turbine? Was Henderson at the controls again? Didn't he learn anything from the last time?"

"Henderson was killed in the explosion, his body is in the street."

"Good heavens," Helena said. "Rest his soul."

A week later Richard Thomas was recuperating at the Conrad ranch after the family insisted he take his medical leave with them. He received excellent nursing care from Helena, but mostly from Christina. All the Conrad men and Markus visited the explosion site several times. It had been roped off and was under military guard.

"I saw a lot of explosions during the war, and I was in the turbine house when the old turbine blew. This was not a turbine explosion. First of all, the turbine is intact, just buried under all the debris." He pointed to a blackened pile of stone and charred beams, including part of the outer wall. "The explosion happened outside the building. Much of this side of the building is now on that big pile inside."

"My God you're right." Wolfgang said. "But how could that happen?" An uneasy thought occurred to both men, though only Wolfgang said it out loud. "Sabotage."

"What?" Tomas asked.

"This was deliberate." Markus said.

Commander Northrop and the Windhoek Constabulary concluded the same. The search was on to find the culprits who murdered Henderson and injured several dozen citizens. Inevitably, one Markus Mathais came up on a potential suspects list. Markus filled in for Richard, informally, at the Telephone and Telegraph Company for the week Richard was absent. Inquiries were made around town by both the military and civil authorities and in that process both agencies visited the offices with general questions as to what they saw, etc.

Later in the next week when Richard was back to work. Commander Northrop visited him. He was quite formal, stern even, in his questioning.

"Why would you allow Mathais to run this office after what happened? You put Mathais in charge and gave him complete control of the entire telephone and telegraph system here...and the emergency power supply, too. That was poor judgment on your part, Mr. Thomas." His voice was cold and harsh.

"What if he's the man we're looking for and carried out another attack?" The commander had an involuntary tic when stressed, a sort of half wink, that he soothed by rubbing his temple with his index finger. That finger stayed at his temple during the questioning.

"You must know he's a suspect in the death and injuries and explosion."

"I'm sorry Commander Northrop, but I have every confidence in Markus, Mr. Mathais' integrity." Richard was careful with his words and tone.

"You are right. He was in a position of authority here at the company, but as you see, nothing happened during his time in charge."

"That alone is no proof, he could just be biding his time. I put you in charge of Mathais but not so you could put Mathais in charge of the whole damned company. I must rethink our agreement concerning that man. We'll talk again, and soon." With that, he and his adjunct left. Richard sat back down in his chair, leaning his still bandaged forehead in his hand.

"What am I going to tell Markus?" he said aloud.

CHAPTER XX

A Mysterious Death: February 1921

Three children found the body near the outskirts of town, stabbed in the back and front. The ghastly sight sent them screaming down the main street into town, and within minutes, adults started to gather around the gory scene. The news spread like a savannah wildfire. Everyone rushed there, including the commander and a dozen military men. Richard and Markus arrived late and joined the outer edge of the crowd surrounding the body.

"Lieutenant, have your men move the people back fifty feet from the body. We don't want to disturb any evidence that might be around."

"Yes, sir." The military doctor examined the back of the corpse and then rolled the body on its back.

"He looks familiar, but I can't place him." After a long moment of considering the face, Commander Northrop exclaimed, "Christ! It's Perkins, Captain Perkins! He got out of the brig a just few weeks ago."

Richard and Markus had worked their way through the crowd and heard Northrop's comment.

"Perkins! Did you hear that Richard, it's Perkins!"

Everyone at the ranch was dumbfounded by the news of the murder so soon after the second explosion.

"This means more trouble with the authorities for us." Tomas commented with a frown. He puffed more rapidly on his pipe as the family sat around sipping drinks that night. "Everyone agrees the power plant explosion was sabotage, and everyone knows what we thought of Perkins. We're in the middle of this."

"Who would do such a thing...both things, I mean. Why blow up the power station and then kill Perkins?" Michael asked.

"I don't think the same person did both crimes as I can't think of a motive to do both, unless Perkins stumbled upon the criminals and they hunted him down." Markus offered.

"Is there no end to all these horrible events?" Helena said. "The war, the deaths of my brothers, and now the explosions, trials, and this murder!" *Once again I almost feel like God is punishing us. Are we, am I, not worthy of God's grace?* She thought.

Christina, Wolfgang and Tomas immediately understood the true source of Helena's stress: the terrible secret still hidden from Markus. Christina came to her, sat down, put her arm around Helena and said, "Now, now sister, you have two beautiful babies, and a wonderful husband, and all of us. The bad times will pass."

Markus, struck by Helena's melancholy, also sat down beside her.

"Christina's right: we've been through a lot, and the bad times never last forever." That evening, lying in bed together, Markus spoke quietly to his wife.

"My love, I fear I know the people responsible for the explosion and the murder. May I share with you?"

"What? Yes, yes, dearest, tell me your theories." She fluffed up her pillow and turned to face him.

"I think Perkins blew up the building to get even with me. Or maybe he wanted to strike back at the military that kicked him out of the service. He was a career soldier after all. Likely both, if my suspicion is correct."

"*Ja*, I can see him doing this. He was an evil man and God punished him, just like..." She stopped herself before she could mention Llewellyn's name.

Markus caught the unfinished sentence. "Just like...?"

"Oh, I was going to say, just like in the bible, when...oh, never mind." She hurried on with, "And your theory about Perkins's murderer?"

"This may surprise you, my love, but I think Wilhelmina and her girls are at the very least involved with his death. I would never tell anyone else this, but they hated him. They could have hired one of their customers to kill him."

"What? Those women, kill Perkins? I can't imagine."

Tomas's dire prediction came true sooner than expected. Sambolo and Petre saw it first, the next day. A large dust cloud on the road leading to the ranch. This time it was made by a military Rolls Royce open touring car. It stopped in a sliding dusty cloud. Two officers and three enlisted men with rifles got out and approached the ranch house. Tomas lead the way out the front door to greet the military men. Commander Northrop greeted Tomas Conrad and inquired whether Markus was home.

"Yes, do come in." Markus appeared with Helena and the baby.

"Markus Mathais," began the commander, "You are a suspect in the explosion of the powerhouse and in the death of Captain...that is, Mr. Perkins. However, the investigation has just begun and we have insufficient evidence to formally charge you, at this time, so you are not under arrest.

"Given the circumstances, you are dismissed from your job at the telephone and telegraph company. You are ordered to stay away from that company and any strategic installations. You are to report for questioning tomorrow at noon at my office. Is that clear?" Helena made to protest, but Markus held her back with a squeeze of her hand.

"Yes, I understand. I'll be there...but I had nothing to do with either of those crimes."

The commander ignored him. "That will be all."

CHAPTER XXI

The Midnight Ride: February 1921

It was near midnight. Richard Thomas came galloping up to the ranch house, slid off his horse and pounded on the front door. Everybody in the house was up in minutes and gathered in the middle parlor, lit with candles.

"What in heaven's name is going on?" Tomas asked rubbing his eyes.

"Sorry to disturb you all but I had to come." Richard sat down on the edge of an upright chair without being asked. "I just got fired today, but that isn't important at the moment." All eyes were on him.

"I was at the pub feeling sorry for myself when I...overheard...a bunch of soldiers talking about you." He was looking at Markus.

"Two of them were really pushing anti-German talk. They said they were looking to "find" someone who'd swear they saw you at the powerhouse just before the blast, and that you were seen leaving the site where Perkins was found."

Everyone gasped. "That's ghastly! That's a flat out lie! They can't get away with that!" Richard said, before the family descended into arguing.

Tomas spoke up over the noise. "Oh yes they can, and they probably will. We have to do something but I don't know what."

Richard spoke, nearly shouting "I don't like relaying this, but I had to." He looked around at staring eyes. "They said this time there'd be a hanging." Christina let out a muffled shriek as Helena clutched baby Charlotte, eyes brimming with tears. "That's what they said."

"These confounded South Africans, we should drive them out of our country!" Wolfgang said, then realized Richard was South African. "Er, sorry, Richard." Richard waved him off as if to say, 'it's nothing'.

Tomas interjected, "Now don't be foolish, son. They won the war."

"I know, Papa, I know." Everyone was quiet for a few moments. Wolfgang broke the silence. "But we have to do something to help Markus. Should we hire a lawyer, a good one?"

"Against a military tribunal?" Markus said. "And there aren't any, anyway."

"What, then?" asked William. They looked around at each other.

"I...have an idea, but it's a pretty radical solution, I mean it would keep you safe, but it's a drastic move." Richard offered.

"This family's good at drastic moves!" Michael blurted out and instantly regretted the comment. Wolfgang gave him a warning look.

Tomas asked, "What's your idea, Richard? We need some good ideas."

"Well, there's a Portuguese freighter leaving in a couple of days for Portuguese Angola up north, before it heads on to Lisbon. Markus, maybe, you could take the ship up north till this thing settles down, until they find the real culprits. Right now, folks in Windhoek are looking for somebody to blame. Things'll be dangerous for anyone falling under suspicion. They want blood."

"What? Leave the country? No! I don't want him to go." Helena said. "What about our cabin up in the hills? Nobody knows about it. We could..."

"If the two of you turn up missing," Tomas injected, "the authorities will start a manhunt and the first place they'll look is our property, thinking you both won't go too far from home with your two babies. And I don't want people going up there." He caught his mistake and to ensure Markus didn't pick up on it he added, "It's not suitable for a baby."

Everyone had an opinion on what to do. Finally, Tomas said, "For now we wait and see. But Markus can't go into town alone. Some of us have to go with him tomorrow. Richard, my friend, thank you for bringing us this important news. I'm sorry you lost your job because of us. We'll repay your friendship somehow."

"It's nothing, it's the right thing to do." He said to the group while looking at Christina. She returned his smile.

The next morning Tomas, Wolfgang, Michael and Markus crowded into the Studebaker's cab for the ride into Windhoek. Commander Northrop's questions were nearly identical to the ones he'd asked when the turbine exploded. Ominously, two soldiers had come forward with information they claimed was pertinent to both investigations. They were to be questioned later that day.

Markus overheard that he would be detained to await trial if the afternoon's testimony provided damning evidence against him. It was expected to.

"You are not in detention right now solely out of consideration for your wife and family, and because there is no place you could go in South West Africa where we cannot find you. I'll ensure you get a fair trial when—if—it comes to that. Dismissed...for now."

The four members of the Conrad clan walked out of the headquarters in the early afternoon, only to be met by several soldiers. "Blimey, if it isn't the explosives expert himself! Poked anybody with your pen knife lately?" All three men hooted with laughter.

"Hey Kraut, the war is really gonna be over for ya soon!" One of the soldiers made a strangling gesture with his hands and again the laughter.

"Bastards..."

"Just keep going, Wolfgang," Tomas insisted as they headed for the truck.

"Gonna bring your own rope, German?" someone shouted after them.

CHAPTER XXII
After Midnight: February 1921

"M aybe Richard is right, dearest." Helena whispered as the two parents lay, side by side, in the early hours of the morning. "Could we go up to Angola with the kids for a month or so?"

Markus rolled toward her. "Yes, we probably could, but that has its own complications. First, how long would we have to stay...weeks, months? Second, How do we even know the authorities will ever catch the real criminals. If they don't, when we come back will I be arrested? And third, my dear, if I leave they will surely see that as a sign of guilt." He looked at her, still radiant after two children and all the stress of the last five years. "If I go, I have to go alone. You and the little ones will be much better off here at the ranch."

"No!" she said emphatically. "You're not leaving me...or our children. I lost you for near five years! I'm not seeing you off to an uncertain future again. Besides, our children need you too." Silence as they snuggled closer and finally drifted off to a fitful sleep.

Sambolo heard them first, horses coming up the road. It was well after midnight with a three quarter moon. He jumped into his pants, gave Petre a shake in the next bunk, and ran toward the ranch house. He came up to the back windows of Tomas' bedroom, banged on the window and did the same to Wolfgang's window, next door. Wolfgang leapt out of bed, opened his window and leaned out, just in time to see an unknown number of horsemen circling the house.

"Jesus! Trouble!" By the time he'd gotten on his pants, grabbed his rifle and cartridges and entered the hall, Markus and Helena were up.

"What is it...what's going on?" Helena was startled to see the rifle.

"Riders and it looks like trouble."

"You in there!" a voice shouted. "Bring that dirty kraut outta there or we'll burn down the whole damn place."

"Oh my God!" Helena said, as everyone crowded near the front door.

"Helena," Markus ordered, "Take the babies out the back to the barn. Tomas please go with her and take a gun. Christina go with them." Richard had stayed the night in a spare bedroom and was up too and left with Christina and the others.

Markus opened the front door and stepped out onto the front porch. "What do you expect to accomplish with your midnight ride way out here?" He said in a calm voice.

One of the riders shouted, "The commander says two men saw you at the murder and at the powerhouse. You're a murderer, you damned German bastard, and we're gonna take you in...save the army the trouble of comin' out here to get ya." He and the others laughed gruffly.

"Tie him up boys! Here's the rope." He threw a coiled rope onto the ground in front of the porch.

A tremendous blast shattered the night air. All eleven horses shied and several reared up, tumbling one rider to the ground.

"Nobody's going to tie up anybody tonight." Michael shouted to the riders. He stepped out of the shadows near the edge of the house. "If anyone touches Markus, I swear on the graves of my two brothers, I'll shoot them dead, right here and now." Everyone was startled by Michael's gun shot and turned to stare at him.

"You better stay outta this, you dumb kid. There's eleven of us and that's an old double barrel shotgun." The riders had regained their composure and laughed nervously.

Bam! *Bam*! Two more startling shots rang out, and again the horses reared and shied in fright. "Christ!" blurted the lead rider.

"This is an eight shot Winchester rifle, I've got six more shots left." Petre shouted as he stepped out from around the opposite corner of the house.

"Have you reloaded, Michael?"

"You're darned right I have. I'll take the big guy if trouble starts."

Wolfgang was now on the porch, too, with his rifle pointed at the riders. Everyone froze for a moment as Markus slowly walked off the porch, picked up the rope, and handed it to the lead rider.

"You've had your fun, scaring my family to death. It's time for you to go."

The rider took the rope, pulled sideways on his reins, and spurred his horse. The others did the same. As they left, one of them shouted back,

"Anyway, you damned Kraut, the commander's coming for you tomorrow."

Having heard the three shots, Tomas and Christina came running from the barn, both carrying rifles, in time to see the riders depart in the moonlight.

"It's near four-thirty and no one's going to sleep any more tonight," Helena said, "Let's make breakfast." All agreed, returning to the house, talking about the latest intrusion into their lives.

"We better figure something out soon." someone said. Petre began the usual morning preparation with Sambolo fetching new honey from the pantry larder. The kitchen was actually one large preparation, cooking and roasting room. There were three smaller rooms joined by a hallway: a wild game and butchery room, a baking room, and a tiled wet room kept cool with water races on shallow foot wide channels of open water running all the way around the edges. For a big family like the Conrads, it allowed simultaneous preparation of various foods.

"I never get tired of the smell of baking." Helena said, trying to take her mind off the night's events. She and Petre peeked into the wood fired oven. In the parlor, Christina and Richard sat together on one sofa and the other four men sat on assorted chairs, sipping coffee.

Wolfgang said, "I would not have trusted those drunks to take anyone into custody. Not the way they were throwing that rope around."

"What are we going to do now?" Christina asked. "Word is that there're two men who'll testify against you, Markus."

Markus had been silent for a long time since the riders left. "Much as I don't want to, I think we should consider Richard's idea. If I could get on that Portuguese ship without being detected...When did you say it was leaving?"

"You're actually considering going away?" Christina asked.

Richard spoke up before Markus could reply. "The ship leaves in two days, I believe. I'll contact the captain by telephone and make arrangements...see if it's possible, if that's what you want. As for getting you on board, we'll work that out later...if you really choose to go."

"Don't worry about getting a spot on board. I know the captains. Enough money will get you on board and buy their silence. I'll help with that." Tomas offered.

Helena walked into the room and waved a hand in front of her face. "Papa, your pipe is smoking too much. So what are you talking about?" There was a moment of complete silence in the room.

Markus broke it by replying, "Just the night's events and what to do next. Do I smell fresh Kaiser rolls?"

Portuguese freighter

CHAPTER XXIII

Last Of A Life: February 1921

After the early morning breakfast with the sun just coming over the hills, Markus and Helena retired to their bedroom still in their clothes from the night.

"I talked with your father and brothers, my love. We all agreed it's best I go up North to Angola, probably Luanda, until this mess can be straightened out. I know you don't want me to go, but with the anti-German feeling running high, everyone agreed it's too dangerous for me to stay here."

He looked at her. She said nothing for a moment, then turned to him. "We are not going to be separated, again. I lived in fear for almost five years not knowing if you were alive or dead out there in East Africa. Our family will be together no matter how long we have to go. God will protect us." Her voice was firm and clear. He knew by the tone her decision was settled.

"Helena, if you are truly committed to this, I will not deny you. It may be dangerous, or the Portuguese may simply arrest me and send me back. I have no idea what to expect...or how long we have to be away."

"I know darling, but we will be together. I have faith in the lord. It will all work out for us."

"Then it's decided?"

"Yes, it's decided. Now get some sleep my love."

The next day at Markus' suggestion, Richard took an early train on the old German rail line to Swokopmund on the coast. He was to check on the Portuguese freighter. Meanwhile, at the ranch, they expected the Commander and his men to come to arrest Markus at any time. Lookouts, Sambolo and Michael, were up on the roof with binoculars watching for tell-tale signs of dust far down the road. A horse was saddled in the barn at the ready for a quick escape.

In the house and after a short sleep, Helena and Markus laid out clothes and other provisions for their secret escape north. Wolfgang found several old leather suitcases and dusted them off, while Tomas volunteered his newer satchel for the baby clothes. As Petre helped close the tightly packed bags, Markus, on impulse, threw in the packet of letters he had promised to deliver to the daughter of General Albuquerque, an old friend from the war. Markus figured that since he was going to a Portuguese colony and she lived in Lisbon, Portugal, he would send them on from there.

"I don't want you to go. When are you coming back?" Christina said through tears. She followed her sister, the sister she nursed back to health after the terrible incident in the barn. Now she felt helpless and fearful. Helena came to her and took her in her arms. The two women swayed gently back and forth as the older sibling tried to reassure her.

"We will probably be gone for just a few weeks or possibly a month. This whole nightmare will be cleared up when the Commander and the court get all the facts, you'll see. But you must be strong now. You'll be the lady of the house. You must look after father and the boys. Can you do that?" Helena asked, then answered her own question. "Of course you can, dear sister. You took such wonderful care of me. Put your faith in the Lord as I have done...but also, be strong just now."

Richard returned on the night train. It pulled into Windhoek station and was met by Wolfgang driving the truck. Wolfgang peppered him with questions all the way on the bumpy ride back to the ranch. Richard responded to his many queries with a litany of answers. "The freighter, the *Brazilian Goddess*, leaves tomorrow on the late tide...Yes, the captain will take four passengers, no questions asked, for a price...One hundred Old Imperial Gold Marks or the same in South African...No, per person and no bargaining...First port is Namibia picking up ivory, Small, dirty, primitive, dangerous...Yes, Luanda is better, but not by much, it's got a clean hotel run by a Jew. Lisbon is the next port of call...in Portugal, two weeks sailing away...Yes, Luanda is the best, the nearest coastal town to stay in for a while." The truck pulled in to the ranch, and the family stayed up late that night so Richard could repeat the facts to all the Conrads.

Tomas whistled through his teeth when he heard the price. "Fortunately, I've got the money from that recent sale of cattle. It's half in coin and half in South African paper. There's half again as much in Imperial gold in a separate sack for your expenses. That gold is good in any town."

"Thanks, Papa," Helena said.

Richard took a long drink of beer and said, "I'm surprised you're still here, Markus. I thought you'd be up in the hills. But I did hear that the Commander was delayed in arresting you for some other urgent business. That's a lucky break for us, but we've got to get you to the ship by early afternoon."

"Let's load the truck tonight and get an early start tomorrow. It's a long drive to Okabandia, about eighty kilometers. We can board the train there without being seen. It's too dangerous to board in Windhoek," Markus suggested.

That morning, before sun up, everyone was finishing breakfast when Tomas announced it was time to go. They spoke the last goodbyes as everyone went out back to the truck. "I tied an extra drum of petro on the back." Wolfgang said as he slid in behind the wheel.

Helena came over to Sambolo and whispered, "You're my precious friend, Sam, thank you." She turned and in a loud voice, "We'll be back in a month or so."

Christina still held little Charlotte. "Come back as soon as you possibly can, sister." She handed the baby over, then unwound a scarf from around her neck. "Here, Helena, my lucky scarf. I want you to have it." They hugged tearfully.

"All aboard, we've got to go." Wolfgang said.

There was just enough room in the cab for Wolfgang, Helena holding the baby, Rupert next, and lastly Markus, his arm hanging out the door and a rifle between his legs. Michael clambered up to the flatbed, wrapped his rifle in a blanket, and sat near the cab back window. The Studebaker truck rumbled to life and with waves, they bounced down the lane toward the road to Okabandia and into a dangerous and unknown future.

Tomas and Christina, arm in arm, watched the dust trail grow smaller and smaller, both lost in their own thoughts. Tomas brushed a tear as he reflected on the last half dozen years.

I lost Arnold to the war, I lost Norbert to that murderer Perkins, Humboldt to that terrible disease, and my poor Helena was attacked by Llewellyn...Markus came back scarred by war, accused of terrible crimes, and now he and Helena flee to another country with the children. Of the ones who remain, dear Christina is growing up too fast, Michael is becoming a man, and Wolfgang...what would I do without Wolfgang. He's the strong one now.

Christina wept quietly for a few moments, thinking, *This is terrible, they're going all the way to Angola and with the baby...I should have gone with them, whether Helena allowed me or not...but that would have left dear Papa alone when he's already been through so much...we all have...and Richard, my Richard...I do love him...do I love him?*

CHAPTER XXIV

Flight To The Sea: February 1921

L et's wait in the truck till the train pulls in. It'll only be in the station about five minutes." Markus pulled his hat low over his eyes, hunching forward in his seat.

"Okabandia is one of the sleepiest little whistle stop towns on the way to the coast." Wolfgang said, trying to relieve the tension in the truck.

"I've gotta go potty." Rupert said looking up to his mother. Markus looked across to his wife, "I'll take him out to this side of the truck." He opened the door, swung his legs out, then paused and pulled his legs back in and slammed the door.

"It's one of those men, the night riders that came to the ranch. Looks like he's getting on our train. Damn!"

"Wolfgang, see if you can get a private sleeping compartment for us. Here's some coin. Bribe the conductor if you have too."

"Daddy, I gotta go pee!"

"Rupert, come here boy. We're going to go pee on the floor of the truck."

"On the floor? Mama will be angry." They both looked up at Helena. The two parents couldn't help smiling at the innocent comment.

"It's all right, just this once. But we won't do that at home, will we?"

Wolfgang climbed back in behind the wheel of the crowded cab.

"I got you the compartment. The train leaves soon, so I'll pull the truck up near the loading dock." He pointed.

"Let me carry the bags on first. Helena, I suggest you go on next with the kids, but wait a few minutes. I'll pull down the shades so you can see which compartment it is. Markus, there're some empty crates where I'll park the truck. Pick one up and carry it on. If anyone is watching, they'll think you work here at the station."

"Right, good plan, Wolfgang." Markus said looking past his wife in the cab.

"Thanks for everything. You and Michael have a safe ride home."

"Yes brother," Helena said. " Thanks for bringing us down and look after everyone while we're gone." She bent sideways and kissed his cheek, smiling.

"*Ja*. Michael, did you hear that? Take care of everyone until I'm back. You're taking the truck back to the ranch. I'm going to Swokopmund."

"What? No. You don't have to go with us, Wolfgang." Helena said.

"You still have to get on the *Brazilian Goddess*. I'm not leaving you four until I see you safely sailing into the sunset." He was smiling. Markus knew Helena's brother was right, and possibly needed. Danger still lay ahead.

"Thanks. We appreciate that. Yes, we still do have to get on that freighter. I just wonder where that night rider is." Markus said.

"Well, we made it on. Let's close the door curtains," Helena said ten minutes later, peering down the aisle of the first class compartment car. They had said their goodbyes to Michael and followed Wolfgang's plan to get on the train unobserved.

"Are we moving yet? little Rupert asked.

"No, dear, not yet. In a little while."

"How soon?"

"Soon...here's your bunny."

"He wants to look out the window."

"In a little while, dear."

The train jerked into motion and the four adults breathed a sigh of relief.

"How soon to Swokopmund, darling?"

"It's about three hours."

The conductor came by checking tickets. Wolfgang left for the dining car to bring back food for the group. "Four inches of hard salami and what's left of that cheese." He said to the dining car steward. "And half a loaf of the rye bread and four apples, *ja*, and three beers and a ginger."

"We can deliver to you compartment, sir. What's the number?"

"Eleven." Wolfgang scanned the other tables in the dining car...several couples, a half dozen single men at different tables, most with their backs to him. *Is that him? I can't tell. Better leave.* Wolfgang thought.

They finished their light meal as the train pulled into one of several stations along the line to the coast.

"Better to keep the shades closed at these stations."

"*Ja.*"

A knock at the door. "Yes, who is it?"

"Steward to pick up the tray and utensils, madam."

"Just hand it to him, dearest." The door slid open.

"Here you are, it was very..." Helena didn't get to finish as the night rider burst into the compartment sending the tray and empty beer bottles flying. He had a gun and it swept the little room.

"I thought I saw one of you Conrads back at the Okabandia station and then again in the dining car. Ha! I got me a real catch," he smirked.

"Hands in the air. By rights I could shoot the murderer, so just sit tight till we get into the station."

"Are you the mean man? You leave my papa alone!" Rupert ran toward the man, who grabbed the child and roughly pushed him back.

"Don't touch my son!" Helena shouted as she pulled Rupert to her. In that instant, with the distraction of the child, Wolfgang leaped the five feet to grab at the man's gun hand. A struggle pursued, the gun fired into the floor, and the three men wrestled on the floor as the train pulled into the station.

The conductor and another passenger saw the commotion and intervened, pulling Wolfgang off the night rider. In that instant, he broke away, ran down the aisle and leaped off the train just as the doors opened to the platform.

"Stop him! Don't let him get away!" someone shouted, but it was too late.

After detraining, Helena asked, "What are the chances he can alert the authorities?" She spoke as the group hurried through the crowded train station and on to the waiting rental hacks. They all climbed in, dragging their luggage.

"Oh, he'll alert the police alright, and probably telephone the Commander back in Windhoek," Markus said, "he wants the credit if we're caught."

"Let's just get you on that ship...it sails in a few hours," Wolfgang added. They arrived at the docks, always a confusion of horse-drawn wagons, and trucks loading and unloading cargo in clouds of blue exhaust. Clusters of burly men milled around waiting for work.

"There it is...the *Brazilian Goddess*!" Wolfgang pointed. It wasn't much to look at, as long streaks of red rust coursed down to the water line from drainage ports. It's white superstructure hadn't seen fresh paint in many a voyage. The gang plank was just now swinging into position.

"Let's keep back over there near that wall, we're less conspicuous." Markus said. "When you get on board, I suggest you stay in your second class compartment until the ship is far out to sea." Wolfgang advised. "Don't take any chances."

They waited for an officer, usually the purser, to position himself at the foot of the gangplank, indicating time to board. Wolfgang handed Markus boarding papers and an envelope full of South African cash.

"This will get you aboard. I'll say my goodbye now. Better I stand off a bit. I'll wait till I see you safely off."

"Dear brother, what would we do without you." she hugged him tightly.

"Look out for everyone till we get back."

Little Rupert wedged in, asking, "Aren't you coming with us? I thought you were coming with us."

"Not this time, little man, maybe next time. We'll go riding when you get back, ok?"

"Thanks so much, Wolfie. You and Michael have a safe ride back to the ranch, and tell everyone not to worry, it'll all work out in the end. I'll send you a wire when we get to Luanda." With that Wolfgang stepped into the crowd and was gone.

"Wait here with the kids, I'll see if we can board." Markus was back in minutes. He looked around, scanning the crowd for the night rider.

"We can go." He picked up the two suitcases and the satchel and the little family headed for their ship. As they reached the top of the steep gang plank, and stepped onto the steel deck, far down the dock a commotion could be seen.

It was Wolfgang in a fight with another man! Some of the crew and an officer leaned over the railing to watch the altercation.

"Keep moving dearest, there is nothing we can do."

"But Wolfgang..."

"There's our cabin, go on!"

"Oh boy, I want this bunk!" Rupert exclaimed, jumping onto the bed, oblivious to the concern of his parents.

Markus quickly closed the cabin door. "We mustn't draw attention to ourselves, my love. I suspect Wolfgang arranged that little fight for our benefit. It was a great distraction."

"You think so? I hope you're right." She sat on a bunk, unpinning her hat.

Markus looked out the porthole, moving his head way to one side and then the other. He pulled the little curtain shut and came over and sat by

Helena.

"This is really the best solution...going up to Luanda for a while, don't you think?"

"Yes, of course it is. I just don't like leaving Papa for, what, a month? He's getting on and he's had so many tragedies so close together. I mean, we all have, but somehow I feel it affects him more...seeing his two sons..." Tears were in her eyes and she began to cry. As she sniffled, she added, "and what happened to me, us, and you. He is too good a man to deserve all these bad things." Markus held her tightly in his arms. "And now this having to run away to a different country. We didn't do anything. Is God punishing us?"

Markus tightened his hold on his wife. "No, no, my dear, things will get better." Suddenly, pounding on the cabin door.

"Jesus!" Markus exclaimed, as the back of Helena's hand covered her gasping mouth. Markus jumped up and went to the port hole. Peering out, he let out another "Jesus!" But with a different tone of his voice.

"Leopold! My God, it's Leopold! Leopold!"

"Who?"

Markus quickly stepped to the door, opened it, and in fell Herr Leopold, Markus' benefactor and friend from Portuguese East Africa.

"My God Leopold, it's so good to see you! What are you doing here?"

"I was going to ask you the same thing!" he said, smiling, as he eyed Helena. "I thought I was seeing things when I saw you down on the docks. Then, when you came up the gangplank, I knew it couldn't be anyone else. Is this your family?"

"Yes, yes. This is my wife Helena, and my son, Rupert, and Charlotte."

"Dearest, this is Herr Leopold of the Leopold Trading Company. He helped me...saved me, during the war. Do come in. Here, sit down."

Helena wiped a tear while Leopold sat in the only chair in the cabin, and looked around the cramped quarters.

"*Ja*, so you survived the war. I had a feeling you would, after all the other dangers you lived through." He let out a mighty laugh, and Markus joined in. Helena sat transfixed, her eyes wide on the two laughing men.

"So what are you doing on this sorry excuse of a freighter?"

Markus' smile faded to a serious frown. He was silent for a moment and Leopold noted the grave continence.

"Leopold, I wish I had a drink for you, because if you really want to know why my family and I are here, it'll take a while." Markus commenced to relate all the events that led up to their boarding the *Brazilian Goddess*.

"That's quite a story..." He looked at Markus' lovely wife, at Rupert, at Charlotte and then at Markus.

"I'm sorry, I *am* sorry for your present circumstances...if there is anything I can do, you know, Markus, you just need to ask." He slumped lower into the chair, silent for a moment.

"As a matter of fact, there is something I can do for you, you two...four, and I will not take a 'no' from you, Markus. I am traveling alone, and I'm traveling first class." He pointed up with his finger.

"I mostly sleep and drink on these trips...very boring. I walk the deck some, but most of the time I get good and drunk and sleep...makes the time go faster."

He shifted in the chair. It creaked under his weight.

"What say we switch cabins. All I need is a bunk. You need lots more." He stopped. Markus was about to say something when Leopold held up his hand as if to say, 'Halt!' "So, it's settled. Grab your bags and let's go up one deck!" Helena and Markus were too flabbergasted to protest so they followed Leopold's command.

They had just reached Leopold's first class cabin, and were about to enter, when they looked across the expanse of water to the other freighter tied up alongside theirs. To their shock, the night rider and three policemen were on board walking swiftly, looking, and appearing to be checking all the public spaces on board.

"It's him!" gasped Helena.

"Quick, quick inside!" Leopold physically pushed the family through the cabin doorway.

"Stay here. I'll see what they're up to. Lock the door, close the curtains and don't open it for anyone. I'll give a signal, three knocks, then one, then three more, when I come back." With that, Leopold stepped out and was gone.

It seemed like forever till Leopold returned. The seven knocks sounded and Markus opened the door. In stepped Leopold carrying two sealed bottles. The broad smile on his face marked a man who knew he was about to indulge in his pleasures.

"They were in your cabin," he began. "I leaned on the railing outside your cabin and heard them talking. They knew it was your assigned cabin, but because you weren't there and your luggage wasn't there, they figured you hadn't gotten on board yet. They left the ship to search the dock and put two of the police at the gangplank. Your 'payment' paid off. The officer down there didn't say a word!"

"Herr Leopold...my friend...you've saved me again."

CHAPTER XXV
Playing It Out: February 1921

M inutes before the *Brazilian Goddess* was to sail, the night rider clamored back up the gangplank, this time with twelve South African soldiers behind him.

"Search the ship! They've got to be on board!"

The captain of the ship, a rotund man of sixty, who had started his seafaring days before steam replaced sail, asked, "What is the meaning of this? Get off my ship!"

"I demand to see your passenger and crew manifest."

"Who are you to be demanding anything?" the red faced captain said.

"We're looking to arrest a German murderer who we believe is on your ship. Where's your manifest?"

The captain, knowing the stranger had no legal authority, warmed to the banter, and decided to play out this cat and mouse game.

"Why do you think this murderer of yours is on my ship? I couldn't help noticing your search party looking around on the freighter across the way. You know there's another ship, a Dutch freighter, a few hundred yards to the south of us. Did you look there? After all, the Dutch took in old Kaiser Wilhelm after the war...and they speak German." He smiled craftily.

The night rider and the South African officer, craned their necks to look across the choppy water to the Dutch freighter. Just then the *Brazilian Goddess'* first officer blew the ship's horn and crew members prepared to cast off.

"All ashore! All ashore that's going ashore!" someone announced. In frustration, the search party headed down the gangplank and ran toward the Dutch ship, just as it also sounded it's horn.

In their stateroom the Mathais family felt the subtle increase in vibration from the ship's turbines and a slight tilt of the *Brazilian Goddess* as she got under way.

"I think we can relax now," Markus said as Leopold entered. Helena, the children and Markus were all exhausted, physically and emotionally from the strain of the day, and it appeared on their faces.

"Why don't you all relax. Take a nap. I'll be in my new cabin with my two friends here." He hefted the bottles. "Join me later, then we'll all go to dinner. Seven sound good?"

"Wonderful, Leopold, just wonderful," Markus said, sprawling backwards on the bed.

"*Ja*, but first this calls for a drink, a toast, to celebrate outfoxing the fox!" Leopold cackled.

CHAPTER XXVI

Worse Than War: March 1921

T he slow freighter plowed north toward its next destination, the city of Luanda, Angola. It was the first time sailing for Helena since her visit to Germany several years earlier. She was distracted from her worries by the brisk sea air and the novel living arrangements on board. After smooth sailing for several days, they approached their destination. On the bridge, the ship's captain stared hard into his binoculars for a long time.

"Christ! I haven't seen that in years. Take a look." He was talking to his first officer as the *Brazilian Goddess* neared port.

"I've never seen it before," said the first officer. "But...is that what I think it is?"

"You know damned well what it is. It's the signal flag "Lima", the yellow jack! It's cholera. Luanda's got the plague!"

The captain took back the binoculars and scanned the waters ahead. "I knew Angola's been with it for several years, but it's been inland and up north. Now it's on the coast! There's no way we're going near those docks. I won't let the *Goddess* become a death ship." he spat out.

"Officer Blanca, don't allow anyone aboard. Some of those lighters will come alongside, and look...see those people on the docks, see them? They see us...they'll be clamoring to get on board. I would too. It's damned contagious. Prepare to repel all boarders." he ordered, as much in exasperation as in anger. "Have the crew get the fire hoses out. We won't be able to pick up that load of ivory and skins from here and we can't take on coal, damn it. What's our fuel supply? How many days can we stoke the boilers with what we've got? Call the engine chief, get him up here." He peered through his binoculars again.

"If anyone wants to get off in this hellhole they can, but nobody reboards. Tell our special guests we've arrived where they wanted to go...but also tell them I said their kinder will be dead in two weeks if they go ashore."

"What?" Markus said mere moments later, when Leopold came huffing in with the bad news.

"You can't go ashore here, too dangerous, your kids..."

"But we had plans, made arrangements..."

"Look, people are dying out there...it's cholera, and it's bad. I mean it's a bad outbreak. I've seen it before. Some people die within hours of contracting it. Did you know that? Some take a week or two." Leopold looked at them and added in a gentle voice, "One of my favorite composers, Tchaikovsky, died during the cholera outbreak in St. Petersburg. Did you know that?" he shook his head, and continued, "Just being near the coast and at a dead stop is dangerous. People are desperate...they see a ship, any ship, and try to get aboard. The captain damn well better sail as soon as possible." Leopold sat down in his former compartment.

"You'll just have to choose another country further up the coast."

"But we were only going to be gone a month. Can't we find an island or just stay on the ship...?" Helena trailed off as everyone sat in silence to contemplate this latest challenge. Both children were sound asleep on the bed. "Can we send a wireless to Papa to let him know what's happening to us?" she asked. "He'll be worried when he hears...they all will be."

Markus, sitting on the bed with Helena, turned and took her hand. "No, dear. By now the commander knows we've fled. If we send a wireless to your papa, it will surely be intercepted and could get him into more trouble. The whole family will be taken for accomplices anyway. It's my fault. I should have left alone, or stayed. At least you and the children would be safe at home." His shoulders slumped as he stared at the floor.

Leopold, watching him awhile. "No, best to keep a family together in a crisis. You did the right thing, Markus."

"Yes, yes you did, my love...and besides, you know I wasn't going to let you leave us behind." She leaned in to him, holding his arm.

Markus tilted his head back up to catch Helena's gaze. After a moment he smiled faintly. "Then let's send a message to Thomas...maybe in some kind of code he can figure out. I don't think they'll check his wireless messages."

"*Ja, ja*, let's do so...but we don't know where we're going."

"Not yet, but we can send another wireless later. What do you think, Leopold?"

"Who is this Thomas?"

"A friend."

Yellow Jack flag

CHAPTER XXVII

Yellow Jack: March 1921

I t's all along the West Coast of Africa. It's going to kill thousands...French Equatorial Africa, Cameroon, Togo, Liberia," Leopold informed his friends. "The captain says we have to pull into Portuguese Guinea, we're almost out of coal. He says we'll be dead adrift if we don't, so he's got to."

The captain, ever pragmatic, knew the danger but needed the coaling station. "Taking on coal from lighters is going to take a long time...triple the watch. I don't want any unauthorized boarders. It's bad enough the coal has to be loaded by hand into the bunkers below, *that* can't be helped, but keep the crew away from them. When they're finished use the fire hoses and wash down the floors and shovels. What a damned sorry mess this is!"

Later, in the galley, everyone not assigned work duties were called together. The Mathaises and Leopold sat in the cramped quarters as other crew members and a few other passengers stood around waiting for the captain.

"There are several ports up north we could stop at. They usually have freight going to Europe, but..." he hesitated, "most of the hold is full. I've got most of my freight, I can still break even on this voyage. I'm making for Lisbon. We've got enough coal in the bunkers, so there'll be no more stops till home port."

Although he was adamant, he still glanced at the Mathaises with a sympathetic eye. The rest of the crew and passengers were fine with this news.

"Lisbon! Lisbon? But we agreed..."

"You had your chance to get off at Luanda. Of course, it would have probably killed your entire family, so now you're going to Lisbon. You should be grateful."

He looked around. "Crew dismissed." The crew smartly returned to work, while the passengers milled about and slowly shuffled out of the mess until only the captain, the Mathais family and Leopold remained.

"Oh, now, now, don't feel so bad," said the captain. "You're really not so far from home. There'll always be plenty of ships going south. You'll be back in Africa again soon enough, don't you worry." He smiled comfortingly, trying to put the best face on the news. "And I won't charge you any more for the longer...the additional voyage."

For the next week, Helena walked the decks in a daze and slept fitfully for long periods. Markus and Leopold spent hours together drinking and speculating on what would happen and how to handle the charges against him.

"If there's a competent investigation and a fair trial you should be completely cleared of those charges." offered Leopold. "I'll do whatever I can to help." Markus thought it was generous of his friend but didn't see much that Leopold could do.

Finally, the Portuguese coast emerged from the endless horizon with Markus, Helena clutching Charlotte, and little Rupert huddled together, gripping the railing of the old ship as the *Brazilian Goddess* sailed into Lisbon harbor. It was a sight Markus remembered from what seemed a lifetime ago, when he and Levi returned from China and the whole happy world seemed open to them.

Passing the ancient white stone of Belem Tower that had guarded the Lisbon Harbor for centuries, Leopold pointed out the rows of famous Portuguese explorers and other heroes carved on monuments nearby.

Markus tried to cheer his wife up. "I've fond memories of walking the city with Levi and Katherina. We'll be safe here for as long as we have to stay, so we should try to make the most of it."

"*Ja*, and you will be my guests at my home for as long as that may be. I'll have it no other way."

Helena turned to Leopold, "Leopold, my new friend, you are a most kind and generous man."

"Yes, well, I have been mightily entertained by your husband's exploits and adventures, and I want to see a happy ending to your present difficulties."

As the ship edged toward the dock, the captain approached Markus. "You've got a telegram waiting for you at the harbor master's office." It read:

To Markus Mathais
Wolfgang in prison Stop Tomas under house
arrest Stop Happy you are safe Stop More
later Stop
Signed Richard Thomas

German South West Africa

CHAPTER XXVIII
The Offer: March 1921

B ack at the ranch in South West Africa, Tomas Conrad sat in the overstuffed chair in the parlor of his house, listening to two South Africans present their proposal. His hair was unkempt and he hadn't bothered to shave for several days. Christina, and Michael, his last two children still at the ranch, sat nearby. Petre was off to the side at Tomas's request.

"This is a fair offer, a generous offer, especially as to the fact that you're...well, Germans. We really needn't offer so much, but to complete the sale of your ranch expeditiously, we are willing to pay a premium. We have the papers right here. You can look them over, or have your banker examine them. So, what do you think?"

The South African doing all the talking, his red hair hanging over one eye, hesitated, then added: "It's a good offer, but we need an answer soon. I can't guarantee how long it'll last."

"I agreed to listen to your...your proposal, only because the commander in town insisted I do. Now I have listened as I was so ordered. The answer is no, and it will remain no, as long as I have a living breath. My wife is buried here, three of my sons are buried here, and the third was murdered by one of your military officers. I hacked out this ranch from the wilderness and raised my family here. I will never, ever sell. Now get off my property. Michael, kindly see these...these gentlemen to the door."

"You're making a big mistake mister Conrad. You should not expect such a generous offer when I see you next. I'll leave the papers in case you change your mind before that time."

Michael got up and moved toward the two men and gestured toward the door. "You'd better leave now."

"And take these damned papers with you!" Tomas shouted after the South Africans. He collapsed back into his chair coughing. Christina came over to her father and knelt next to him.

"Papa, Papa, don't let them upset you so, it's not good for you. Don't worry, we'll never sell the ranch." She couldn't hold back the tears as she laid her head on his knee.

Outside, the two South Africans turned to Michael, stepped closer, and said, "Michael, is it? Look Michael, three of your brothers are dead, another is imprisoned for helping a criminal escape, your brother-in-law fled the country, isn't coming back any time soon, your father is under house arrest, and you've got no one to work the ranch except your sister...and a couple of blacks," he allowed with a smirk. "Be reasonable, talk to your father. I bet you can get him to come around." He looked back toward the house. "Do that and I'll see to it that you get a generous gift. That part can stay between you and me. No one needs to know." His smirk expanded into a full blown grin. "Got it?"

Michael stared at them and said in an ice-cold tone, "It's time for you to go."

Both men shrugged their shoulders and got into their open-air Rolls Royce. As they did, the quiet one spoke for the first time. "He's a cool one, isn't he?"

That evening, around the dinner table the last three Conrads at the ranch, and Richard, who rode in after work, talked into the night.

"Maybe Wolfgang will be out of prison soon. He hasn't been tried yet for helping Markus," Michael offered.

Richard, more a realist, countered, "He'll soon stand trial on that charge and probably others."

"Can we get my brother free with some kind of bail?" Christina asked. She was holding Richard's hand under the table. "I mean, before the trial."

"If it could be done, and that's a big 'if', it would cost a lot of money. Commander Northrop let Markus come home before his trial and we managed to get him and his family out of the country. The commander was apoplectic. Papa," he nodded toward Tomas, "would have to mortgage the ranch to cover a bond like that." Tomas, returned to his normal temperament, had a different suggestion. "Perhaps we should concentrate on proving what really happened at the powerhouse."

At that same moment, Commander Northrop was reviewing the facts of the now weeks old investigation into the powerhouse explosion and the murder of ex-Captain Perkins. Evidence taken from the blast site, as well as taken from and around the corpse, painted a disturbing picture.

First: unlike the previous incident, the turbine did not explode. We found it completely intact under the rubble, he thought. *Second, the southernmost wall was blasted into the building, suggesting the explosion occurred outside the building. That explosion brought the building down. Third, and most distressing, there were fragments of at least two artillery shells found in the debris and embedded in the wall of the building opposite the blast.*

His artillery officers reviewed the evidence. "To work the shells, one needs specific training in handling them, how to open them and secure the fuse. One also needs a specific wrench to work that mechanism. Furthermore, the culprit knew where we kept the artillery shells and how to access them."

Commander Northrop raised his hand. He'd heard enough, there was only one conclusion that could be drawn. "There is only one man who met the criteria. Our very own cashiered and disgraced officer, the heavy weapons expert Captain Perkins, released from confinement just a week or so before the blast."

He looked at his men. "Gentlemen, this knowledge must be kept strictly secret. Meanwhile, we continue investigating both incidents." His officers nodded.

Again Sambolo was the first to see the dust cloud on the road leading to the ranch. He knocked and opened the front door. "Hello somebody?" He called out, "Motorcar coming up the road."

Tomas, trying to nap on the parlor couch, heard Sam's voice. "What? What's that, Sam? Come in, come in, what did you say?"

"Motorcar coming, sir." Tomas got up, adjusted his suspenders, ran his hands through his hair, coughed, and went toward the door.

Michael and Christina were up a rise of land off to the side of the ranch house. They too saw the auto.

"Let's get down there, Papa's all alone." Michael said.

"Yes. I just hope this isn't more trouble." They spurred their horses to a canter so they pulled up in front of the house at the same time the open-air Rolls Royce came to a stop.

They both slid out of their saddles and walked briskly to bracket Tomas as he emerged from the house. Sambolo and Petre kept back but watched intently.

Commander Northrop and two of his officers got out of the vehicle and approached the group. He spoke in a very formal manner, "Good day, Herr Conrad, young lady." He nodded at Michael.

"I'm here on official business and must ask to inspect part of your house. It will not take long, I assure you. Won't you show us in?"

The Conrads stared at the Commander a moment, then Tomas said, "Inspect the house? What for? We don't have anything to hide. Can't you just leave us alone?" He backed up clumsily. Christina took his arm, and looked intently at the three officers. She thought she detected a different mood in their formal yet unbelligerent attitude. Something had changed since the last time she had exchanged words with the commander.

"What are you looking for, Commander?" Michael asked politely.

"Please, shall we proceed?" He put his hand out in a gesture to indicate the family was to proceed first. They all stopped in the parlor.

"Please direct me to Frau Helena Mathais room."

"What? She hasn't done anything! She's not here." Tomas shouted.

"Papa, let them see her room. I can't imagine what this is about, but let them do what they came for."

"Thank you, Fraulein Conrad." The commander said.

The group proceeded down the hall, save Tomas, Petre, Sam and one officer. Michael and Christina edged into Markus and Helena's bedroom and watched as Commander Northrop scanned the spacious room, stopping his cursory survey at Helena's dressing table. He approached, bent over and looked intently at the collection of lotions, perfume bottles and vials. Michael and Christina looked at each other perplexed. *What on earth is he doing.*

The Commander opened a drawer in Helena's lovely little table below the mirror. He stirred it around, then closed it. He opened the second drawer too. He stopped and stared hard for a moment, and lowered his face to within inches of its contents. Standing back up, he took from his pocket a folded piece of paper about six by four inches. He bent over again and out of sight of the two Conrads, seemed to scoop up something, lift it to his nose and smell it.

Christina, unable to contain herself another moment, blurted out "Truly sir, what are you doing?"

"All in good time miss," he replied. With that, he folded the small paper and put it carefully in his uniform pocket. "Now then," he said, "where is your room Miss Conrad?"

"My room? You want to search my room...for what?"

"Please Miss Conrad, it won't take long."

The group filed down the hall to Christina's room. She passing in first, and quickly picked up her night gown from the bed and hung it behind the door. Again, the commander quickly sought Christina's dressing table, almost an exact duplicate of Helena's. Again he bent low as if he was sniffing out some particularly irresistible smell. Looking over the objects on the table, he stopped at a small round and lidded jar some four inches in diameter. This he picked up, unscrewed the lid and looked inside. He raised it to his nose. Setting it down he again took out another piece of paper, the same size as the first, folded it in half, picked up the jar and tapped a pink powder into the crease of the paper. After writing Christina's name on the bottle with a pencil, he dropped it in his pocket. He quickly glanced through the two drawers, straightened up and spoke. "That will be all. Thank you for your cooperation. Miss Conrad." They all filed back down the hall again to the parlor where the commander thanked Tomas for his cooperation.

As he was about to leave Tomas asked, "*Ja*, so did you find what you were looking for, Commander?"

"I do not know yet, Herr Conrad. You will be informed at a later date."

Before the Rolls pulled away, Tomas asked Christina what they were looking at. "My cosmetics...and Helena's!"

Later that day, Christina telephoned Richard and described what had transpired.

"Richard, can you come out this evening for dinner, and stay over? Petre and I are making those little meat pies you are so fond of."

"Oh, Shepherd's Pie! Mmm...And yes, I am very fond of them." He paused for a moment and before she could say goodbye he said, "You know Christina, that's not all I'm so fond of at the ranch." He heard a little giggle before he hung up. Her gentle voice caused a warm feeling in him.

There was animated discussion at dinner between mouthfuls of antelope meat pie, about what the commander could possibly want or need with samples of the two women's cosmetics.

"What could that possibly have to do with the explosion at the powerhouse?" Richard asked, looking to Tomas.

"I haven't the slightest idea about that, but they better not try to drag my daughter into this unholy mess." He paused to fill a small glass from the Bombay Gin bottle sitting near him on the table.

"Thanks for bringing this Richard." He raised his glass lightly as a toast.

"You and this gin are about the only two things I like about our occupiers."

"Papa, Richard is no occupier, he's our truly dear friend, right?" She looked at Richard and they exchanged smiles.

"Of course, of course. Richard, you know how much we appreciate what you've done for Markus and us all. You're like one of the family."

CHAPTER XXIX

A Shocking Encounter: March 1921

Two weeks passed and still they heard nothing from Commander Northrop concerning the strange visit to the Conrad women's bedrooms and the gathering of rouge powder by the commander. Michael and Christina rode into town on several occasions to visit their brother in prison. They brought him a basket of his favorite food treats and a book newly published on the geography of Africa.

Wolfgang also could not figure out what, if anything, cosmetics had to do with his upcoming trial—His concern was that, somehow, Northrop would implicate the women in the explosion or in Perkin's death.

"Have you heard from Markus and Helena?" Wolfgang asked quietly.

"Yes, a wireless message from the ship to Richard. They couldn't stop in Angola because of a cholera outbreak, so they were going north to another port," answered Richard.

Sister and brother left the prison and walked around the little town they knew all their lives, asking shop keepers and the postman and others if they had heard anything about the investigation of the explosion. No one had heard anything.

On this particular trip, Michael suggested a visit to an establishment that he thought Christina should not visit.

"I'm going, and that's settled. I don't care what people think. Besides, how will anyone know I visited there anyway? I want to hear whatever you hear. Papa always says two heads are better than one."

"*Ja*, OK, if you insist, but I'll bet they will be as shocked as anybody, seeing you walk through the front door." They left their horses at the local stable in town and walked the considerable distance to the house at the edge of Windhoek.

There was no front door. They walked around to the side door, and knocked. They were met by a very young and skinny woman in a very sheer dress. She was not wearing any undergarments. She and the Conrads stood speechless for different reasons. Finally the skinny girl, averting her eyes and backing into the shadows, said, "Oh, you have the wrong house, Miss. There is no one here that you would want to see." She tried to close the door quickly, but Michael was quicker and reached his arm out and stopped her.

"Please, please, go away!" she said in a plaintive voice from behind the door.

"Heidi? Is that you?" Michael said in disbelief.

"Please, please Michael, just go away...Please!" He staggered backward, bumping into his sister and almost falling over.

"Yes, yes of course, I'm sorry, I'm..." he stuttered. The young woman closed and locked the door, but not before both Christina and Michael heard her whimpering. Michael and Christina were dumbfounded by the last few moments. Christina, of course, was shocked by the near nudity at the front door. Even more shocking was how the young woman recognized Michael, and how he'd recognized her!

"You've been here before haven't you?" she accused. "How disgusting! I never thought a brother of mine would..."

"Wait, hold on, Christina. I've never been here before in my life! Didn't you recognize her? That's Heidi Roth, from school, from the level behind us! My God, I can't believe she's...she's working in a brothel."

"What? But she's younger than me. I thought..."

"Whatever you thought, you were wrong. Poor Heidi, she must be desperate." They looked at each other and at the locked door.

"We should leave," Christina said. The pair walked slowly away and were quiet until finally Christina said, "I'm sorry, brother, to accuse you of... patronizing her at that place."

"Oh, forget it. I can see how it seemed that way to you. I just can't believe Heidi is working there. Her family must be hurting for money, but still, can't her mama and papa get jobs? I mean, Windhoek is growing and the farms and ranches around here are...I just don't understand it."

"*Ja*. Well, just like you predicted, we had a shock, but we didn't get to talk to...what's her name, the lady, the 'Madame'." She put a special emphasis on "Madame".

"Markus told us her name, I think it was...Oldendorf. Wilhelmina Oldendorf." They walked back to the center of town and stopped by the

Dutch café for lunch. "Why don't we try calling Frau...that is, Madame Oldendorf? What do you think?" asked Michael.

"We'll have two of the luncheon specials, please. OK with you, Michael?"

"*Ja*, fine. Oh, fraulein, is George the owner in?" George came out from the kitchen and greeted the Conrads.

"I haven't seen many of your folks lately...sorry about Wolfgang, when's the trial? I'm sure he'll get off...he's a fine young man. What can I do for you?"

"May we please use your telephone?" Christina asked.

"Of course, it's back in my office. Follow me." Both got up and followed along.

"Maybe you should make the call." Christina said. Michael cranked the phone.

Gladys, the town telephone operator, asked, "Name or number please."

"I'd like to be connected to Wilhelmina Oldendorf, please."

"George, is that you? You know your wife told me not to connect you to that women ever again!"

"Gladys, this isn't George, it's Michael Conrad. Please just connect me."

"Does your papa know you're calling that woman?"

"Gladys, please! Just connect me. Thank you!"

The telephone rang at the house with no front door. "Hello, may I help you?" It was a sultry voice of a mature woman.

"Yes. May I speak to Madame Oldendorf, it's important."

"Speaking."

"Hello Frau, that is, Madame Oldendorf, this is Michael Conrad. We've never met, but you may remember my brother-in-law Markus Mathais, he..."

"Of course I remember Markus. A fine man, once more wrongly accused I'd say. What can I do for you, Michael?"

"*Ja*, so I'd like to talk to you concerning...well several things. Could we meet in town somewhere, perhaps at the hotel lobby or at the Dutch Café...I'm actually calling from there now."

"Yes, I'll be happy to meet with you, but best we not meet at the Café, poor George is in enough trouble as it is, but that's another matter. What's this all about?"

"Well, it's...complicated. Could we meet soon?"

"I could meet tomorrow...or even today if you like."

"Wonderful! What time can we see you at the hotel today?"

"Yes, give me one hour. I'll meet you in the hotel lobby. How will I recognize you?"

"I'll be with my sister, she's..."

"Ah, you two were here at the house earlier today...one of my girls was very upset. Maybe you could tell me what that was all about, when we meet."

"Yes, I'm sorry about that...we are both wearing white shirts."

The lobby of the Bismarck Hotel was quiet with a few guests sitting, smoking and reading the newspapers. Several gray haired South African officers with chests full of medals seemed to be waiting for someone. Michael and Christina found a large Victorian sofa upholstered in wine red velvet. It was soft to the touch and as they sat waiting for Madame Oldendorf, Michael absentmindedly smoothed his hand back and forth across the cushions.

Wilhelmina Oldendorf swept through the open double doors of the hotel and strolled across the lobby toward the two Conrads. One of the officers tipped his hat to her and she smiled back. Christina saw the exchange and rolled her eyes in disapproval. She immediately brought back her smile as Michael stood up and extended his hand in greeting. Introductions and light chatter followed.

Finally the Madame asked, "So what is so important to bring you two young Conrads all the way from your ranch to my establishment to talk to me?"

Christina spoke first, "We wanted to know if you had heard anything about Commander Northrop's investigation into the explosion and the murder of Captain Perkins. We've asked all around town, but nobody seems to know anything. Even my...our friend Richard Thomas hasn't heard anything."

"It's true, I do hear a lot that never reaches the public ear." The madame smoothed her long dress and looked around the lobby. "The fact is, I heard from...a client... that several artillery shells had gone missing. He felt certain they were used to blow up the powerhouse. Quite interesting, don't you think?"

"*Ja, ja*! Anything else Madame..."

"Oh, call me Wilhelmina...Markus did, and I liked it." She smiled at them. "No, there's nothing more to tell except I had a disruptive visit by Commander Northrop recently. I had to shoo several clients out the back door...he wanted to search the entire house! Heaven knows what he was looking for, but he did a strange thing. He took bits of some of the girls' face powders in little paper folders. I have no idea what he wanted those for."

"What? You too!" Christina burst out, "He came to the ranch and did the same thing with my cosmetics, and Helena's too!" This led to a moment of discussion that left all three with questions but no conclusions.

"He is definitely looking for something and it involves us women." Wilhelmina said with a sigh. She looked at Christina, "Don't you worry, though, dear, you're as pure as desert sand."

"Do you know anything at all about whoever killed that Perkins?" Michael asked.

"Only that they think he was killed by a group of people on account of how many stab wounds there were on his front and back. That's about all I know." They lapsed into silence, digesting the information.

"What have you heard from Markus...are he and his family all right?"

The Conrads shared their latest news to her and then Michael asked, "May I ask you Madame...that is, Wilhelmina, about one of your...assistants, Heidi? I knew her in school, and I just couldn't believe, that is I was so surprised to see her today."

"Ah Heidi. Poor lost soul, dear Heidi. I was going to ask you two about your encounter with her today...now I see why she was so upset. I'm sure she was very embarrassed seeing you. It reminded her of the old days, when she had a good home, poor as it was." Michael and Christina both sat straight-backed on the edge of the sofa, their full attention on the sad implications of the madame's words.

"Please forgive me, but why is she working as...at your business? Can't her parents find a suitable job for her? Surely their ranch produces enough to, to..."

"You don't know do you? Her parents are both dead. I found her half-starved and begging for food around town. She was so desperate she was selling herself out behind the stables for a few marks at night. I heard about it from several women who complained to me that she was taking their business. I mean, a young pretty girl like that? She's a man's dream. I took her in. At least she's safe with me." Christina's face paled. What she'd heard was far outside her experience and values, but even she had seen firsthand what a despicable man could do to a woman.

"Dead! How did they die, do you know?" Michael asked.

"Yes, yes, I know. Heidi told me every terrible detail. Her mother contracted influenza and died within a week. Losing his wife tore her father apart. All three of them worked hard at their ranch, but it never amounted to much. When she died, he took to drinking, but what really killed him was getting a notice of deportation. I'm sure some South African wanted his land and paid a bribe to get her father's name on the list. That's what killed him, even if it was his own finger on the trigger."

"He killed himself!" Christina blurted out. "How terrible for Heidi."

"I'm sorry to give you this sad news about you school chum. If I can help in any way with the trial or anything else, just give me a call. You know where to find me." She let out a little funny laugh and the two joined in.

"And if we can ever be of any help to you Wilhelmina, just call on us."

After Madame Oldendorf left, Michael and Christina sat there drained from the tension of the conversation. Finally, Michael said, "I had no idea the Roths were dead! I wondered about them on occasion because we stopped seeing them at the livestock auctions. Poor Heidi."

"Truly this is a cruel, brutal world. How can God let all these bad things happen...our brothers, Helena, Markus and poor little Heidi." Christina brushed a tear from her cheek, "What can we do?" she said.

Michael took her hand. "I don't know...maybe we could get her a job? I mean, you know, a real job." He thought a moment. "Why not ask Richard, maybe he knows someone in town."

"*Ja, ja*, that's what we'll do." She squeezed his hand. "We should get back to the ranch. It's almost nightfall and Papa will be worried."

CHAPTER XXX

A Slow Fellow, An Unexpected Visitor: April 1921

Richard arrived soon after Michael and Christina stabled their horses. At dinner, the two told of their visit to Madame Oldendorf and the tragic tale of Heidi, their school chum. Tomas exclaimed, "So that's what happened to the Roths. It's terrible, *terrible*, and that poor girl..."

Christina put down her fork and dabbed her mouth with a cross stitched napkin. "We must do something to help her. Richard, we thought maybe you could inquire around town if there are any positions she could fill. What do you think?"

"Yes, of course. What a terrible story, and I'm sorry that some profiteers grabbed her parent's land. They should be brought to justice." He took a draft of beer as he looked at the three Conrads.

"Finding a suitable position for this young girl...no, this young woman, may be difficult given her present circumstances. Explaining her current circumstances to prospective employers... It's a tall order, but I'll see what I can do." Christina smiled proudly.

After dinner the little group retired to the parlor, where Michael played with one of their dogs, Tomas read the newspaper Richard brought out to the ranch, and Christina sat at the piano, plinking out some simple tunes.

"Tomorrow is Saturday. Can you stay for the weekend?" she asked Richard.

"I must be back in town Sunday afternoon. I'll go in when you all go in for church. How's that?" He grinned, nudging her as they sat close on the piano bench.

"Grand!" she said. "Want to go for a walk? Papa, we're going for a walk."

Tomas stirred from half-sleep, " *Ja, ja,* take your wrap." Christina slipped the shawl off the hook by the door and they were out the door into the cool night air. She took his arm with both hands and held it tight.

"It was a real revelation to talk with Madame Oldendorf and see Heidi today." They were out by the big tree near the barn.

"Did I tell you what Heidi was wearing? It was almost nothing at all, a summer dress, with hardly anything..." Richard turned, reached up and touched her cheek. They came together in a most willing embrace, a long tender kiss that went on a few moments, her hands up around his back. He pressed her to him and it warmed their passion for each other.

His hands swept down over her back making circular motions as their gentle kisses continued. It had a passionate effect on her as a wonderful energy surged through her body.

"I love you Richard." she murmured between sublime kisses.

"Yes, and I you." They separated a bit and stepped closer to the big tree. He came up behind her placing his hands on her upper arms. He kissed her neck and she tilted her head to receive his lips. His hands moved over her body and rested gently on her breasts. He squeezed them tenderly as she arched her back, turned and passionately kissed him. He whispered, "We could do this every evening, you know...for the rest of our lives."

"Oh...? How do you mean?"

"If I asked your father if we could..."

"Are you proposing to me, Richard dear?" She turned around and faced him.

"Would you like to get married...would you marry me, dearest Christina?"

"Oh Richard, I just knew we should, and yes, I will!" They both kissed and giggled and swayed as they stood there in the dark under the big tree by the barn.

The two lovers scurried back to the house, Richard being pulled by Christina. "Papa, are you awake...Papa? Richard has something very important to ask."

"What? What time is it...I should be going to bed." He scratched his beard and looked up at the two young people.

"What was that? What did you want? Has Michael gone to bed?"

"Papa, Papa, this is important. Richard wants to ask you something." She turned to Richard and pulled him in closer to her father slumped in the chair.

"Herr Conrad," Richard began, "Christina and I...that is, could you, I mean I'd like to marry your daughter." He stared at the old man in the overstuffed chair.

"What! You want to marry my daughter?" He pulled himself up in the parlor chair, coughed several times, and looked at the two with a faint smile on his face. "You woke me up for that?" He burst out laughing at his joke. "I was wondering when you'd get around to asking her...or me for her hand. You're a rather slow fellow, aren't you...Mister Thomas?" Again he laughed at his little joke and the two lovers laughed with him.

Michael came into the room from the kitchen munching on a roll with a slab of meat hanging out of it. What's all this laughing about?"

Christina came bounding over to him. "Richard and I are going to get married! Isn't that wonderful?"

With a mouth full of food he couldn't talk, but he had a big grin on his face as he hugged his sister.

Two days later completely unexpected visitors arrived at the ranch in Commander Northrop's Rolls motorcar. Petre spotted the car coming up the road and alerted Christina in the kitchen. She went to wake her father from his nap, while Petre hurried to the barn where Michael and Sambolo were shoeing a horse.

"Quick, Papa, the commander is back again!" Tomas rolled out of bed still in his clothes, adjusted his suspenders and went to the parlor. Michael came in still wearing his leather blacksmith's apron. Petre followed him in. "Now what? Is he going to collect some of my shaving cream this time?" Tomas said in a disgusted voice. When the knock came, he gestured for Michael to open it.

Michael yanked the door open. "Now what do you..." he started.

"Wolfgang! Wolfgang! It's Wolfgang!" Christina shouted. She and Tomas rushed to the door, throwing their arms around him.

He smiled and laughed, saying, "I'm home! Finally, ha." Petre came up and welcomed him back with a pat on the back and a hearty handshake.

"But how...how did you get out...get released?" Michael asked looking between his brother and the commander.

"I'll let Commander Northrop explain that." Wolfgang grinned as he turned to the commander. All eyes intensely focused on the man.

"Do come in, commander...and your other officers, please." Tomas ushered the group into the parlor. Christina kept hold of her older brother, hugging his arm and constantly looking up at his face.

"I'm so happy you're home...we were so worried." A tear trickled down her cheek.

"Sit down gentlemen, sit down, please." Tomas continued. Petre moved up several chairs for the group of seven. Sambolo looked on from the dining room doorway.

Commander Northrop approached as if ill at ease, but indicated for his two officers to sit.

"I'm sure this visit comes as a surprise to you and your family..." He looked around at the gathering, "but our investigation, which I feel has been thorough, has turned up certain 'facts' that have convinced me, and the military council investigating the second explosion at the powerhouse, that the evidence against Herr Mathais and Herr Conrad here was circumstantial at best." He nodded toward Wolfgang. "The Council agreed it is not necessary to hold him any longer. Therefore, we release him from incarceration unconditionally." Everyone was smiling and glad to have Wolfgang back home and hear that Markus was also cleared.

Petre brought in cool drinks for everyone as the commander continued, "I have here a copy of the transcript of the Council's deliberations detailing the evidence compiled. I felt you were entitled to a copy." He handed it to Tomas. "The evidence points to former Captain Perkins as the culprit who, probably alone, although we don't know that as fact, blew up the powerhouse using stolen artillery shells. He had access to them and professional knowledge as to how to detonate them. His rationale for perpetrating this crime is still conjecture. However, based on what we uncovered, it is highly unlikely that Wolfgang here, or Mathais had anything to do with it. We are pleased to release them both."

Again everyone thanked Northrop, asked questions and made comments on the unexpectedly happy event. After the room quieted down, Northrop continued, "However, the murder of Perkins, and it was murder, has not been resolved, and it is known that several members of your family held deep anger toward him. Rightly so, it could be said, on account of your son's unnecessary death." The Conrads' mood sobered on being reminded of Norbert. "That investigation continues, I must remind you. I hope no one here is in any way involved in that crime. As bad as Perkins turned out to be, it was still murder."

Tomas hastened to say, "Yes, of course, but no one in this family had anything to do with that."

"I hope so, Mr. Conrad. I know your family has been through a lot since the war. As for Markus Mathais and his wife and family, they can return without fear, except with the caveat that the murder investigation is ongoing and everyone, and I mean everyone, is still a suspect."

"Yes, yes, we understand," Michael said, and turning to his father, "We must wire Markus and Helena in Lisbon right away!"

"They went all the way to Lisbon?" the commander asked incredulously.

Royal Portuguese Flag

CHAPTER XXXI

In Lisbon, A Promise Kept: May 1921

L eopold was true to his word and offered Helena, Markus and the children a suite of rooms on the second floor of his 400 year old stone villa overlooking Lisbon harbor. It was a grand old mansion, small, but full of a lifetime of collecting African and Islamic art and specimens from the wilds of the dark continent.

The front entrance hall had two enormous elephant tusks on either side of the archway leading to an inner patio. Animal hides covered the floors: zebra, lion, leopard and a grotesque gorilla skin, head attached, sprawled in one of the rooms. Arab rugs and textiles and African masks covered the walls between heads from every animal that lived in Africa.

"Are they going to bite me?" asked little Rupert, as he hid behind his mother's skirt. As soon as he was shown he could touch the animal rugs without bites, he cut loose and ran through the rooms jumping and rolling on first one animal rug and then another.

A week after arriving in Portugal, a telegram arrived, in response to one letting the Conrads know the details of their near-brush with cholera and Leopold's generosity.

"Wonderful news, dearest! Wolfgang is out of prison, and we're both exonerated of all charges related to the powerhouse explosion!" Markus exclaimed, summarizing the lengthy first half of the telegram to his wife and Leopold. Helena was so happy with the news, she hugged first her husband and then Leopold.

"We can go home! Oh, Leopold, can you find us a boat going south?"

Leopold smiled at Helena's happily expectant face, then nodded at Markus. "Markus, why don't you finish reading the entire telegram."

"About that... Dearest, there's still a problem back home."

"What? What is it?"

He began to read the last part of the telegram. "Everyone is still a suspect in Captain Perkin's murder, leaving a threat and a danger to our entire family..." He frowned. "I think that means us especially, dear."

"What? But none of us had anything to do with that dreadful man's death! When will this all end?"

"Best be patient, Frau Helena," Leopold advised, "Best to let the authorities sort that crime out before going back home and drawing undue attention to yourselves. Anti-German sentiment is still strong since the war, and probably in high places."

"Leopold is right, dearest. Let's wait and see how things develop."

This didn't sit well with Helena but she knew her husband and Leopold were right. "But for how long? How long must we wait?" The two men were silent.

A few days later, after exchanging telegrams with his mother in Munich and with Levi at Kalvarianhof, Markus proposed an idea he had been harboring since arriving in Portugal. They were in their bedroom, the children asleep in an alcove, when Markus broached the topic to Helena. "I was talking to Leopold and he said there is an express train to Madrid, then on to Paris and then to Munich...we could be to my mother's in two or three days. We've come so far...I would really like to see my mother and Anji and, of course, Levi and Katherina. It's been over ten years since I've seen my family. What do you think?" He looked for a reaction from Helena, then added, "A quick trip to Munich might be just what we need to pass the time until things settle down back home in Windhoek."

Helena looked up at her husband, at his expectant expression and sighed softly. "How could I object to you seeing your mother after so long a time...after the war and the things that separated you from all you knew back then. Of course, darling...we have to wait before returning home, so let's spend the time with your family and friends in Germany. And your mother and sister will be so happy to meet Rupert and Charlotte."

"Thank you dear, we'll leave soon. I have one important duty to take care of before we leave for Germany. I have letters to deliver."

CHAPTER XXXII

Senhora Angelina de Monhona de Albuquerque: May 1921

I t did not take long for Leopold to discover the residence of General Albuquerque's daughter. It was in a fashionable district above the city, in what once was an elegant home. Now, behind high iron gates in need of black paint, stood the slowly crumbling villa of a once highly regarded general. His mysterious death...murder or suicide or...was never fully explained, but it's effect on his only daughter, now his only heir, was visible to all who passed by and took note of the old walled enclosure.

Leopold telephoned the villa. What sounded like the housekeeper answered. He asked the woman to summon the lady of the house, Senhora Angelina de Manhona de Albuquerque. "Yes, this is Angelina de Albuquerque. Who is speaking, please?"

Leopold replied, and as tactfully as possible, explained that a friend of General Albuquerque would like to visit with his daughter as this friend has something from the General for her.

"What? That seems impossible. My father has been dead for over fifteen years."

"Please senhora, be so gracious as to meet this man and his wife. They have come a long way...from Africa. They feel it is very important to see you...just for a brief meeting, if you would be so kind."

"Africa? Did you say Africa? Are you sure it was Africa?"

"Yes, senhora, from Portuguese East Africa via German South West Africa. It's a complicated story best told to you by my friends." Leopold listened for a reply.

It took a long time, and when the senhora replied, it was in a apprehensive, hesitant tone. "Yes, senhor Leopold," she said in a quivering voice, "I will meet these people. Would you like to come to my home? How soon may I expect them?"

"I have an automobile. We could actually meet this afternoon or tomorrow if you prefer."

"Do come this afternoon, senhor, with your friends, at three. I'll have Rosita open the gate for you." There was silence for a moment..."I can't imagine what this could be about concerning my father."

"We will be at your villa promptly at three, Senhora Albuquerque." With that Leopold hung up and turned to Markus and Helene and relayed the plan.

In the French made open touring car Leopold owned, the three adults and children bumped and swayed along the narrow curving road. Leopold relished swerving the turns at just a bit more speed than was safe.

"It's up this road a ways, we'll be there in ten minutes."

"Leopold, what happened here in Lisbon to the General that led him to disappear?" Helena shouted over the sound of rushing wind and road noises as she watched Leopold grip the wheel tightly.

"I've heard so much from Markus of Albuquerque's story in Africa and his tragic death there. However, the mystery of his supposed death...murder or suicide, here...it's such a strange story. And, of course, his emerging in the most distant lands of the Portuguese Empire, Portuguese East Africa...it's a story that can now be told."

"*Ja*, well, it comes down to Portuguese politics from before the Great War. The Portuguese king and his heir apparent were assassinated, and then General Albuquerque was swept into the intrigues of court. Between that and the revolutionary forces that sprang up he started making enemies, endangering his family, and in the middle of it he died. That was the story and everyone knew it. His scheme...that's what I think it was...was to secretly escape to the colonies. He arranged things to look like his enemies killed him or drove him to suicide, and they left his family here in Lisbon alone. He basically exiled himself to Africa so his family could live in peace." Leopold adjusted his hat and downshifted as he slowed for a tight curve in the cobblestone road.

"He even arranged a body for his coffin. There's a beautiful tomb here in Lisbon the family built for the general...with an unknown stranger in it. The family never knew." He smiled. "Clever!"

Rosita unlatched the heavy iron gates and with some effort swung the two halves open for the waiting automobile. Senhora Albuquerque stood motionless as the vehicle crunched across the gravel drive in front of the ornately carved and weathered doors.

Markus hopped out and assisted Helena and the children as Leopold came round. The little group from Africa stood looking up to the general's daughter as Leopold made introductions. Passing through a large entry hall, they were led past a stately reception room with furniture draped in white cloth.

"We don't use most of the rooms since mother died several years ago. Here, we will be comfortable in my parlor," she said leading them into a small but lovely space showing signs of daily use. The little group sat on an assortment of Baroque chairs and couches, covered in red velvet, soft to the touch. "Rosita, please bring our guests coffee." Angelina ushered everyone to seats.

Little Rupert spied a large open box of toys in a corner of the room. The Senhora noticed, "Yes, my son's toys when he was your age." She leaned toward the boy. "You can play with them if you like." Rupert looked to his mother and scampered to them at her nod.

Rosita brought in the coffee and a plate of cookies on exquisite china. After Angelina served everyone, she said in a hesitant voice, "Now, what did you want to tell me about my father?"

Markus began as only he felt he could. "Senhora Albuquerque, I knew your father. He was a great and a noble man. I would say I cherished him as one of my dearest, truest friends. He helped me many times and even saved my life more than once. This all happened in Africa, during the Great War. But I should start from the beginning. It was…"

Senhora Angelina's hand went to her throat and her trembling hand rattled the coffee cup into the saucer.

"That cannot be! He died here in Lisbon during…Africa! Africa! Oh," she moaned, "The rumors were true…true!" she sobbed. "Mother could not bring herself to believe them, but I knew, I knew…I felt it, I felt he was still alive." She burst into uncontrollable sobbing. Little Rupert, looking on, ran to his mother.

"It's all right Rupert, darling. Senhora is just sad at the moment." Markus took his son as Helena got up, went over to her on the couch, and sat beside senhora Angelica, offering comfort and Markus' handkerchief.

"We know this must be such a shock to you senhora. I'm sorry that it is, but you deserve to hear the true and noble story of your dear father, and how much he loved you and your mother." Helena signaled to Markus that he should continue.

"Would you like me to continue, Senhora Albuquerque?"

Angelina blew her nose, sniffling a bit, "Yes, Yes, of course, please." Rosita, long time housekeeper to the family and another who remembered General Albuquerque, stood by the door wiping away her tears. Markus began the long, convoluted story of his first encounter with Angelina's father at an isolated military post in Portuguese East Africa. That led to stories of his further encounters with the general and finally to his tragic death, as well as the small bundle of letters given to Markus for his daughter. At the General's deathbed on a muddy rain-soaked battlefield, Markus had promised to deliver the letters to Lisbon.

"Here are the letters you father wanted me to deliver to you, senhora." Markus got up, crossed over to the two women sitting on the couch and in a solemn gesture, using both hands, offered the letters to Senhora Albuquerque. She accepted them, held them in her hands in her lap. Her watery eyes looked down at the tightly tied string, at the dirty, crumpled envelopes, each with her name in a lovely cursive script that even now she recognized as her father's.

She gazed at them for a long time in stillness. These battered missives from the past, from a memory of a man long gone from her life but never from her heart. She sat there and began to cry softly, her head bowed over the bundle, tears dripping on her lap. Helena moved close, put her hand on Angelina's shoulder. "These are a wonderful gift from a loving father. Know that you were in his heart always."

Angelina picked up the letters, held them to her chest. "Yes, and thank you so very much, Senhor Mathais, Senhor Leopold, and Senhora Mathais. Thank you from the bottom of my heart. I will tell my son of the stories you told me of his grandfather...of the truth of his life. You have brought me a wondrous gift from my father...it will comfort me forever."

They were silent driving back to Leopold's home, drained emotionally by the encounter with Senhora Albuquerque, but knowing the pure satisfaction brought by fulfilling a sacred promise.

CHAPTER XXXIII
Munich: November 1921

They're coming, they're coming! Markus and Helena are in Lisbon and are coming by train in three days!" Anji, Markus' sister, bubbled to her mother as Frau Mathais stumbled through the door of her apartment in Munich carrying groceries. "A telegram just arrived from Lisbon, Mama! It's from Markus! Oh, this is wonderful...after ten years, Markus is coming home!"

Fany Mathais, dumping her net bag bulging with potatoes and a fish wrapped in newspaper, exclaimed, "What? When are they coming? Are you sure...are the children with them? Oh, my boy, finally, he'll be home." She read and reread the telegram, as the two of them, danced around in circles with tears of joy. "We must make room for them...where will they all sleep?" She handed the telegram back to Anji.

"Three days, about three days, that means they may be here in two days! Anji, you must call the Levis, they'll be so excited! They'll want to know, to come visit."

And it was a wonderful homecoming. Everyone was at the train station in Munich to greet them: Anji, her husband Johan and their one year old daughter Hannah, as well as Markus' mother Fany, the entire Levi family including Levi, Katherina, and their children, Rebecca and Karl, just born this past November 1st. Also with them were the senior Levis Otto and Friedl, and Levi's sister, Ilsa, and her husband Rolf.

Those who knew Markus before the war were startled by the facial scars he suffered in Africa, and tried to avoid staring during an afternoon coffee reception at Frau Mathais' apartment. There were three deep purple scratches crossing his forehead, nose and cheek at a diagonal, with several lesser lines to each side. He was lucky to have survived the attack of the leopard and not lost an eye. Later, off to one side, Frau Mathais touched with light fingers the long deep scars made by the leopard eight years ago.

"Oh, my dear son, you suffered so."

"Not so much, Mama...most suffered more. I'm fine, really."

"And what's this business about a power plant explosion and you and Helena having to leave your home?"

"It's a big misunderstanding, Mama. We'll return home after our visit. Don't you worry." Levi and Katherina embraced Markus, Levi patted his friend saying, "Here you are, back in Bavaria. We've all looked forward to for...years really. You must come out to Kalvarianhof soon. It's the same old place. We have so much to catch up on, especially in your present circumstances. And look how our families have grown. If the political situation would just stabilize, *ja*?"

In mid-November, Anji drove her brother Markus and his family out to Kalvarianhof. "I'll bring Mama out for dinner on Sunday. That gives you three whole days to catch up on the news with Levi!" she laughed gaily and addressing Markus said, "Remember, you promised to walk in the woods with all of us before the snow gets too deep."

Helena, not used to snow from growing up in Africa, joked, "It gets deeper than this? It's up to my ankles!" Everyone in the car laughed.

To see again the dirt lane through the woods from the village, with a light dusting of snow just covering a carpet of leaves, and the rich damp smell of a winter forest, brought back so may memories for Markus. Wonderful thoughts of he and Levi hunting these woods in the fall, running and playing on sunny summer days and riding the farm wagons loaded with hay or cabbages—these images and more floated through his mind. He recalled the many forest walks with family and friends...and the illicit secret passion of he and Ilsa that one night—true but forbidden love and now a distant memory.

The old manor house loomed before them as Anji's car cut new tracks in the light snow. She tooted her horn and the little family piled out. Markus dragged the battered suitcase with their meager belongings meant for a tropical month in Angola.

Helena wore a light fall jacket that Anji gave her that was a gift from Katherina. Again, warm greetings, Katherina, recognizing her gift on Helena, said, "Tomorrow we are going into Munich to buy you and the children some warm winter clothes. Look at Rupert, that borrowed sweater hangs down to his shoes! And poor little Charlotte." As a matter of fact, Rupert was running around in circles dragging a stick through the snow, having a grand time, oblivious to the unaccustomed cold.

That evening, after a sumptuous dinner of roasted rabbit, creamed potatoes, pickled beets and a carrot salad followed by a five layered chocolate cake with raspberry jam layers, everyone retired happily to bed, except Markus and Levi and Otto. Finishing his Schnapps, Otto said, "Well, I'm off to bed, too."

They sat in the alcove of the kitchen, at the pine table and benches so worn with use, drinking schnapps and smoking cigarettes. The two war veterans reminisced their almost five years of fighting in Africa.

"We survived the bullets and bombs and all those diseases, and even the influenza...lucky I guess...and that terrible spider bite, remember?"

"*Ja*, I do." Markus hesitated a moment, "Do you ever think it will be back to what it used to be, Levi, back before the war, after all the killing and hardships and separation?"

His friend drew deeply, the blue smoke puffing out his nostrils, and when he spoke, smoke came out with the words.

"You've only been here a short time, my friend, and haven't seen what I've seen in Munich. There's fighting in the streets between the socialists, and monarchists, and communists, and now these new agitators the fascists, like the ones in Italy. All of them are against the Weimar Republic. How can a young democracy function when half the country is fighting in the streets!" He crushed out his cigarette and took up his drink.

"So, I hope things settle down soon politically. You've heard, of course, how the allies blame us for the war and that damned Versailles Treaty. It's more like...no, it is a surrender document...it's got most everybody here boiling mad. And don't get me started on the reparations the allies are demanding. Wilson promised no reparations, remember? No taking land, no blaming one party for the war. But the English and French want revenge. They'll bankrupt the country for a dozen years." He looked at his friend for a reaction.

"*Ja*, I'm sorry Markus, you've got your own troubles here in Germany."

"Mama just received a telegram from Richard...he's a good friend, a South African. He gave me a job when I got back from the war. The telegram says...well, I've got it right here, you read it yourself." Markus dug it out of his vest pocket and handed it over when Levi reached over for it.

> To Fanny Mathais
> Inform Markus/Helena Commander Northrop
> claims evidence linking Helena to Perkin's
> death Stop Do not return now Stop Details
> in letter to follow Stop All else fine Stop
> Christina and I engaged to marry Stop
> Signed Richard Thomas

Levi looked astonished "Helena, involved in this Perkins's death? How could that be? Does she know about this?" Levi handed the telegram back to Markus, looking at him intently.

Markus said, "No, no, Mama just gave it to me and asked what to do. I told her to say nothing to Helena until I spoke to you. Mama is also very upset, but I told her she had to be strong and not show too obvious concern when Helena finds out. What do you think? I've got to tell her, and soon. She's going to be very upset being accused like that. And of course, it's another delay in going home...this is just beyond belief...what has happened to us and the whole Conrad family since I got home. We've done nothing!" His shoulders slumped as he shook his head. Levi heard the hurt and anguish in Markus' voice and spoke gently to his friend.

"This surely will be resolved in your favor, Markus." You must tell Helena that, and remind her she is safe and among caring family and friends here. We will do everything possible to help." He hesitated, "What about a good lawyer?"

Markus replied "It's still run by the South African Military down there. It's in the hands of this Captain Northrop and his military tribunal." They both sat in silence, each in his own thoughts.

"Is he...fair, this Captain Northrop?"

"Yes...yes, I think so. He found in favor of my innocence twice now...first when the turbine blew up and when he finally decided Perkins blew up the plant with artillery shells. So, if he gets the facts, I think he'll be fair."

"Well, that's something. Can you think of any reason why this commander would think Helena is involved in Perkins' death?"

"No, no...except that strange business of Helena's cosmetics. He took bits of it in little papers, and bits of Christina's too. You think Helena's powders linked her to Perkins?"

"I don't know, but I'm sure you'll hear. What of Christina, has she been accused?"

"As far as I know she's not under suspicion, but at this point I feel it's almost a matter of time.

Munich

CHAPTER XXXIV
A Bit Of Powder: November 1921

Helena took the news badly. Markus made sure Anji was home in her mother's apartment when Frau Mathais read the telegram to Helena. They were sitting in the large parlor overlooking the park.

"What? Accuse me of...Markus!" she cried, "Why are they doing this to us...I just want to go home...I want to see Papa and my brothers!" She leaned in onto Markus shoulder crying as Anji, sitting to her side, rested her hand on her sister-in-law's back.

"I know this is hard my dear sister...and so unjust. I'm sure your father and Wolfgang and Richard and Christina are doing everything they can..."

"God is punishing me, he must be. Markus, what have I done to deserve this, this...all of it, everything!" She wailed uncontrollably, upsetting everyone in the room.

Markus, a tear trickling down his face, answered quickly, "No, no...dearest, He is not punishing you...you have done nothing, my dearest, nothing." He wiped his cheek with the back of his hand and held Helena closely in his arms.

Frau Mathais rung her hands in anguish, seeing her brave daughter-in-law so distraught. She stepped to them and patted Helena head, "It will all be over soon, it will all work out somehow...we love you Helena, you'll see." She turned away, sat down across from her son and daughter and poor Helena, and slumped in exhaustion, dabbing her eye.

Later Markus called Dr. Rungi, the village doctor and old family friend. He graciously agreed to come into Munich to see what he could do for Helena. Levi called and inquired how Helena had taken the news.

"Badly, I'm afraid." Markus said, "I've sent for Dr. Rungi and he's coming in to town. It's so good of him, I'm sure he never sees patients in Munich." There was a pause in the line, "Wait a minute Markus, Katherina wants to say something."

"Hello, Markus, I've been listening, I'm so sorry for Helena and you..."

"She won't get out of bed, she won't eat anything. Mama is beside herself. Anji stays with Helena all day...I don't know what to do. I called Dr. Rungi, he agreed to come in the morning and..."

"That's a good idea. He helped me when I needed it, do you remember?"

"Yes, he should be able to help. I certainly hope so."

"Would you like me to come in town, I could relieve Anji if nothing else."

"Yes please. That would be...do come. Mama says yes, and stay over."

"I'll be in on the afternoon train, the three-forty. Levi will come, too, but he'll only stay a short while." She looked over to her husband; he nodded agreement. She hung the receiver back on the hook. "What an impossible situation, they've been through so much already. I'll pack a few things."

The three-forty arrived on time in Munich, and the Levi's took a cab to the Mathais' apartment. Anji met them at the door, looking exhausted. "Thanks for coming. You're a godsend." Levi and Katherina stepped into the quiet entry hall. Anji took the small satchel from Katherina and ushered them into the parlor.

"She's quiet now, but she only sleeps a short while. I think she's having bad dreams. Something's wrong. It's more than just being angry and fearful, she seems lost in her own world. Mama and Markus are lying down. They're both worn out. Peek in on her if you like. Can I get you anything...coffee?"

"No, no, we came to help, not be a burden, we're fine. You look like you need a rest, too. Really, why don't you lie down. We'll sit with her."

"Yes, thank you, I'll rest for a while." Levi ended up staying the night, as he and Markus shared brandy in the front parlor till late. Katherina helped Fanny make a light supper for everyone with Anji and Katherina taking in the meal to Helena. She was awake and sat on the edge of the bed to nibble some food, sip a bit of beer, and then laid back down, a hollow look in her eyes. As she rolled over, her back to the two women, she whispered "They want to hurt us like they did Arnold and Norbert and Humboldt. But Papa will protect me, I know it. We just have to leave everything to Papa."

The two women looked at each other, Katherina's eyes wide with concern. "She's been like this for two days. When little Rupert comes around she just hugs him till he wants to get down and play. Same with the baby. Markus has been wonderful with the children, but he's at his wits end about how to help Helena. She is just so melancholy and depressed."

A letter arrived the next day with the noon delivery, just as Doctor Rungi was closing his black bag. "Give her one pill twice a day, with a third one if she has an episode. They should calm her nerves and perk her up. But you must keep the bottle out of her hands. Too many at once can cause problems. I'll telephone tomorrow. Don't you worry, she'll be alright."

"So good of you to come doctor," Markus said.

Katherina also stepped forward and greeted the old doctor. "Herr Doctor Rungi, I will always be grateful to you for helping me before the war, and now here you are helping Helena. You are a true blessing on our family."

"It's so good to see you and Levi happy and your family together after the war. I pray we never see another one like it." He stood to take his leave. "Until tomorrow."

The letter was addressed to Markus Mathais, care of Frau Fanny Mathais. Markus sat on the sofa and opened the three page letter with writing on both sides.

Everyone, including Helena, sat attentively as Markus read the letter to himself, flipping the pages quickly as his eyes scanned each line. He nodded to himself on several occasions and finally looked up. Helena sat next to him, took the letter, and began reading but stopped when her husband began.

"The gist of it is that investigators found traces of women's cosmetics on Perkins' arm and shirt. They assume he struggled with his assailants and it rubbed off there. The powder matches some they found in Helena's bedroom, and on that evidence, she's a suspect. However, three women at Madam Wilhelmina Oldendorf's, er, 'house' also use the same cosmetic...a Heidi something, couldn't read the name, and two other women. They arrested all three on suspicion of murder. Apparently William and Christina knew Heidi and are trying to help her. Richard Thomas, he wrote the letter, says we should stay away as Helena would just be arrested too.

"I seem to recall Helena buying that powder at the dry goods store in Windhoek. There must be a dozen women in town who bought it as well.

Surely that's no reason to arrest someone."

Katherina leaned back and rested her hands on her skirt. "Yes, but they figure she and this Heidi had some motive to kill Perkins that other women with that same powder apparently didn't have."

"If you ask me, that seems like very slim evidence," Levi said, "too circumstantial to arrest anyone on. Here in Bavaria I don't believe that would hold up in court."

"Unfortunately this is happening in a defeated country," Markus offered, "occupied by the victors, in an investigation being carried out by a military court some members of which still see we Germans as the enemy. It's not like justice in Bavaria, even in these times."

"But still, it is pretty shaky evidence, isn't it?" asked Fanny. "What other evidence is there?" There was silence in the room for a long time.

Finally, Markus began, "Mama, it's a long story..."

Later, after everyone had retired for the night, Levi and Markus sat smoking and drinking schnapps. Levi wanted to broach a subject he had been thinking about ever since the Mathais' arrival.

"Markus, have you ever thought about returning? I mean coming back home, bringing your family...living here in Germany again. With your skills and experience, you could easily secure a position, a good position with any number of firms." He waited keenly for an answer from his friend. Markus crushed out his cigarette and emptied his glass.

"*Ja*, well, it's crossed my mind, really several times, but Helena has her family, her brothers and sisters and Tomas, and the ranch. She loves the country life and ranching." He trailed off and was silent a moment. "And I've grown to like it as well...the family, my brothers and sisters in law...and I have a good job rebuilding that transmitting station with Richard. I told you about Richard, he's a fine friend. So, Levi, I don't see moving back here in our immediate future."

"Well, Germany will welcome you back if you ever change your mind. Time for bed."

CHAPTER XXXV

Earlier in Windhoek: March 1921

Y ou can't hold her indefinitely on circumstantial evidence, sir. This is an outrage, she's just a young girl!"

"This 'girl' is nineteen and a woman of the world," he said with emphasis on "girl" and "woman" both. "We can hold her as long as we want. She's suspected of murder, remember?" Michael and Christina Conrad were pleading their case for Heidi Roth with Commander Northrop.

"What would you have me do? We can't just let someone loose who is suspected of a capital offence." The commander's voice was forceful but almost sympathetic. All three were silent for a moment.

"What if you released her to us, if we vouched for her, guaranteed she would not run away or anything...she could stay out at our ranch," Christina offered. She looked at Michael for support. He furled his eyebrows but said nothing.

"Look you two," the commander shook his head, "if I ever got into trouble, I'd want the likes of you two to be on my side." He had a thin smile on his face. "I'll tell you what. If Herr Tomas Conrad agrees to take full responsibility for Heidi, to be held accountable for her every action, I will consider releasing her to his custody while the investigation continues. But," he said sharply, "if any new evidence turns up against Miss Roth, she comes back into my custody. Agreed?"

Both their faces lit up with broad smiles. "Yes, yes, of course. Agreed!"

"Remember your father takes full responsibility for her. We'll have this in writing."

"Right, yes sir, thank you sir." Christina said, extending her hand out.

The commander reluctantly shook her hand, and waved them out. As they left, he thought, *If Herr Conrad agrees with this, he's a saint and a fool...but with those two barking at his heels with pleas of mercy, he'll probably do it.*

Outside the Commander's office, Michael turned to his sister, "You want to bring Heidi out to the ranch? What's she going to do out there? Papa will never agree to being responsible for a, a..."

"A what, a prostitute? Michael! She's suffered terribly, and we practically grew up with her. She's got no one...except Madam Oldendorf, bless her soul. If she hadn't taken her in, even to *that* house, where would Heidi be now? We have to help her, right, Michael?"

"*Ja, ja* I guess so, it's just that...well, we've got to convince Papa. Do you think he'll go along with this? Sign to be responsible for her and all?"

"That's why our job is to convince Papa to let us bring Heidi to the ranch.

Later that week, in Commander Northrop's office, "She's surprised, and apprehensive about your offer," the Commander said while looking over the paperwork. Tomas Conrad, two sons, and his daughter and her fiancé, Richard, looked on. A light rap on the door brought a military police guard into the Commander's office with Heidi in a gray prison dress. Northrop dismissed the guard with a nod.

"Please sit down Miss Roth." He indicated an empty chair next to Christina, facing his desk. He turned to Heidi and, looking her straight in the eye, said, "This is very serious business, young lady. Herr Conrad is willing to take you into his home while you are a suspect in a most serious investigation. It is a grave responsibility for the Conrads, and a very generous offer."

She watched him stare at her. "You must stay out of trouble, any trouble. This includes your current mode of employment." Heidi looked away, then down at her hands. "This agreement states you are to report here on a weekly basis. Any violation of the conditions we spoke about earlier, and you will return to prison. Is that understood?"

In a voice just above a whisper she said, "Yes, yes sir."

"Good. Then we simply must have your signature here, Herr Conrad. That concludes this business...good luck to you with your charge." He nodded toward Tomas. He looked over to Christina and Michael. "That will be all. Good day."

The ride back to the ranch in Richard's car was awkward with Heidi saying very little and Christina being especially attentive. "I got some clothes laid out for you, Heidi, and we have an extra bedroom...Well, it belonged to one of my brothers, but it's just down the hall from my bedroom. We thought you could help in the kitchen and there are all sorts of things to do around the ranch...of course, you know that, being a farm girl yourself."

Over the next few weeks Heidi warmed to her new home and dove into what needed to be done around the ranch house and the barn. Sambolo at first complained. "No Miss Heidi, this is my work, you don't have to muck out the stables."

He finally gave up after Wolfgang took him aside and told him to let her do it. "Heidi needs to feel useful, she needs to work. She came from a poor farm family where everyone worked all day, every day."

In the kitchen and the rest of the ranch house, it was the same thing. Petre observed Heidi taking every opportunity to be useful, clearing the table after meals and doing the scullery work in the sinks. "She works very hard, this Miss Heidi, maybe too hard."

The whole Conrad clan took special care to make the young woman, fresh out of prison, feel welcome and useful. Heidi soon began to smile and to laugh at simple jokes and mealtime banter.

"Let's have a family picnic after church this Sunday," Christina suggested. "Maybe up among that pretty grove of trees you spared from the axe, Papa. Remember those pretty trees?" It was decided, and Petre and the women prepared a generous spread to be picked up after church.

The Conrads filed into St. Joseph's parish church in Windhoek as usual, with Heidi attending for the first time. Christina and Heidi wore colorful dresses and hats and worn white gloves. The familiar hymns were stirring, the candles twinkled on the altar, the sun streamed through the stained glass windows in a rainbow of colors, the smell of incense and the jangling of the offertory bells all contributed to an otherworldly experience. It always put the parishioners in a warm, friendly mood as little groups of neighbors gathered in front of the stone church after the Catholic mass.

The usual friends exchanged greetings and light conversation, although several male parishioners scurried off on seeing Heidi with the Conrads. Both Christina and Tomas noted the swift exit and surmised that they probably had visited Madame Oldendorf's establishment and had seen Heidi there, or worse. Several ladies in a small group stared at Heidi disapprovingly. Heidi drew in close to Christina and Wolfgang, and as one, the Conrads turned their backs to the ladies.

In his kind way, Tomas announced, "Time to go on that picnic you all have prepared."

Just as he spoke, a commotion broke out on the side of the church. Wolfgang was first to recognize his brother Michael swinging wildly in a fight with one of the other young men.

"Keep your dirty mouth shut or I'll shut it for you!" he shouted. The two rolled on the ground jabbing at each other, as Father Lorraine came out of the rectory attached to the church.

"What is going on here, stop this immediately! For shame, fighting on sacred ground!" The two fighters were pulled apart by onlookers. Everyone looked to the priest for direction. "What do you have to say for yourselves? You first, Fritz." Fritz was nursing a very bloody nose. He squinted and dragged his sleeve across his face.

"I just said, Father...I just commented on Michael's new girlfriend and...and her present...er, former employment...I didn't..."

"You called her a whore, you bastard!" Michael lunged at Fritz but was intercepted by strong arms.

"Stop it you two! Into my office, now! By all the saints, I'll have none of this!" The two young men quieted and sheepishly followed the priest into the rectory.

"It's my fault. I shouldn't have come." whimpered Heidi, "I've been bad, I'm dirty...I want to go...I..." She starting to cry. Wolfgang put his arm around her and held here tight, saying, "No, no, you're a lovely young woman, and as good as anyone in church this morning." The Conrads began to file back to Richard's car.

"What about Michael?" asked Christina.

Tomas answered. "We'll just wait for him. Father Lorraine won't keep them long, although he's going to expect them in his confessional before next Sunday."

Michael reappeared moments later, his right eye swollen almost shut. "Father Lorraine gave me a cold cloth...and one to Fritz. I'm fine, really."

Heidi was very quiet on the ride back to the ranch, and the quietness was awkward. Christina tried to cheer her by saying, "Oh, don't pay any attention to those people, they're not even good Catholics."

"Yes, but... this happened because of me. Michael is hurt because of me."

Heidi refused to attend Sunday Mass for several weeks. It was agreed that one of the Conrad men, either Wolfgang or Michael, would stay behind. Heidi and whomever stayed behind went for horseback rides in the morning and then helped Petre prepare Sunday dinner in the early afternoon.

On this particular Sunday Michael and Heidi rode out up to the pretty grove of trees Tomas had saved. "It's so cool up here, let's rest the horses." The two slid out of their saddles and tied the reins to low branches.

"I love it out here, away from town and people," she said, "I like the dry season and the wet season. All the colors change and the birds change as different ones come and go." They walked in among the ancient trees.

"Look, see there, with the blue wings and red neck, a, a, oh, I've forgotten the name." The little bird hopped around as the two watched intently. "I never thanked you for standing up for me at the church." She turned to Michael, both standing close. "Thank you Michael, it was brave of you." She leaned in and gave him a quick kiss on the cheek. She pulled away, and headed back to the horses. He touched his cheek and watched her as he followed toward their mounts.

"Here, let me give you a boost up." He cupped his hands for her to step in. As she raised her leg his hands parted, slid up her sides and pulled her to him in a spontaneous kiss. He was swimming in passion. She did not resist but finally pushed gently. Michael broke off the kiss. Heidi took a little step back.

"I...I've wanted to do that, to kiss you, since you came to the ranch, even before," he said. He looked down, then slowly looked up.

Heidi brushed her wind-tossed hair away from her face. "Your father would not like it...if he knew you kissed me." Quickly she followed with, "but it was kind of you to do it, Michael...I mean, it, it was...very special." She turned away from him and added, "Your father would send me away, if he found out, send me back to prison." She looked down, a tear on her cheek.

"No, no, Papa would never do that!" He came up to her and brushed away her tear. "He wouldn't." She looked up to him and he swept her into his arms.

In the shade of the trees Michael was consumed with desire for the young body he held, she feeling the same but fearful of the consequences. She let him run his hands over her body, over her small breasts and shoulders and backside. Finally she whispered, "Everyone will be back from church soon and I have to help Petre." He gave her a last kiss and this time, cupped his hands to help her remount for the short ride back to the ranch house.

It wasn't long before Christina noticed the glances, the body language, the way they moved around each other. *I know something's going on between those two. Should I say something, ask him?* She decided to say nothing, and watch and wait.

Wolfgang noticed the closeness building between the two almost as quickly. He came to Christina, saying, "Can you see it too? I'm sure

Michael is infatuated, what with an attractive young woman living just down the hall from his room."

"Well, let's keep an eye on them. It's the best way to keep Michael out of trouble," she said.

CHAPTER XXXVI

The Wishes of Love: April 1921

They were laying in the hayloft of the barn, their secret meeting place. They had a hidden light blanket there. Everyone was in town or out somewhere on the ranch. Michael still had his shirt on, Heidi lay nude next to him. They had been making love, intense love for months, every chance they found to be together.

"Michael dear, I...we are going to have a baby." Heidi was on her back, one hand on her tummy and looking up at him. Her perfectly white skin was always an erotic sight. Michael was hard for her as soon as she slipped out of her dress or skirt. He was on his back next to her, staring at the heavy beams above them. He was silent for seconds then sat up.

"What? Are you sure? How can you tell? I mean, I love you, but are you sure?" He reached over and put his hand on top of hers. She sat up, coming very close, her apprehension clear to see. He took her head in his hands and kissed her. Tears rose in her eyes. He kissed them gently and could taste the salt. Her arms went around his neck as he eased her down. They made love tight against one another, trying to say without words that they would stay together, no matter what. They whispered to each other their hopes and fears.

"We'll get married, like Christina and Richard are going to do in September. What do you think, Heidi, maybe about the same time...or should it be sooner?"

"We have to tell your father, and Christina. I'm so worried what they will say."

"Yes...yes, of course. It's going to be a big shock to everyone. Maybe we should just say we want to get married. What do you think? I mean, nobody knows. They can't know, right? I mean, nothing's showing now, not for months, right?"

"Michael, there may be complications. I saw some at...at Madame Oldendorf's. But sometimes there isn't anything till later." She looked at her lover. "Oh Michael, I do so want to marry you...let's ask to be married, and then, later, we can tell them. Or maybe we won't have to tell anyone. Oh, I don't know what to do. Michael?"

"I'll talk to Papa. I'll say we want to get married right away...no, I'll just say soon. I'm sure he'll let me do what I want, let us, and he likes you, you know that. So does Christina and everybody. It'll be all right, I'm sure of it."

"But what if they find out about...me? There might be a scandal, Commander Northrop might put me back in jail!"

"Heidi, Heidi, that's not going to happen! Don't think like that. It's going to be all right for both of us." They laid there in each other's arms, in their own thoughts, in the loft of the old barn, for a long time. Finally, "It's time to go."

In the ranch house, the two lovers encountered Christina reading a book in the parlor. They were holding hands...actually Heidi was holding Michael's upper arm with both hands. Christina nodded casually at them, and then took a second look. Michael looked at Heidi, then back to Christina. "We have an announcement to make. Heidi and I are..."

Christina interrupted him. "You want to get married, am I right?" She smiled. I knew there was something special between the two of you!" She grinned happily at the two young lovers. Heidi stood sheepishly but with a smile on her face. Michael beamed like a tourist hunter bagging his first antelope.

Christina asked excitedly, "What did Papa say, Michael? Did you tell him? When did you decide to get married?" She stepped toward Heidi and hugged her. "Oh, I'm so happy for you...for both of you! Wolfgang and I, we both thought there was a, an attraction between you. Wait 'til Helena hears her little brother is engaged! Won't it be grand, two weddings!"

Tomas Conrad walked in on the conversation smiling broadly and exclaimed, "I can tell you when Michael and Heidi asked me...it was five minutes ago in the kitchen. Petre was a witness, am I right Michael?" Tomas let out a mighty roar of delight, and slapped his youngest son on the back. He winked at Heidi.

"Now maybe I'll get more grandchildren around here. And just in time, we can use more ranch hands! Ha!" They all laughed and came close into a happy group hug. Christina, always the observant one, noted the twitch in the eye of Heidi as she glanced at Michael when Tomas mentioned grandchildren.

Wolfgang chose that moment to walk in. "What's all the merriment?"

"Your youngest brother here is engaged to our darling Heidi! What do you think of that?" Tomas again let out his characteristic hoot.

"What? Really?" He looked at all the beaming faces. His face lit up, too. Well I'll be! Congratulations Heidi, Michael!" He hugged Heidi gently and gave his brother a bear hug that lifted Michael off his feet. Turning to his soon-to-be sister-in-law, he said, "I always knew Michael would get in trouble, living so near to a pretty woman!" he gloated, as laughs again rang through the house.

CHAPTER XXXVII

Commander Northrop: July 1921

I t was late in July of 1921 when Commander Northrop steered his tan army vehicle to a halt in front of the ranch house he had visited so many times before. Petre answered the door and ushered the Commander into the parlor. Everyone was there, seated, waiting for him as he requested in his phone call.

"Good day Herr Conrad," he began, nodding to everyone else. Heidi sat with Michael on the couch holding hands that were nervous with sweat. She was nearly shaking and the Commander took note.

"First of all I want to say that I bring good news," he began in a very formal tone. "That is, it's good news for your family." He looked at Heidi and gave the slightest smile. Everyone came to rapt attention.

"As you all know I have been conducting a very extensive investigation...two really. The first and most important is of course, concerning the death...murder of Captain Perkins, late of the South African Army. A number of people are suspects in that crime. Certain motives and circumstantial evidence links these suspects to the crime." He paused, cleared his throat and continued. "After months of inquiry, no further evidence has been obtained linking any of these suspects...these people to the crime. As chief investigator and military judge presiding over this case, I have concluded that it would be unfair to hold the several people concerned to any restrictions that have been imposed. Therefore, I am here to tell you that Miss Heidi Roth and Frau Helena Mathais and her husband Markus, and the two other women held in custody, are free agents and are no longer held to any restrictions. As time slips by, I fear this crime must remain unsolved as other pressing needs occupy the court's time."

A silent pause followed the commander's words as the significance sunk in. Heidi radiated a smile as she hugged Michael. Christina practically shouted

"Helena and Markus can come home...we can all be together again! Isn't this wonderful Papa, everybody can be together again!"

"Yes, yes," Tomas said, "This is wonderful news. We'll wire Markus and Helena first thing tomorrow."

The commander raised his hand slightly as he had something to add. "There is also the issue of the mysterious disappearance of Captain Llewellyn, who was billeted here at the Conrad ranch for several years. No word of his whereabouts has ever been determined and so that case remains open. Again, given the passage of time and our limited resources, no further efforts will be undertaken to find him at this time."

Michael and Christina looked at each other, Tomas caught the look and winced. *Don't react you two, we don't need that case reopened.*

Northrop moved to the edge of his seat, looked at Tomas, and continued. "I wanted to personally deliver this news to you, Herr Conrad and your family. We've had our issues, and more than a fair number of...stressful... encounters. I want you to know, from the perspective of the court, you and yours are once more regular members of the community, free to come and go and pursue their worldly ambitions. I regret the discomfort you've experienced during these investigations. I assure you it was not my intent."

He paused, looked around at the staring faces, and got up. "Thank you for your time, all of you. Now if you'll excuse me, I must return to my duties in town."

"Yes, of course." Tomas said getting up, as did the others. "Thank you for coming, for personally delivering this wonderful news. It is such a great relief for all of us." He, Wolfgang and Richard escorted Commander Northrop to his car.

Through the open car window, Tomas said: "We always felt you acted fairly in your inquiries. We did, and still do, appreciate that. I just wanted you to know."

Northrop looked out at the old man standing beside the car, looked away and then said, "Thank you for those kind words. Auf Werderschen."

As the commander's car made a wide arc in front of the ranch house, stirring up a haze of dust, Wolfgang looked across the vista before him, studying west at the far horizon. He stared for a long moment, then touched his father's arm.

"What do you make of that, Papa? Way off to the west, do you see what I see?" Tomas turned back and squinted in that direction, as did

Richard.

All three men stared for several minutes. Finally Richard said, "Is that smoke? It looks like it's coming up on the far side of Windhoek."

"*Ja*, it looks like fire. What's over there, the hotel?" Wolfgang said.

"They look like storm clouds to me." Tomas offered.

"This time of year?" Richard asked. "We never get clouds like that so early."

Wolfgang added, "*Ja*, the rain isn't due for a few months. Besides, even if those are storm clouds, the chance of them making it this far from the coast...?" He didn't finish the comment as he turned to go back in.

CHAPTER XXXVIII
Munich: August 1921

To Markus Mathais
Good news Stop Commander Northrop lifted
all restrictions/accusations on Helena and
Markus, Heidi Roth, and others Stop Free to
return home Stop Christina and Richard to
marry Stop Heidi and Michael engaged Stop
Love, best wishes to all Stop
Signed Wolfgang Conrad

"Markus, we just couldn't wait for you to get home! There's a telegram from Wolfgang with the most wonderful news! We can go home! God has finally blessed us." Helena could not contain her happiness as she handed the telegram to her husband, throwing her arms around his neck even as Markus struggled to read the telegram.

Katherina, who was visiting the Mathais family, had already telephoned her husband at work and then called the Levis at Kalvarianhof, and her parents and brothers in Potsdam as well. "Everyone is delighted for you and your family, and they want you to know it." Kathi said to Markus and Helena.

Rupert, overhearing the conversation, joined in with, "I want to go home too. I want to see Opa and Oma and my friends at school. When are we going, Mama? When are we going?"

"Soon dear, soon."

Markus picked up Rupert with a grunt. "Oh, you are getting to be a big boy. Did you hear Mama? We'll be going home very soon. Are you happy about that?"

"Yaaaaay!" Markus put his son down and Rupert ran away to play.

Markus looked at Helena. "I believe we both feel the same way as Rupert, don't you think, dearest? It's been wonderful being here again with Mama and Anji and her husband, and for you to be able to visit the Levis, but after everything...just knowing it's safe to go home...it just sounds like God sent us a miracle, it's almost too good to be true."

For the first time in months Helena was truly happy. She was free from suspicion of murdering ex-captain Perkins, and certain to return to the ranch and the family she so loved. She shared newfound joy in bed that night with a passion she had not felt in a very long time. Afterwards, turning to face her husband, she said, "Oh, Markus, I am so happy we met before the war, that we shared good times before all the pain and fear that befell us. For so long now I have been afraid...But God has not forsaken us. He has seen us through it all." She stretched over and kissed him.

He smiled and caressed her shoulder and back with long and sweeping motions. His feel of her body, so familiar, smooth and warm and soft, never ceased to stir him. As she lay there slumbering in the semidarkness of their room, he realized anew how much he loved her, appreciated her tender delicateness and her trust in ultimate goodness.

CHAPTER XXXIX

Love, Joy, Dust And Mud, Windhoek: August 1921

A double wedding indeed took place in late August, in little St. Joseph's Parish church in Windhoek, between Christina and Richard, and Heidi and Michael. The wedding announcement in the local German newspaper read:

Windhoek Marriage Announcements

Herr Tomas Conrad takes great pleasure in announcing the betrothal of his daughter Christiana Maria Conrad of Conrad Ranch to Mister Richard Thomas of Windhoek. Herr Conrad also announces, with great pleasure the betrothal of his son Michael Conrad to Miss Heidi Rolf of Windhoek. The double wedding will take place at Saint Joseph's Church, Windhoek, Saturday, August 5, 1921, at one o'clock.

Reverend Father Lorraine will perform the holy ceremony, with a reception dinner following at the Bismarck Hotel, Windhoek. Honeymoon plans for these couples have not been announced. This writer and all of our newspaper staff wish these four fine citizens of Windhoek happiness and good health in married life.

As a wedding gift to Saint Joseph Church, Herr Tomas Conrad has pledged funds for a memorial window in memory of our young men who served in the Imperial German South West African Colonial Army and especially all those who gave their lives in the Great War.

The Catholic church was packed with well-wishers, even spilling out onto the stone front steps under a heavy overcast sky. The church was lit with dozens of candles and the golden glow was made even more effervescent because the usual sun was far behind dark clouds. A profusion of white flowers with overflowing green foliage transformed the small altar and aisles into a veritable garden of coolness in a land of summer heat. The two brides floated down the aisle on the arms of their escorts as if a soft white cumulus cloud had graced the church.

The crowd included many locals who would not normally socialize together, including Commander Northrop, Tomas Conrad's distant ranching neighbors, Richard Thomas's South African colleagues and Christina and Michael's old school chums. Even Wilhelmina Oldendorf and several other women from the Madam's establishment attended. They sat in the back of the church, off to the side, behind the last pillar, and near the confessional.

"I'm sad Helena and Markus could not be here, but they will be coming soon...all of us together again...how wonderful that will be!" A smiling Christina said to her new husband after the ceremony and above the noisy chatter of the many guests as they made their way to the Bismarck Hotel.

The two newlywed couples sat under a huge colorful chandelier made of Bohemian glass, a rainbow of pastel colors brought from Prague to be the most dazzling object in the hotel. It twinkled brightly. The entire sumptuous scene reminded the attendees of the *Belle Époque*, lost since the Great War. For most, it was a moment to forget the hardships and tragedies of the past and see youthful beauty and the hope for the future.

As a soft thunder rumbled outside the elegant dining room of the Bismarck, Tomas beamed with a happiness he had not felt in years. Madam Oldendorf, finding an opportunity, whispered into Heidi's ear "Dear, we are all so proud of you and wish you every happiness. If there is ever a time you are in need, for anything, we will be here for you. I will be here for you." She kissed Heidi on the cheek, dabbed at her nose with a scented lace handkerchief, and slipped back to her girls.

You could smell it, even in the hotel, the heavy moisture in the air and the tingly electrical energy just before a storm. The first drops were huge, as much water as in one of the sterling silver tea spoons on the banquet tables. They spattered the sand on the streets and disappeared without leaving even a moist spot. The drops could be heard on the roof tops, slowly patting and splattering the dust into muddy rivulets. It was as if someone was throwing bits of gravel. It went on in scattered bursts, spaced out every few seconds, slowly at first.

Most everyone was in a doubly happy mood, first because, of course, the beautiful double wedding, and second because of the nearly miraculous rainstorm in the dry season, so strange and so welcome. Toasts were made to the brides and grooms and to the heavens above for showering them all with its precious water.

"The wild flowers will simply burst out of the ground," someone offered. Heads nodded in cheerful agreement. These country folk and small-town people knew the beauty that hid in their semi-arid land, just waiting for the coming of rain.

The newlyweds, both couples, stayed on in the hotel for two nights, luxuriating in the bliss of married love. They agreed to meet for lunch and dinner and for a stroll about town, later canceled because of the rain. It was no matter to the foursome as they chatted about their futures and gossiped about the people who attended their weddings. On the third day, after lunch, Christina and Richard hurried the short distance to a little house Richard had rented.

Heidi and Michael, knowing the road to the ranch would be very hard to traverse in the ranch truck, chose to hire a closed carriage and driver with a pair of stout horses to see them safely home. Seeing them preparing to leave the hotel, the manager advised, "Drive slowly, there's going to be deep mud and washouts, reckoning this storm. I haven't seen anything like this in a long time!"

German South West Africa

CHAPTER XL

Home Safe?: August 1921

B efore the wedding, while riding the ranch truck to town, the Conrad clan passed two groups of surveyors heading cross country, their small trucks packed with surveying gear and camping supplies.

"The South Africans are making new maps now that they've taken over our colony," Wolfgang said to no one in particular, as the wedding party glanced at the workers. "That's going to be quite a task but I guess it needs to be done."

"Well, the old ones are those war maps drawn up in 1904," Richard commented.

"A lot has changed since then...new roads, longer rail lines, bigger towns. We could use new maps." Around Windhoek and all across the former German colony, South Africans worked to update the charts.

Michael and Heidi jostled merrily in their closed coach as the two horses plodded along, splashing through the mud as flashes of lightening and crackling thunder sounded around them. The telephone line was still up so Tomas knew his son and new daughter-in-law were on their way.

"It's the third day since this storm rolled in...I can't remember one this long this early," Tomas murmured to himself while gazing out the window toward the road.

He was startled with the sudden bang behind him, of the parlor door to the back garden, forced open by the wind. Petre came rushing in and closed it.

"Here they come!" Conrad exclaimed, as Wolfgang, Petre and Sambolo scurried to the front door, gathering up several umbrellas from the hat rack. Sambolo was ahead of everyone out the door, as he grabbed the bridles of the two horses and lead them to the barn.

"It's like the great flood...it's biblical!" shouted Michael with a laugh as he stomped his boots on the front porch while Heidi shook raindrops from her hair.

"Come in, come in," Tomas said gladly. "It certainly has cooled off since the rain started."

"Here's a pile of your foreign newspapers, Papa. Richard gathered them up for you. Lots of disturbing stories from Europe, as always. Heidi and I read some coming back from town." He handed the pile to Sambolo. "They're a bit wet."

Tomas glanced at a week's worth of reading as he hugged Heidi.

"That must have been quite a ride for you two...I haven't ridden in a closed carriage in years." Turning to Petre he said, "Pay the coachman generously Petre, he had to ride up top, and give him a nice meal." Turning back to the newlyweds, he added: "Home, safe and sound...good! I've moved my things out of the back bedroom. You two will need the space."

CHAPTER XLI

The Saddle: September 1921

I 'm glad Helena and Markus are coming home soon, what with the turmoil in Germany right now. Ebert's Weimar government isn't getting any support from those radical factions over there, and now the Bolsheviks are trying to take over. If it isn't the Communists, it's the Monarchists...their coup in Berlin lasted, what, a week? "Conrad was talking to Wolfgang as the two sat by the wooden table in the garden outside the middle parlor, after the week long rain storm.

The sun was shining brightly and, as predicted, the arid land was a profusion of orange and blue and white wild flowers surrounded by bright green shoots of grass. A scattering of white puffy clouds still lingered making for a spectacular vista across the landscape of the ranch.

Heidi and Michael were riding the high country behind the ranch house, enjoying the day and checking on the grazing cattle. They had stopped to share a bottle of beer Heidi retrieved from her saddlebag, when a faint sound made them both turn.

They held still, straining to listen. It became clear as Michael pointed across the rolling landscape to a black speck moving down the far slope.

"It's a motor vehicle... there, see? Probably a truck," Michael said, shielding his eyes from the sun with his hand. They took off their hats and fanned themselves.

"Look, they're turning this way. Let's ride over and see what they're up to."

"Yes, let's!" Heidi said, turning her horse and spurring it into a brisk walk.

The truck slid to a stop on top of a sweep of wild flowers and other newly sprouted greens. As the engine died to a stop, two men eased out of the truck.

"You must be part of the survey team," Michael greeted, as he reined in. "This is my wife, Heidi."

Greetings were exchanged as Heidi offered them her last bottle of beer. "You gentlemen have quite the task, mapping the entire colony."

"Yes ma'am, but we don't call it a colony anymore." There came an awkward moment while the surveyors traded the beer between them. "Sorry, just the way it is." Again a long pause.

"You're from the Conrad ranch, right? You sure have a pretty spread here. We saw lots of game mixed in with your cattle." His arm swept out and all four took in the vista that stretched to the far hills.

Michael asked, "So how far into the Kalahari will you go in mapping?"

The one with the bottle replied. "All the way to the non-existent border!" They all burst into laughter, because everybody knew there was no settled demarcation between German South West Africa and her neighbor to the East, Bechuanaland, in the deadly Kalahari desert that is their shared border.

"How is your work going?" Heidi inquired. "Roaming these vast lands must be interesting...you're seeing sights most people never will see."

"Well, young lady, it's a job. Pay's good, food's bad...he's the cook," pointing to his companion with a beer bottle in hand, "but we do see a lot...and on occasion discover something interesting."

"Really?" Michael inquired, adjusting himself in his saddle.

"Yes, like this saddle," he pointed to the open bed of the truck, "we pulled it off a horse carcass way back up in the hills. Found it in a washed out gulley. It's military all right. Thought I'd take it back to town, turn it in."

Neither Heidi or the two surveyors noted Michael's shock. He managed to say, "Well, it's time for us to head back. Keep up the good work." With that, he turned his horse and called over his shoulder, "Heidi, let's go."

"Goodbye then, and thanks for the beer."

CHAPTER XLII

The Return Of A Nightmare: September 1921

eidi noticed her husband's almost complete silence on the ride back to the barn. He was off his horse in seconds, handed the reins to Sambolo, who had heard them coming and stepped out of the stable doorway. There was no usual greeting from Michael as he hurried into the ranch house. Sambolo looked at Heidi, who raised her eyebrows and shrugged her shoulders.

Michael bumped into Petre in the kitchen and asked, "Where're Papa and Wolfgang?"

"Hello Michael. Tomas and Wolfgang are at the table in the garden. Would you and Heidi like something to drink?" Michael didn't answer as he hurried to the garden.

The two men were reading the assorted newspapers scattered on the table. Michael came right to the point as he approached his father and brother.

"Papa, we've got big trouble!" He blurted out as he slipped onto the bench and leaned halfway across the table toward his father.

"What? What's the problem Michael?" Wolfgang sized up Michael's demeanor instantly and knew his younger brother didn't exaggerate.

"They found a saddle...the saddle...and the remains of the horse. The surveyors did." He was breathing hard in the telling.

"What? The horse up by the cabin? God, are you sure?" exclaimed Tomas.

"It was a military saddle. I saw it from a distance but what else could it be?"

Wolfgang injected, "Did they find the body?"

"No, no, They would have mentioned that! What are we going to do Papa? If they go up there and find the body, we're all going to jail...maybe worse!"

Just then, Heidi came out the parlor door. "Hello Papa, Wolfgang. What's all this intense talk?"

The three men silently looked at her, and then at each other.

"What?"

Michael got up quickly and came over to Heidi. "It's too complicated. I can't...that is we can't tell you right now. Please dear, we've important family business to discuss. I'll tell you soon, I promise." He looked at her with pleading eyes.

"It's about that saddle, isn't it? I know it is. Michael, you got so strange out there with the surveyors."

"Yes, well, that's part of it. There's more, a lot more. But right now we've got to figure things out. It's a long story, and I'll explain it all...just not now!" He looked to his father for help, then to Wolfgang.

Tomas half stood up. "Heidi my dear, we really need to talk over some...issues...that are very important to the whole family, including Helena and Markus. So please, give us some time to collect our thoughts. We will have a family gathering and explain it all very soon."

Curious as she was, Heidi resigned herself to wait for an explanation of the mysterious saddle and why her family reacted so strangely to the news. "Of course, Papa, so long as you *do* explain. And Michael, I didn't mean to press you so, but really..." She was interrupted by Michael closing the distance between them.

"Thank you, dear, I promise I will explain." He gave her a light kiss.

As she turned to go, Tomas said. "Heidi, would you please ask Petre to come over here? And if you see Sam tell him to join us too."

After Heidi left, they returned to their discussion. Petre joined them and was quickly brought up to speed. He understood all too well the danger they were all in.

Michael continued, "Heidi knows nothing at all of this! Should I tell her? She's completely innocent. I don't know what..."

Tomas cut in. "She'll find out soon enough, either by us or by the authorities, if it comes to that. We must decide what to do now, immediately, before the surveyors have a chance to show that saddle around and Commander Northrop gets wind of it...and he will."

Wolfgang added, "We have to go up to that washout and see if that bastard's body is still there."

"God, Papa, this is extremely dangerous for us all." Michael added.

Tomas shook his head slowly, eyes downcast. He spoke in a low, stressed voice.

"*Ja, ja*, of course. Will this never stop...? *Ja*, it's late afternoon now, too late to go up...first thing in the morning then." Michael looked at Wolfgang, then at his father. He suddenly realized how old his father was, and in what an emotional state he was in. It brought a tear to his eye, quickly brushed away.

"Papa, this is too important to wait. I think Wolfgang and I and maybe Petre should go up now, so at first light we could look around, do a thorough search. What do you think? Papa?"

There was a long pause.

"*Ja, ja*. Whatever you think...go up there, tonight then, and take shovels in case..." He broke off, still looking at the center of the table and running the back of his hand under his nose.

Michael and Wolfgang looked at each other again. They nodded together.

"We'll take care of it, Papa, don't you worry, we'll take care of it." Wolfgang said gently, reaching across the table and laying his hand on this father's arm. Michael nodded to Petre and tilted his head toward his father.

Petre got up, came around to the old man. "Tomas, maybe you ought to lay down for a while before dinner." He eased him off the bench and they passed through the garden door without seeing Heidi.

She had been watching, first from the front parlor window facing out to the garden, and then closer from the middle parlor window closest to the door. She snatched bits of the conversation among the four men, but what was most troubling to her was the agitation that built in them all, especially her father-in-law. Fear rose up in her throat. She clutched her hands together and simply could not wait any longer. She stepped back through the open door.

"I'm sorry, but I heard bits of your conversation. Enough to know you are going up to that old cabin later. Whatever this is all about, it concerns me, too. Michael, I'm your wife. I want...I need to know what's going on. What is it that's got Papa so upset? What's got all of you so upset...I'm going with you this afternoon. I want to know."

"Heidi dear, I...you..."

Wolfgang interrupted him. "Let her come Michael. She has a right to know since it threatens the family."

British military truck

CHAPTER XLIII

Vultures Of A Kind Descend: September 1921

They left late in the afternoon, pack horse on lead rope, loaded down with shovels and supplies for their overnight in the cabin. They decided to have Petre and Sam stay behind so Tomas was not alone. During the two hour ride Heidi was told the whole tragic story of Helena's encounter with Llewellyn, Sam's heroism, and the subsequent burial. She was shocked to tears but after a rest stop on the trail, she recovered her composure.

"This is worse than anything I've ever experienced at...at madame..." Heidi stumbled.

Michael cut in. "Yes my dear, I understand, you don't have to explain, we'll get through this, we're a strong family. We'll get through this." He brushed a tear from her cheek and gave her a little kiss.

They approached the cabin just as the sun set on the horizon. Wolfgang dismounted, saying, "Too late to check out the gulley this evening. Let's get a fire going and make some supper. I'll tend the horses." Everyone unsaddled their horse and helped unload the packs.

The cabin was small but had a stone fireplace, four bunks, a table and two benches. It was dusty but water tight. A stew pot and large metal coffee pot were soon cushioned in a bed of glowing coals, steam rising up.

Heidi spoke, "Michael, I'm glad you called Christina and Richard before we left. Maybe they will hear something in town in the next few days."

"*Ja*, and I'm sure we'll see the authorities soon. We'd better have a good story. This damned discovery is going to start up the whole awful affair again...and with Helena and Markus arriving in a week or so. Who knows what effect this will have on her and on them. Nothing good, that's for sure." He shook his head back and forth and kicked an ember back into the fire. "*Mein Gott*, will this never end!"

They all rose early with a quick breakfast of rolls, honey and coffee.

They left most of the gear in the cabin, took their shovels, and rode fifteen minutes to where the Conrads had buried Llewellyn and his horse.

The grave was gone. The four-day storm had completely transformed the dried out gulley where the Conrads had buried the rapist and his horse. The heavy rains had cut a new and deeper gully, carrying the bodies away.

"Jesus! I can't believe it's gone! We've got to ride downhill, find the horse and rebury it!" Michael said angrily, wheeling his mount around in a circle.

"No, Michael, we can't do that. The authorities will be looking for the horse. We can't touch it now," Wolfgang counseled. "They'll know we were involved if we bury it again. Let's look for the horse and find Llewellyn's body. It's downhill somewhere, either between here and the horse or just past it. Let's go!"

The three riders could smell the rotting beast before they saw it. Or what was left of it. A half dozen red headed vultures were pulling at the bones and hide of the half buried horse. What had been exposed to open air was picked clean, and the ravenous birds were now pulling what they could out of the dirt. The entire hind quarters of the horse was gone, the bones scattered here and there. Part of the ribcage was visible, the curved bones standing upright like a white picket fence.

"See any trace of the body?" Heidi asked tentatively, bringing her hand up to cover her nose and mouth.

Wolfgang dismounted, took the shovel tied to his saddle, and probed the dirt around the horse. "I don't want to disturb the soil too much. We can't leave any trace that someone touched this mess."

Heidi asked, "What if he's under the horse?"

"I hope they won't dig up the horse. Or what's left of it," Michael answered.

Wolfgang walked around the far side of the carcass and said, "They probably will dig up the horse. They'll bring some blacks up to do that."

"Yes, probably you're right, but nothing we can do now." Michael said, "Let's look downhill. This washout goes on down for quite some distance."

After three hours of fruitless searching their little group decided there was nothing to do. Wolfgang said it aloud. "Let's head back to the cabin, get our gear and head home."

The shock was palpable among the three when Heidi, Michael and Wolfgang came up to within eyesight of the cabin. Three military trucks were parked nearby with half a dozen blacks milling around. More were in the cabin. Wolfgang was the first to speak as he pulled up his horse. "Jesus, just what we need. They're already here!" He turned to his two companions: "Let me do the talking. Don't offer anything. We need time to talk with Papa in private."

CHAPTER XLIV

The Dig: September 1921

W ell, what have we here...and with shovels." Commander Northrop stepped from the shadows of the doorway of the cabin into daylight, followed by three other officers. "Wolfgang, Heidi and Michael!" He shook his head in a strange mixture of surprise, sadness and anger. The three rode up and dismounted.

Wolfgang nodded cheerfully. "Hello Commander, gentlemen. We haven't seen you since the wedding." He nodded to the three other officers. "Commander Northrop, I expect you are here regarding a horse. A military horse, I imagine, the surveyors said the saddle was military make. We were just..."

Northrop interrupted him: "Indeed, Wolfgang, and I'm curious as to why you are up here and with shovels."

"*Ja*, of course commander, we came up here after hearing about this discovery. After all, it is on our ranch. Michael here, and Heidi," he turned slightly and nodded in their direction, "they waved down the surveyors and saw the saddle. We're always interested in anything that's on our property." He stopped and looked at the black men watching them. "I see you brought some men to dig, although there isn't much left what with the buzzards and all."

For a long moment Northrop sized up Wolfgang suspiciously. "Well, we want to find out whose horse it was, yours or ours...that is, German or South African. Care to show us where the carcass is?"

"We'd be glad to, Commander."

Michael, Heidi and Wolfgang lead the two military trucks down a fairly steep hill paralleling the washout. One of the trucks slid and almost turned over. The red headed vultures waited till the last minute to fly up as the trucks arrived. It wasn't long before the six men with shovels uncovered the remains, put a rope around one of the two remaining legs of the horse and pulled it free. The smell was awful. Swarms of flies clouded the air causing the Conrads to back off.

Northrop ignored the smell and flies, got out of the lead truck, and walked close to the carcass. He poked and prodded and finally stood up straight, took several steps away from the horse and said, "There's a bullet hole in the head. Someone shot this animal. Why?"

Everyone was silent. Finally one of the other officers said, "Sir. Could be any of several reasons for shooting a horse...broken leg, probably." He hesitated, then added: "But what happened to the rider?"

Commander Northrop ordered the six workers to dig deeper into the washout around the dead horse. "I want to see anything you find here. Anything that doesn't belong. Dig deeper, especially where the animal was found. I want a thorough investigation of the site as well as further downhill. Lieutenant, you're in charge. We will leave one truck...work the area until dark and report to me this evening."

"Yes, Commander." Northrop returned to his vehicle, got in, and leaned out. "You won't need those shovels, Wolfgang, we will do all the digging. This investigation is only beginning. Good day."

The ride back to the ranch was an easy downhill walk for the horses. "Wolfgang, you handled that beautifully with Northrop...and they didn't find the body, so probably they won't either." Michael said optimistically.

"*Ja*, well, as the Commander said, this is just the beginning of his investigation and if I know Northrop, and I do, he will reexamine every detail of our testimonies. If there is a bottom to this for him, he will get to it. We have to be very careful, very cautious. We shouldn't change our routines and we have to watch what we say in town."

Heidi asked a profound question: "What about Markus? You said he knows nothing of...of what happened to Helena or what Sam did, or what you all did with Llewellyn. He must be told the whole story, as painful as it is going to be for both he and Helena."

Michael spoke up. "Who's going to tell him, Papa? You Wolfgang? Helena? Or maybe we should all gather, all of us and recite the entire story. We don't have to go into too much detail about what happened in the barn. But the rest, every detail must be revealed. It's the only way he can protect himself and all of us."

Silence for a moment, then, "And he and Helena will be home in a week."

CHAPTER XLV

A Scrap Of Paper: September 1921

W hat have you found Lieutenant?" Commander Northrop sat at his desk at Windhoek's military base, as a full moon lit the landscape in a soft evening glow.

"Yes, sir. We didn't find a body. Seems like we dug up half the mountain...nothing further downhill either."

"So, is that it, your full report?"

"Yes sir, that's it," he paused a moment. "Except...Besides part of the bridle sir, we did find one thing. This scrap of paper."

Northrop straightened up. "Let me see it, Lieutenant." The officer handed over the wrinkled, crumpled find. It was less than a quarter sheet of typewriter paper, covered in dried dirt, faint traces of a few printed letters still visible. He examined the fragment closely. "Could you read any of this printing, Lieutenant?" He turned the paper over and held it to within inches of his eyes.

"No sir, just a few letters...most of it's gone, being buried and all."

"Bad light in here. I'll examine it in the morning. Good work, Lieutenant, you are excused, good night."

"Good night, sir." The Lieutenant saluted and left.

It lay on his desk, this scrap of crumpled paper, like the last missing piece of a puzzle, and Commander Northrop stared at it for a long time, a very long time. *I need to know what this paper says.*

CHAPTER XLVI

A Name, A Signature: September 1921

The commander was at his desk early the next morning, having secured a large handheld magnifying glass from his aide. He moved his desk lamp close as he sat leaning in over his desk, near a steaming cup of tea. The crumpled paper fragment lay in front of him. He held one edge with one hand and used his other palm to press down and flatten the paper on his desk. *Careful, don't wipe off anything.*

He brought the wood handled magnifier across the paper, staring intently for a few seconds. He shifted in his chair, adjusted the lamp, and picked up the fragment, holding it so the light lit up the back. He studied the upper left corner of the paper, an inch or two from the top edge. *Looks like a capital letter...a "P" or "R" or "B"...what's the next letter...no, I can't tell.*

He moved the magnifier down the left side of the four by seven inch fragment. *Numbers...pieces of a word or two. Names? What's this? The number four and "Co"...an "r"...or is this an "n"? Maybe an "m". Anything more?*

"It's a list of some kind...but what of?" he said aloud. "*Cor* or *Con* or *Com.*"

Northrop moved back to the top corner and the first mysterious letter. He turned the paper over gently, again using the glass to examine it. *Aha, a water mark...this is military stationary!* He sat up, put down the magnifier, and thought for a few moments.

"Lieutenant!" he called out.

Within a half hour, Commander Northrop had a stack of every form used by his staff since the end of the war. By eliminating all except those forms with a heading with the first letter either P, R, or B, he reduced the pile to a dozen or so. *Now let's see which of these forms have lists under a title that starts with a P, R, or B.*

Six forms had lists under the three suspect letters. The first read, <u>Barracks Assignments: New Arrivals</u>. Moving down to line number four, he saw a name: Wilbur Keel, Private.

No, that doesn't fit, it starts "c, o" something.

Next form: <u>Radio Repair Parts Requisition</u>. His finger traced down to line number four: Fuses, 220v, one dozen. Again, no match. He discarded two more forms for not fitting the proper letters. His eyes had only just started to scan the fifth form when he knew he had the one. *Recommendations For Repatriation And Deportation* read the title. With heightened interest, Northrop's finger glided down to number four. There in the bold cursive of Captain Llewellyn's handwriting, was the unmistakable name: Conrad ranch family.

Astonishment knocked him back into his chair. His gaze came off the page to an inner vision. *My God, the Conrads did it! They must have. They were going to be deported so they killed him! Could that be true? Christ! I can't believe it!*

"They lied, the whole bunch of them!" he blurted.

"Sir?" The Lieutenant had just stepped through the door.

"What? Ah, nothing Lieutenant, just shut the door." He studied the fragment on his desk, and then the military document. To his surprise he noted further down the page another recognizable name: Roth farm family! He studied the name.

The Roths, damn! That Heidi girl, her father's farm was unjustly seized, but it doesn't absolve the Conrads of murdering one of our officers. If they did it. Bad as he was...What am I going to do, I can't overlook this, can't let it pass. Is this, this scrap of paper, enough evidence,? Christ! What a mess!

Northrop mulled over what to do for several days. He dispatched a larger search party and even visited the site again himself. Everyone at the Conrad ranch saw the vehicles crossing the landscape and knew what it was. Potential trouble.

"Stay calm and do what we always do." Tomas advised. "They'll come to us soon."

German South West Africa

CHAPTER XLVII

The Homecoming: September 1921

Commander Northrop did indeed take his time with his customary investigative thoroughness. A week passed since he deciphered the scrap of paper found with the horse that had a bullet in its skull. He had no doubt the Conrads had something to do with Captain Llewellyn's disappearance. At the very least, they knew more than they said. But he was conflicted about Tomas Conrad and his family.

There is something that just doesn't feel right. They're decent folk, the entire family, taking in that girl from the brothel and all. But they know something, I'm sure of it. It's time for a visit to the Conrad ranch, and possibly some arrests.

Meanwhile, Helena and Markus' ship arrived in Swakopmund harbor with waves from the dock and cheers from the crowded decks, as passengers hurried down the gangplank. Markus and Helena were greeted with subdued joy that neither of the two arrivals noted. Most everyone focused on young Rupert who masterfully entertained with his eager questions.

"Is this Africa? Where are all the animals? Papa came home brown...why isn't everybody brown? Oh, there are some really brown people over there! They must have been in Africa a long time." On and on he went, until Wolfgang took him in hand and asked, "Would you like to see a camel, Rupert?"

"Yea!"

"We thought we would take the train directly to Windhoek," Christina said. "Papa and Petre will have the truck, and my Richard has just purchased an auto from one of his friends, so he will be there too," she continued with pride.

It was early evening when they arrived at the ranch to a lovely dinner of local game and an enormous salad from their fruit trees. Helena recited Grace before the meal with everyone offering the *Amen*.

"Oh Papa, it is so good to be home...to be with everyone again. God has finally blessed us. I missed you Papa, and dear Christina..." First she looked across the table with a smile and tear in her eye. She looked next at brother Michael and then Wolfgang, both had broad smiles on their faces.

"A toast!" Tomas proclaimed, half rising from his chair at the end of the table. "First, to our newly arrived world travelers from Bavaria!" He raised his schnapps glass and let out a roar of laughter. "And second to my entire family," His eyes swept around the table. "We have so much to be grateful for, so much..." His voice trailed off as he settled back into his chair with a trail of moisture down his cheek. Richard, sitting next to him, realized it was an awkward moment, raised his glass high, and shouted out, a bit louder than necessary, "To the family!"

German South West Africa

CHAPTER XLVIII

The Call: September 1921

With Markus and Helena still asleep after their long journey and the past evening dinner, most of the Conrads gathered in the front parlor, talking in low voices and discussing what to do.

Wolfgang came to the point. "We simply must tell them what is going on here...with the discovery."

"Yes. We are all in agreement brother, but when, where?" Christina asked.

Silence held the room until Michael offered a suggestion. "Maybe we should tell them separately...I mean, several of us could talk to Markus...fill him in, away from Helena, so if he is too upset, we could deal with that alone." Looking around, he continued. "And several of us could talk with Helena. She is likely going to take it hard, but she has to know what's been found."

Tomas was the next to speak. "We don' t know what Northrop knows. Has he found the body? They've been digging up there for days."

"Papa, I think we would have heard about that for sure, it would be all over town. No, I don't think they found it." Wolfgang's words were emphatic.

Heidi spoke up for the first time: "Whatever we tell Helena and Markus, alone or together, it's going to be very upsetting, just dreadful. Is there any way we can say nothing at all?" She looked around the parlor at the family she had grown to love. They all looked back at her in silence.

That silence was broken by the ringing of the telephone. Petre answered it. "It's for you, Tomas, sir. It's Commander Northrop."

He took the telephone...a long pause: "Yes, yes, when? Tomorrow? Yes, we can do that, Commander. About two then. All right, good bye."

Conrad slowly replaced the receiver onto the hook. He turned to the group, all staring at him intently. "He's coming out to the ranch tomorrow afternoon...that is, they are coming out, two trucks." The old man stood there with slumped shoulders. In a tired voice he said, "They want us, all of us, to be here in the house at...two, two o'clock."

He turned away from the group. As he shuffled off, he said over his shoulder, "Let's see what he has to say. It's all we can do so...I'm going to bed."

CHAPTER XLIX

The Pain Of Truth: October 2, 1921

The entire Conrad clan waited in the front parlor: newly arrived Markus and Helena, Tomas, Conrad, Michael and Heidi, Christina and Richard, Wolfgang, Petre and even Sambolo. They heard two trucks pull up in front of the ranch house, and through the window saw Commander Northrop and six armed Military Police get out of the vehicles. Those six waited by the trucks while Northrop and two other officers approached the house.

Earlier, Markus, with Helena nearby, had asked Tomas, Michael and Wolfgang what was happening. The three answered noncommittally, with Tomas simply saying, "We're hearing what he has to say."

Helena was very quiet now, her eyes darting back and forth between the men. She stroked the gold cross on her chest in nervous anticipation.

"I thought this whole business was settled? Why are there police accompanying Northrop...and why is he calling a meeting in the first place?" There was tension and exasperation in Markus' voice.

Christina, greeting the Commander and his companions at the door, guided them into the front parlor. All eyes were on the three officers as they came in.

They stood stiffly in front of the group as Tomas greeted them on behalf of his family and offered three chairs. Reluctantly, Northrop indicated his men to sit. He also took a seat, cleared his throat, scanned the group, and began.

"I regret having to call this meeting on a subject that has vexed me and caused your family great stress. However, new evidence...that is, information has come to my attention concerning Captain Llewelyn's disappearance in February, 1919, that throws serious doubt on certain statements you and members of your family made then." He was looking straight at Tomas.

Markus was at the edge of his seat, his head turning back and forth, one to the other, as Helena gripped his upper arm tightly. The rest of the family sat stone-faced as the commander continued.

"As you know, a military horse was found half buried on your ranch near your cabin high up in hill country, a week ago. Of course you knew about the find as I met several of you there." He looked at the three. "Through extensive searching by my investigators, an important paper was found near the horse, that establishes that the horse was almost assuredly Captain Llewellyn's. I have identified this paper as an official military document. It's significance is very clear, and may implicate members of your family, Herr Conrad, in the captain's disappearance."

"What? That's absurd!" Markus charged. "Haven't you..."

Michael and Richard both interrupted Markus saying, "Let the commander finish."

Markus looked perplexed but settled back into his chair. No one noticed the tear trickling down Helena's cheek.

The two officers had risen in their chairs, and Northrop motioned for them to sit. He continued sternly, "The paper I am referring to is an official military form. The title is *Recommendations For Repatriation And Deportation*."

Christina gasped. The others noticed, and Northrop nodded grimly. Markus again spoke up forcefully. "I still don't understand...what has this got to do with us?" He paused, his eyes grew wide in horrified understanding. "You mean the Conrad name is on that list! What? Why?" He shouted.

Helena, who had sat quietly but apprehensively and in a state of near panic and despair, blurted out in a low anguished voice almost inaudible, "Because I wouldn't give in to him." Markus turned to her.

"What? Dear, what did you say?"

Helena half rose from her seat and in a crazed, hysterical outburst of shattering screams that caused everyone in the room to shutter in transfixed horror, she shouted, "He raped me! He raped me! Because I wouldn't give in to him!"

She collapsed to the floor in front of everyone, repeating the tragic refrain over and over between sobs. Markus leaped up as did half the onlookers.

"What? No...! No...!" He was down on the floor, his arm around his wife. "I should have been here...it's my fault!" he said in an anguished voice. "I should have been here for you!" He was crying, the entire family was in tears, kneeling and crying and reaching out to Helena and Markus.

Northrop and the three officers were stunned into immobility for a few moments by the scene. "Good God!" he blurted. "What..."

He was interrupted by a lone figure from the back of the room. Sambolo, tears streaming down his face, ran forward. He shouted at the three officers. "*I* kill him! I kill Lle...el en! With my pitch fork! I hear screams in barn...that man rip Helena's clothes...he on top of her...I stab man in back with my pitch! I kill him!"

Northrop leapt to his feet. "What? You killed Captain Llewellyn? You?" The three officers rose from their chairs.

They flinched back when Michael jumped up and, wiping tears off his cheek with his sleeve, shouted, "No! That's not true!"

Heidi screamed to interrupt him. "No, Michael, no!"

"I killed him, I killed that filthy bastard. I beat him to death with the dung shovel. It wasn't Sam, he only stabbed him. I beat him to death and I'd do it again, that dirty rotten..." he broke down in shudders of tears as Heidi came to him.

Christina turned to Northrop and between tears and a breaking voice said, "It's true! We had to stop him...stop him from...we were on horseback...Michael and I, just returning to the barn. We heard Helena's screams...we knew it was her...we ran into the barn just as Sam stabbed Llewellyn in the back. Then Michael... Michael..." She couldn't go on. Richard came to her and folded his wife into his arms. They swayed back and forth in a sea of tears.

Michael repeated in a low voice, "It was me."

Commander Northrop sat rigidly in his chair. Watching this family come apart, he knew he had the truth he'd sought, the painful truth of Captain Llewellyn's fate.

Only Petre saw Tomas suddenly sit upright in his seat, his left hand grabbing his chest. As Petre came the few steps to him saying, "Tomas sir...Tomas!"

Conrad rose slightly and tumbled sideways to the floor, clutching his chest. He landed almost exactly next to Helena. She screamed. "Papa, Papa, no...Papa!"

Everyone leaped up including Northrop, who went down on his knees to roll Tomas onto his back.

The meeting descended into a confused babble. "Heart attack...the stress! Get a pillow...some water...call the doctor!"

Helena's thin fingers clutched at her father's clothes as others tried to help. "Papa, Papa...it's my fault...God is punishing me, not you, Papa!" She was hysterical. Markus, Christina and Heidi pulled her away, trying to comfort her by saying: "No, no...Papa will be all right, you'll see...Papa will be all right."

Northrop, still kneeling, said to one of his officers, "Call the base, use their house phone, get our military doctor out here at once...at once!"

CHAPTER L

Death By A Thousand Cuts: October 2, 1921

Commander Northrop stayed until the military doctor arrived, almost at the same time as the Conrad family's doctor. They did what they could, but it was hopeless. Tomas Conrad, patriarch to the Conrad clan, who had seen his wife Gretel, die early on, and the death of his three sons: Arnold from war wounds, Norbert from a careless accident by the South African military, and Humboldt from influenza, joined them in death that evening.

A pall of anguished weeping hung heavy over the Conrad ranch that night. Even Northrop was physically shaken by Tomas' death and the horrific story that had unfolded.

He spoke quietly to Wolfgang, Richard and Petre. "I'm leaving now, but I want you to know I am suspending any further action and investigation into... *this*... based on what transpired here today. I am truly sorry for the tragedy that has befallen your family. If there is anything I can do, let me know. Please inform the other members of your family of my decision."

Wolfgang walked Northrop to his car, saying, "I'll let everyone know. I hope this tragedy will be the last my family sees for a long time."

Commander Northrop extended his hand. "It will," is all he said.

CHAPTER LI

The Departure: October 1921

I t was the largest funeral in Windhoek that anyone could remember. Tomas Conrad had always been highly regarded by the ranchers, farmers and townspeople, and today, his old friends crowded Saint Joseph's church to overflowing. It was a sight to see Madame Oldenburg and several of her girls sitting near Commander Northrop and a half dozen officers with Petre and Sambolo close by them. After the funeral mass, a long procession of assorted vehicles snaked their way along the winding road to the ranch and the family's burial plot. Under a bright, late morning sun, the mourners gathered near the tombstones of Gretel, as well as Arnold, Norbert and Humboldt. Tomas Conrad was laid to rest next to them.

Helena, surrounded by comforting family, recovered from her sorrow enough to speak, briefly reciting a poem she'd written:

We say he has passed
Like a ship passing over the horizon,
But I know Papa is here with me,
In my heart, in my mind, in every breath I take.
He comforts me, as God comforts me.
I speak to him and he hears me,
His voice rings pure love in my heart.
Papa, you are at peace now, and surely in heaven.
In heaven with your Gretel, my Mama,
And your boys, my brothers,
Arnold, Norbert, and Humboldt.
As you are joined together again,
Over the horizon, I am comforted,
Knowing God has graced you with life,
And now, with a loving place beyond the sky.

It was brief but caused many a tear, as Father Lorraine closed the burial with a prayer. Most of the people walked the short distance to the ranch house for a luncheon provided by neighbors and friends. It was a lively group telling funny and daring tales, most exaggerated, about Tomas' early days building the ranch.

"You remember that time a steer came into this house—*ja*, this house—and went down that hall...woke up Tomas with a fright! There, see that? That gouge in the wall was made by the damned steer!"

"How about that well? Remember that story? Old Conrad spent most of a week digging that well...pretty damned deep it was, but not a drop of water down there. The dirt walls weren't even damp. Brother, he cursed that hole in the ground like you never heard. But guess what? A week later there was water in the bottom of that hole and there's been water ever since. Where'd it come from? Nobody knows, but some think his cursing scared that water right outta the ground!" And so it went, late into the afternoon. With the sun approaching the horizon, the crowd thinned out until all were gone except family.

𝕭𝖆𝖛𝖆𝖗𝖎𝖆

CHAPTER LII

Kalvarianhof: Late Fall 1921

S now fell in a continuous white cloud at the manor house as the wet flakes clung to every tree and twig in the surrounding forest. News of Tomas Conrad's death arrived in a telegram from Markus.

Levi imagined how devastating Tomas Conrad's passing must be for the entire Conrad clan. In his mind's eye he could see his friend and Helena. He also knew Markus well enough to know there was more to the story.

"The telegram's real short. Somehow it seems peculiar for Markus, I just feel there's something else going on. I ought to write him a letter."

Katherina peered over her husband's shoulder and said "He's been through so much...the both of them, poor Helena. At least her faith is strong. That will be a comfort to her. Losing her mother young, her brothers in succession, and now her father? It's too tragic."

Levi flipped the pewter lid on his beer stein up and down, unfocused eyes on the salt-glazed gray tankard while Katherina served herself a bowl of potato soup. She added, "I'll write to Helena too. I wish I could be with her. Thank God she has Christina and Heidi. Strange that he should collapse like that. The way Markus described him, he always seemed like such a strong, vigorous man."

"Yes, but it happens all the time. He was in his late fifties if I recall." Levi went back to his afternoon newspaper as Katherina finished her rapidly cooling soup.

"Oh, Willie is picking up Rebecca from gymnasium, she forgot her boots again...that girl!" she smiled. As she was getting up, Levi stared at a blurry photo in the news and pointed.

"Look here, dear, this is Count Harry Kessler. I mentioned him; he's the diplomat I'm going to meet in Berlin in a few days. He's quite a man. Gustoff Liebermann gave me a very detailed account of his past. He's an aristocrat of the old school but with progressive ideas and a wealth of diplomatic and business experience. Seems he knows everyone of consequence in Berlin, Vienna, Paris, London...pretty much everywhere...here in Bavaria, too. Liebermann thinks he's a valuable contact for his company to get government work. We'll see."

Katherina leaned over the paper. "He certainly is a handsome man." She smiled at his expression. "Even if less handsome than you!"

She leaned ever closer and kissed her husband as he patted her on her back side. "Are you sleepy tonight dearest...maybe we should retire early!" They exchanged knowing smiles.

Two weeks before Hanukkah, while Otto and Friedl snored away in an early afternoon nap, the telephone rang in the front hallway. Levi was at his desk in the music room upstairs, and hurried down.

"*Ja*, hello Anji. Merry Christmas to.." He was interrupted by her nervous voice.

"Yes, yes...Levi, I wanted you to know, Mama...you know she hasn't been well. She was in a lot of pain this morning. The doctor was...is here. We're taking her to the hospital. I thought you would want to know. I haven't contacted Markus. Do you think I should? She's been in the hospital before, but this time...she's so weak she can hardly sit up. She won't eat and her abdomen is so swollen on account of her illness...I don't know what to do."

Levi's face took on a serious countenance. "I'm so sorry to hear, Anji. I think it's best Frau Mathais remain at a hospital 'til she recovers, of course. I'm sorry to hear she's gotten poorly, we saw your Mama in the Oktoberfest tents last September. She seemed fine, but...thin."

Anji's voice was stressed as she asked again, "Do you think I should write Markus...let him know? I don't want to upset him so soon after Tomas died."

"I think you should send him a telegram, he will prefer knowing." He hesitated, then said, "If there is anything we can do... would visiting Frau Mathais cheer her up?"

"No, not now, she needs rest and care by the doctors. It's kind of you to ask. Later though, and I'm sure letting her know will be a comfort. Thank you Levi. Extend my greetings to your parents and Katherina. *Auf Wiedersehen*."

"Who was that dear?" Kathi asked from the middle parlor, putting down her embroidery. She walked up to Levi as he replaced the receiver on the wall mount.

"It was Anji. Frau Mathais is ill and is to be hospitalized. Anji's worried of course, the way she described her mother doesn't sound good. She wanted to ask whether she should telegraph Markus, and I said she should." Katherina took Levi's arm.

"After all Markus and Helena have been through this past year, I hope she gets better. Do you think she will?" A grimace twisted Levi's face as his wife looked him in the eye, and he shook his head slightly. He didn't need to speak.

HMS Newcastle

CHAPTER LIII

The Long Way Home And A Revelation: December 1921

Anji's first telegram arrived at the ranch eleven days before Christmas, 1921, just as the Conrads were decorating the *Tannenbaum*, the Christmas tree, with little red candles in brass holders that clamped to outstretched branches. The news deeply concerned everyone in the extended family, but since Anji suggested they wait and see, no immediate plans were made.

And then Anji's second telegram arrived.

> To Markus Mathais
> Mama very ill Stop Doctors say one month
> or less of life Stop Can you come brother
> Stop
> Signed Anji Mathais

It arrived in Heidi's hands as she picked up the mail at the post office in Windhoek. "Telegram for Herr Markus Mathais," the postman announced as she walked in. She knew what it said just by seeing the sender. Gathering the rest of the mail, Heidi hurried through the rain to the Dutch café where Michael waited.

"Will Markus go?" she asked her husband while he ruminated on the telegram. "And what will Helena do? We should get back to the ranch."

"I've already ordered. Let's eat first." He paused as the waiter put down two plates of Weiss wurst, sweet mustard, potato salad and Kaiser rolls. Two half liter glasses of beer were already on the blue and white tablecloth. "It's difficult to say. Markus maybe. They returned from Germany so recently, and it's a long way to his mother's home."

Later: "The quickest route home is a British ship out of Wales Bay. It leaves on Thursday. We have four days to get ready and over to the coast." Markus ruffled the newspaper as he scanned the notices of ship arrivals and departures. "I'll telegraph the shipping agent." They were in the middle parlor, sunk into the overstuffed couch.

"Markus, I have something to..."

She was interrupted by Wolfgang. "I'm going too, as a representative of the rest of us Conrads," he announced as he put down his newspaper. This came as a real surprise to Helena and Markus.

"Really, Wolfgang? That would be wonderful," Helena said as she snuggled next to her husband. "Going to Europe is quite the adventure." Helena paused, "Oh Markus, I'm sorry...I didn't mean to make light of your mother's illness."

"It's alright. Of course. Wolfgang will find the trip to Germany exciting. It's an adventure for me every time I go home. I'll see Mama and we'll see the sights in Munich...it's a great opportunity for Wolfgang."

Michael and Heidi had overheard Wolfgang's decision. Heidi, looking at Michael, said, "I think it would be good idea to have Wolfgang represent the family. We can manage the ranch with Petre and Sam while you're gone. Christina will come out and help keep track of the cattle. Don't worry about that."

"Good, thanks," Wolfgang smiled.

Turning back to Helena, Markus asked, "I'm sorry you were interrupted...what was that you were about to say?"

She turned to him, put her hand on his chin and turned his head to her. "I think we are going to have another baby...I'm not sure yet, but it's been two months and..."

"Really? I mean are you sure? That's wonderful dearest, when?"

"Christina, Heidi and I went into town and saw the doctor. It's almost for sure, I mean, I know it's for sure."

"Oh, another child, another bright star from heaven for you and me."

"Yes, God is blessing us again, I'm so happy!"

"But what about the trip? You can't go now, you have..."

"No, no no...I'm going...I'll be fine. The doctor says I'm as healthy as can be, and there are plenty of good doctors in Munich."

"Are you sure, dearest?"

"Yes."

CHAPTER LIV
The Long Way Home Continues: January 1922

The British freighter *HMS Newcastle* sailed from Britain's Wales Bay on the Southwest coast of Africa on a day of showers and brisk winds. Christina and Heidi came to see Helena, little Rupert, Charlotte, Markus and Wolfgang off to Germany via London, and a short ferry ride across the channel to the express train to Munich.

"Give our greetings to everyone, sister dear," said Christina as hugs, kisses and farewell's were passed one to another.

As the freighter's lines slipped their moorings and splashed into the water, Heidi asked over the low steady blast of the ship's horn. "How long do you think they will be gone?"

Christina replied with a shout and a tear at the edge of her eye. "No one knows. Months, I imagine."

The *Newcastle*, with about twenty paying passengers, rode low in the water with a full cargo in the relatively light Atlantic seas south of the equator. Wolfgang took several days to get his sea legs but marveled at the beauty and immensity of the ocean. "It reminds me of when I'm on the highest point of the escarpment back home and looking out over the endless rolling lands as far as the eye can see. Really it's like these great swells the ship rolls with. And the air, that salty, heavy air and always a wind...nothing like the dry dusty air we have most of the year."

He was thoroughly enjoying himself as Markus and Helena looked on. "Maybe you missed your calling, Wolfgang. It's not too late to be a sailor!" Helena offered. Everyone was amused, including Charlotte and Rupert. "I want to be a sailor too, when I grow up, can I Papa?"

"*Ja*, you can, but what about your pony back home?"

"I'll bring him along and I'll ride him all around the ship...around and around and around!" Neighboring passengers, hearing Rupert's story, joined in by saying things like, "Now that will be a real seahorse, *ja*!"

Passing north of the equator the winds picked up, the swells grew and the temperature dropped on the open ocean. The ship's captain announced, "We will be arriving tomorrow in Freetown, Sierra Leon, a British crown colony. The ship will be there for one night to pick up cargo. Passengers may disembark for a walk but must be back aboard by sundown. We depart on high tide in the morning."

The passengers hung over the portside railing as the *Newcastle* eased to its berth, observing the dusty, shabby port that seemed uncharacteristic for a prosperous British colony. Wolfgang led the way through the narrow passageways to the gangway.

"Isn't it warm here? One of the crew told me it's because winds from the Sahara Desert blow this way in February. I heard we should see what's called the King's Gate in town. Something about slaves."

"What are slaves, Mama? What are slaves?" Helena looked at Markus.

"Slaves are people that are controlled...that are owned by other people, Rupert."

"Can we own people, Papa?" Charlotte listened intently.

"No, son, it's not right to own people...but you can own your pony. Now let's take a look around this town."

They wandered down the narrow dirt streets, past several mosques and a church that looked similar to the Catholic church in Windhoek. "Let's go in, just for a moment." Helena said. The cool inside was refreshing, protected by the thick stone walls. A large candle burned inside a hanging red lantern near the alter. To the side hung a large painting of a black Virgin Mary standing on a sharp tipped sliver of a quarter moon. Her gold crown seemed to sparkle in the dim light. Helena knelt for a few moments with Rupert on one side and Charlotte on the other, as Markus and Wolfgang walked the two short side aisles. "I said a prayer for Frau Mathais and for our safe voyage."

"Thank you, dear wife." Markus offered with a smile, adding, "I think it's time to return to the ship...Rupert and Charlotte look tired."

As the four headed back to the *Newcastle*, they spotted the King's Gate, and walked over. "Look here," Helena said, pointing to a plaque. "It says, 'Any slave who passes through this gate is a free man.' What do you make of that?"

"*Ja*, well, the Portuguese shipped slaves to the Americas from all along this part of the coast. I've read that after the slaves were finally freed in America, some of them came back to Africa. I suppose either the British or the ex-slaves built this. It's an interesting bit of history," said Markus.

The next morning, a strong smell of diesel vapors enveloped the *Newcastle*'s decks as they headed out of Freetown harbor. That evening, in the small lounge area reserved for passengers, a young crewman cranked up a Victrola phonograph player, placed the disc, set the needle, and stood back grinning. Out of the soundbox came music unlike anything the adults had ever heard before.

"*Vas est das*! What is that?" exclaimed Helena with a smile.

The crewman grinned at her. "Jazz, American jazz! It's all the rage in London, everyone's dancing to it. All my friends are, too." He couldn't contain himself. "Here, you do it like this." He spun around and tapped his feet, threw his hands up in the air and gyrated around the small space.

"They dance like that in London?" Markus exclaimed as he and everyone burst into uncontrollable laughter.

"Do you think they are dancing like that in Munich?" Helena asked. This brought on even more cackles, red cheeks and tears in the eyes.

"*Ja*, thank you for that performance." Wolfgang said grinning and shaking his head. "We don't have jazz in Africa."

"Oh, I'm sure you will, sir," said the crewman as he hurried off to his duties.

A week later, the captain announced, " Lisbon is our next port of call, arriving soon."

Royal Portuguese Flag

CHAPTER LV

A Visit To The Past: February 1922

The captain announced that the *HMS Newcastle* would be in port for two nights. It gave Markus the opportunity to make two telephone calls he had been thinking about since he learned the ship was to stop in Lisbon. The first was to his dear friend Leopold, who helped him in Portuguese East Africa during the great war. The second was to Senhora Angelina, the daughter of his other Portuguese friend and savior General Augusto de Monhona de Albuquerque.

"Hello? Yes...he is not here right now, would you like to leave a message or a telephone number? I'm sure he...Oh, he just walked in. One moment please."

Leopold took the receiver from his housekeeper. "Yes, this is Leopold. Who is this? No! Markus my friend, you're in Lisbon again. I knew you couldn't keep away." He let out another roar of approval. "What brings you here?"

Markus proceeded to explain their reason for the trip home to Bavaria, and his delight that his friend was in Lisbon.

"Can we meet? Our ship is here for two nights. I also want to call Senhora Albuquerque...possibly visit her again. What do you think?"

"As a matter of fact, I see Senhora Angelina at the opera on occasion. I believe you gave her a renewed interest in life with those letters from her father. Why don't I give her a call and we can all have dinner here at my home. Say tomorrow evening, early, about seven...I'll pick you up at the dock. What ship?"

For Wolfgang to see an ancient city like Lisbon for the first time, one of the richest cities in the world two centuries ago, with its cathedrals, monuments, medieval and Renaissance castles, streets and hillside villas, was awe inspiring.

"*Ja*, so this is what a European city looks like...Wunderbar!"

Leopold contacted Senhora Angelina and with her son, Carlos, she agreed to the invitation warmly. Senhora Albuquequere greeted Markus, Helena and Wolfgang as they all gathered at Leopold's villa. The two young boys took an immediate liking to each other, despite the language barrier. Charlotte went along with whatever they did. Warm conversation over Portuguese wine led to the dinner bell. The banquet table, in a gold encrusted Baroque dining room, dazzled the eye. It was set resplendently with a mix of fresh cut pink and white flowers. Sparkling candelabras, and Meissen china with a different important German cathedral on each plate, made the whole evening unforgettable for the Africans.

The six guests and Leopold sat at an oval table covered in a hand embroidered cloth of infinite complexity. Leopold had obviously hired a footman in full livery, to help serve, accompanied by his housekeeper cook, she in white starched apron and bonnet.

Wolfgang sat stiffly as he viewed the array of sterling cutlery at each setting. Three forks, two knives, two spoons, two wine glasses and a water glass! *What do I use first? We had wonderful parties at the ranch but nothing like this!*

"I enjoy the old ways," Leopold began. "The ways of my parents long before the Great War. It was a splendid era, no matter the politics of the time."

Angelina looked down for a moment, remembering her father. Leopold took note and changed the subject. Taking up his wine glass, he proposed, "A toast to friends old and new. To the heirs of two great families..." he said with a look at the two boys. "And to the elegant splendor of the past I so cherish. And to a bright and promising future for all my friends here at my table." Salutes and affirmations resounded all around followed by a return toast to Leopold from Markus.

"To our dear friend Leopold, my great benefactor in Africa during the war, and who assisted my family and my friend Levi. It is through his generosity that we are together again tonight with Senhora Albuquerque, and Carlos, too, in the beauty of this home. Thank you, Leopold."

The sumptuous dinner drifted into the late evening with Portuguese wine flowing along with warm heartfelt reminiscences. The two boys and Charlotte, excused from the table earlier, sat half asleep on a couch with heavy books in their laps. "It's late and we must go. Thank you dear Leopold for bringing us all together again. And Markus, I will be forever grateful that you delivered my father's letters to me. If there is anything, anything I can ever do for you, please do not hesitate to ask."

CHAPTER LVI
The Return: February 1922

T he *Newcastle* nudged the dock at London, England in mid-February 1922. The harbor was jammed with ships from all over the world bringing goods from Britain's dozens of colonies.

"I've seen a lot of harbors, Wolfgang, but this is truly amazing...all these ships!" Markus had his hand on his brother-in-law's shoulder as he spoke. The next day, the travelers took the sea ferry to Bremerhaven and took an overnight sleeper rail car to Munich.

"There are so many people everywhere. Windhoek is so small compared to these European cities." Wolfgang smiled in wonder of it all.

"Wait till we take you around Munich, my friend," Markus said.

Anji, Markus' sister, and her husband, Johan, with Levi, Katherina and his sister, Ilsa, and her husband, Rolf, met the new arrivals at the train station.

Broad smiles greeted everyone as Anji said excitedly to her brother, "Mama will be so happy to see you! I know it means so very much to her that you came all the way from Africa...and Helena with the children."

"Of course, dear sister, and thank you for the telegrams. Mama will sure enjoy seeing her grandchildren."

Another European city, and a German one at that, captured Wolfgang like nothing else could. *The ancient architecture...the automobiles everywhere...the people in their modern fashions...and all these shops...look at all these interesting items for sale...we've got nothing like this back home.*

"We drove to the train station, so everyone has a ride to Mama's apartment." Anji nodded toward Levi. "Mama's apartment overlooks the Englishergarten, Wolfgang, that's a big park in the center of town. Markus, Helena and the children will stay at Mama's, and Wolfgang will stay at the Levi's, out at Kalvarianhof." She turned to Wolfgang with a big smile. "You'll love it: it's a real German farm and the woods and, of course, their beautiful home."

Markus kept a loving face when he entered his mother's bedroom, but thought, *Ah, Mama, Mama you have declined so much since I last saw you...Mama dear, you have seen me through so much, and now...and now...* A tear formed in his eye at her touch. She saw the scars of battle and age and the streaks across his face from the leopard attack.

"You home again...it's a tiny miracle. We have to thank God for that," she said in a weak voice. "Come sit by me."

And so it went for several weeks, long bedside visits, as Frau Mathais told family stories for everyone's enjoyment. But, her condition improved, worsened, and for a time held in this repeating cycle.

March brought blustery winds and snow showers with the promise of an early spring. Levi continued his search for building contracts for Gustoff Liebermann's company in Munich. With a fortunate introduction to Count Harry Kessler, and through him, contacts throughout the upper echelon of the Weimar government, Levi finally secured a building project, one kept very secret by the government.

"The Versailles Treaty forbids Germany from having a military air force of any size." Count Kessler began. "But the rapid advances being made in both airplanes and their ancillary components like inflight wireless communication, compel us, and the German government, to invest in such an undertaking. We simply must keep up with our old adversaries, France, England, Russia and America." Levi and Liebermann listened intently as Kessler continued, "Your brother-in-arms Markus Mathais' extraordinary flying experiences have been talked about in significant circles I hear. I suspect he will be involved in the communication equipment on the airships Count Zeppelin is building. I've been informed they are flying an airship down to an airfield near Friedrichshafen. Marconi is working on the installation of an advanced, experimental wireless system."

Later at Kalvarianhof, "It's a technical site out at the old airfield in the village where you first learned to fly!" Levi spoke enthusiastically to Markus as they sat in the alcove in the kitchen with Wolfgang at his side. Levi, sitting on the blond pine bench and leaning forward on the table across from the two, continued, "*Ja*, I remember your first solo flight in that rickety airplane and how you scared me to death when you didn't come back on that windy day. The mechanic there said you had to be out of gas and probably crashed somewhere, but you'd landed here, in the meadow beyond the barns. We were all so happy you didn't kill yourself that day!" They had a hardy laugh reminiscing.

With his prolonged stay at the Levi's, Wolfgang spent many hours exploring the barns, the farmlands, the crops, the animals and the woodlands around Kalvarianhof. He marveled at the lush greenery of spring, the soil rich with moisture, and the gravelly meandering streams through the forest with darting fish in the shadows.

Wolfgang had a lot of time to think about his life, the ranch back home, about his sister and brother, both married, and about this newly discovered country. *What am I doing with my life. I'm thirty-eight, do I really want to live my life out at the ranch? I love the ranch...at least I loved it before...before...Papa and Mama are gone, and Norbert and Arnold and Humboldt...what a disaster, a catastrophe for the family...my dear brothers, to die so young. Ja, and I almost died in that damnable war, too. Now I'm here, in this other world, the old world they call it. But it's new to me...this world is amazing. But what would I do here in Germany, in Bavaria? I do love it...the energy, the beauty, the modern...everything.*

What he most enjoyed on his solitary walks was the smell of the pine trees. There were other trees on the vast Levi estate, but the pines, planted in dense formations, almost too thick to walk through, made walks especially wonderful. He closed his eyes all alone in the still forest, taking deep breaths and smiling to himself. *This is a piece of heaven...so pure, so clean...beautiful. This is the Germany Markus talked about all the time back home...I can see why.*

REGINA PALAST HOTEL MÜNCHEN

CHAPTER LVII

The Long Goodbye: May 1922

Frau Mathais hovered near death for days, but at times she perked up and talked with whomever was near.

"She grows thinner and thinner and barely eats, but still she holds to life, even as weeks drift into months." Helena said to Markus with a small smile.

It was May and the May poles sprang up in every village and town to celebrate spring. Helena and Markus and their two children were staying at Kalvarianhof for several days as a break from tending his mother.

"I know we've talked about this before," Helena said, "but we must decide what to do. The children should be enrolled in school and I miss Christina and Michael and everyone back home." She looked at her husband, sitting across from her at a table shaded by a Linden tree.

It was a warm sunny afternoon, and she wore riding clothes borrowed from Katherina. The two women were set to ride through the forest to a distant, walled 16th century chapel and burial ground where a dozen generations of village graves lined the walkways. Katherina offered a solution.

"You could enroll Charlotte and Rupert in the neighborhood school in Munich. I'm sure they would accommodate them 'til you're set to leave. I think the children would enjoy it."

"Yes, but how long will it be? Frau Mathais is a hearty soul, thank the Lord, but Markus only has so much leave from his job at the wireless station." Looking to her husband, she asked, "How long can you be away, dear?"

He replied, "Richard sent me that letter last week. There isn't a problem with my being away. Things are quiet at the wireless station, so that's not a concern at the moment." He looked at his wife, "You know how much I enjoy being back here at home again. We don't have to be in a hurry to go back home."

Markus hoped his last comment would be accepted as he meant it. Deep down he was feeling the strong pull of his homeland, of being back in his old haunts and in the vitality of German society, in spite of the war losses and turmoil.

Helena had a decidedly unhappy look on her face as she turned to Katherina. "Let's go," she said. Both women, with the help of Willie the farm hand, mounted up two chestnut horses and headed out across the meadow toward the woods at a brisk trot.

"I know he likes being back in Munich, it is his home...well, his childhood home really. He's been gone from here for so long, eight years is it...but we have a good life at the ranch. It's truly wonderful here, but I miss my home. I'm not worldly like Markus. He's been everywhere...China, those islands in the Pacific, and then East Africa. Travel is not a great adventure for me, I've only been forced to travel away from home." The two women stopped in the shade and eased the reins of their horses to let them munch the tall grass.

"I do love the churches in Munich," Helena continued, patting the mane of her horse, "they're so grand and beautiful and peaceful. I really feel closer to God when I'm there. And the music is so uplifting, I would be happy to stay all day, dreaming and praying and watching that divine light from the stained glass windows." She was looking off in her own world, then said, "*Ja*, I must be boring you, Kathi, sorry."

"No, no, I think it's wonderful that you find such strength in your faith, and that our churches bring you such joy." The two looked at each other smiling. "Let's go find the Chapel you were telling me about!" With that, Helena pulled up the head of her horse, turned him, gave a quick kick with her heels and was off.

Wolfgang, for his part, had taken to riding the train into Munich to experience the city, and more recently, its night-life. He soon discovered night spots featuring the American jazz he heard aboard the *Newcastle*. The rhythms and songs captivated him with an exotic richness he had never known in Africa. Soon he was dancing, solo or with one partner or another, enjoying the carefree life of the big city. *I never saw European blacks before like this, so sophisticated, so well dressed, so enjoying themselves almost as equals in this amazing society. I always tried to treat Petre and Sambolo as equals. But the rest of the blacks back home...they never seemed quite the same. Things really are different here.*

Events moved quickly in the following weeks. The first of June, a letter from Richard brought disturbing news.

Dear Markus and family:

I hope everyone is well and that your mother, Frau Mathais, is recovering. I send bad news. The South African company that took over the wireless station in Windhoek informed me that your position there was to be eliminated with thirty days' notice. I am protesting your dismissal and am appealing the decision but I have been told there is little hope the position will be reinstated. Your talents have been so valuable, particularly with the changing technology. I know this is a big mistake for the company. I'm sorry to give you this news. I'll do what I can.

Christina and Heidi send their love and everyone at the ranch sends greetings and love to all. We look forward to seeing you and Helena and the family soon.

Signed, Richard

Markus stared at the letter for a long time. He was home at his mother's apartment. Anji and Helena were out for a few hours with the children. A day nurse was with Frau Mathais. *I've been fired! I need that job, and the pay. There're no other jobs in Windhoek for me, that's for sure. What am I going to do? Helena is going to be...how will she react? This is damned bad news.*

The women breezed through the door with their net bags bulging. Helena saw Markus from across the room and immediately picked up on his mood. "Is Mama all right?" was her first concern. She came over to Markus as he held up the letter for her to read.

"It's from Richard," is all he said. She took the letter as Anji looked over her shoulder. She immediately understood the depth of this blow to her husband. "Oh darling, I'm so sorry. You've worked so hard at that wireless station."

Anji asked, "What? What has happened?"

With a, "May I?" Helena held out the letter to Anji.

"Of course." Markus replied.

Helena took the news with a certain mild trepidation bordering on stoicism. She and her husband had been through so much in the last half-dozen years that losing Markus's job was, she felt, just another obstacle in their lives.

"Markus dear, you are a highly skilled engineer, I know you'll be able to find another job when we get home. Certainly there are other opportunities."

"In my line of work? Electrical engineering...in Windhoek? The military before, and now the new electric company, are the only ones needing my skills. At least they did need my skills...but apparently not now."

He slumped deep into the soft sofa in the parlor as the two women looked on. Rupert was on the floor pushing a set of wooden railroad cars around the legs of a table while Charlotte watched.

Anji sat down next to her brother. "I know something will turn your way, you're so talented in many ways."

"Maybe if we had gone home earlier..." Helena stopped herself from completing the thought. "Oh, I'm sorry dear, I didn't mean that." She leaned in to him and put her hand on his.

"*Ja*, it's all right, I understand...but I think I would have lost my job anyway. More and more South Africans are moving North and taking the good jobs." He sighed. "We'll figure something out."

Later that evening, Markus called Levi and told him the news. Levi offered, "Why not apply to work at that new research facility by the airport here? With your experience there has to be something for you there, even if it's only until you leave for Africa. Just don't count on the earnings. With this inflation, the mark is almost worthless. It's a good thing you have that South African silver and paper money from back home, I'll bet the bank will be delighted to exchange it for marks...and most of the merchants will take it, too."

After talking it over with Helena, Markus took Levi's advice. He took the train out to the village and entered the newly opened research building. Several men bent over a table within a well-lit office. Architectural plans were being pushed back and forth.

"Hello. Sorry to disturb you gentlemen. I'm looking for someone to talk to about applying for a job here." The three men turned around and eyed the stranger. They noted the deep scars on the stranger's face.

One of the men, wearing a uniform, greeted Markus. "*Ja*, good day to you. We are not hiring anyone at this time...we have so many veterans like you looking for work. I'm sorry...maybe in a few months something will open up." He was about to turn back to his colleagues when Markus spoke up.

"I'm an electrical engineer. I helped set up the wireless station in South West Africa before the war. And I set up a wireless station for General von Vorbeck in East Africa during the war. Besides, I learned to fly at this field back in 1908."

The uniformed man stood erect. He stared at his two companions a moment, then turned slowly around.

"You're not that pilot who flew...that tried to fly across Africa from

Windhoek to East Africa are you? I remember the story in the papers when it happened. And just the other day one of our architects was telling us he knew the man who did it."

"Yes, that was me. Your architect would have to be Solomon Levi, my friend."

The three men came over to Markus, introduced themselves, and asked his name and posting. "Markus Mathais. I'm a former captain, and during the war I was the electrical unit officer of the First Bavarian Army Corps for Lower Bavaria, headquarters in Munich, assigned to special duty in Windhoek, South West Africa. But now I'm just another civilian looking for work."

"Electrical engineer...working that wireless station in Africa, and with von Vorbeck?" The uniformed man, Colonel Helmut Kuhn, said. "Did you actually fly across Africa?"

"Yes. Well, most of the way, and then I ran out of gas and crashed in a storm. Some of the natives were kind enough to take me in for almost two months. They saved my life, really. But that's a long story and right now I just need a job."

CHAPTER LVIII

Through The Window A Saint's Blessing: April, 1922

A job was offered and Markus accepted enthusiastically. Said Colonel Kohl, "You're assigned to assist in the designing of the laboratory for aircraft wireless communication for both lighter than air and winged aircraft. We think it will be a comfortable fit for both of us". A short train ride back and forth from Munich each day was easy.

Helena was quietly proud. "I'm happy for you, dear husband. You see how God provides for us when we need him?" Unspoken went the understanding that the family would return to Africa soon.

Charlotte and Rupert were enrolled in a Catholic elementary school in Munich. Each day Rupert came home brimming with stories eager to tell. "Mama, one of the boys stuck the chalk in his nose. Sister Maria Therisa was not happy about it, but all of us were laughing so much, she laughed too! He had to go to the Mother Superior's office."

Several weeks later, on the cool spring evening of April 22nd, 1922, Frau Mathais' health collapsed. Anji, Helena and the children were by her side and Markus arrived from work just as she breathed her last.

"She died in her sleep," the nurse, an older woman, told Markus. "It was a peaceful passing. I opened the window for her soul."

"What?" Markus asked.

"Her soul. When someone dies, you must open a window to let her soul out."

He stared at her a moment. "Yes, yes, of course, thank you."

"Bless you." Helena added.

Anji knew the old superstition herself, so smiled and let it pass.

"I telephoned the church, darling; the priest will be here soon," Helena whispered to her husband as she lit a cluster of candles in Frau

Mathais' bedroom.

"Did you know, dear, it's Saint Rita's day?" she said, clutching her rosary as she continued. "Saint Rita is the patron saint of long-suffering women. Ironic, is it not? I mean, your Mama suffered a long decline...months. But now she is at peace with God."

Markus said nothing but nodded his head. He glanced at the open window and thought of the irony of that and of Saint Rita. He sat by the bed in silence, holding his mother's fragile hand. *You are free now, dear Mama*. He bent down and kissed her hand.

Father Bernard arrived wearing his vestments and carrying the precious kit containing holy water, holy oil, a small silver chalice and a golden box of hosts. He spoke a few words of condolence to the family and then removed the lid on the holy water jar. Helena, Markus, Anji and the nurse and the children dipped their fingers into the liquid and made the sign of the cross on their chests. Rupert looked on wide-eyed as the priest performed the ancient Roman Catholic rite of extreme unction. The ritual forgave the person of her sins so her soul could pass on to heaven at the second coming of Christ.

"Why is the priest here, Papa?" Rupert asked leaning into his father, and looking a bit apprehensive at the black cloaked man. "I've only seen him in church and at school."

"He is here to help Grandmamma into heaven...isn't that a wonderful thing, my son? Grandmamma will be with Jesus soon. Just like you were taught in school."

Markus hesitated a moment. "Now, kiss Grandmamma good bye, like you kiss her every night." Rupert leaned against the bed and touched his lips to her cheek.
Pulling back he said, "I don't want Grandmamma to leave. I want her to stay."

"Yes, I know, but she wants to go ahead of us to see Jesus. You'll see her again."

CHAPTER LIX

Fear Of All Fears: May-August 1922

Saint Johann's church, built by the Ascum brothers, was a little Baroque church on Sendlinger street in Munich. The funeral mass was short and quiet, except for the beautiful organ music and the angelic boys' choir. Otto and Friedl Levi, Ilsa and Rolf, and everyone from Kalvarianhof attended, including the cook, several farm hands, and Willy, who hunted rabbits for Frau Mathais during the war.

After the service, everyone returned to Frau Mathais' apartment for a light buffet lunch. Although her apartment was large, it was crowded with the many mourners. Five or six young children were enjoying themselves, including Charlotte, who was now two-and-a-half. They scurried around and between the adults, as children do. Passing Rolf, Charlotte fell down but sprang back up again. "Did you trip on the carpet, Charlotte? Maybe you should slow down," he said grinning.

"I didn't trip, I just fell!" And with that she was off again. Gradually the guests departed until only Kalvarianhof friends were left.

"Time to head home," Otto suggested, and all agreed. It was an exhausting day for everyone, and Helena was happy to tuck the children into bed early and hear their prayers.

"I see you skinned your knee today Charlotte. Does it hurt?"

"No, Mama, it's just a little scrape."

"Did you say your prayers?"

"Yes, Mama."

"Good night then, sweet dreams. I love you." With that, she turned off the light and closed the door to the children's room.

That evening, Helena and her husband, under a light quilt in their bedroom, discussed their future plans, including returning to South West Africa.

"I think we should wait until Rupert and Charlotte finish this summer session at school. What do you think, dearest?" Markus asked.

"A fine suggestion. It'll be so nice to be home again. This Bavarian winter is not what I have ever experienced in Africa!" The two laughed at the truth of it. Later, as they snuggled together, she said quietly, "I'm sorry about your mama...I know how close you were to her."

"*Ja*, it was just Mama and Anji and me after papa died. We were never rich, but she was a wonderful mother." He turned to her. "Life is so short...time passes so quickly. Here we are having another baby. It's the kids, isn't it? I mean, that keep us going with their happiness, their joy."

Helena leaned in and kissed her husband. It was one of those kisses that they both knew and understood. Her hand slid across his body, back and forth, down to his thigh.

Amid quiet groans and murmurs, he whispered, "Is it all right? I mean..."

"Yes, just let me..." Her leg crossed his abdomen as he rolled onto his back. She reached down and pulled Markus to her and kissed him. His hands slid over her light nightgown and caressed her back and shoulders. Her full breasts in his hands aroused the both of them with a wonderful rising passion they both welcomed. She raised her behind and pulled her nightgown above her hips and over her head.

"Oh...yes, darling." Markus whispered as he felt her warm bare body press down on his.

Three months later, the Catholic school's summer session was nearing its August end, and the parents were requested to attend a semi-annual meeting at the close of the school day. Markus got off work and with Helena walked the several blocks to the school. They sat in the back of the room on a low bench designed for truly little children.

Children from several grades were enrolled together for the summer session. The large classroom, with neat rows of double seats, accommodated forty students. A long blackboard ran the entire length of the front of the room, above which a large crucifix hung, bordered by a picture of the Pope Benedict XV and the Bavarian crest.

"*Ja*, you have a fine young boy in Rupert, smart and quick with numbers, and always with questions...but many times on topics we were not studying!" A broad smile graced Sister Veronica's face as she spoke.

"And Charlotte is a lovely child full of energy...sometimes too much energy, as her many bruises can attest. Just today she fell down while helping me hang the poems the class wrote on the wall here. She's already quite the literary talent; she helped Rupert write his poem, and it was one of the best in the class. You may want to encourage her to write poetry on her own when she's older."

The walk home was leisurely, and the four of them strolled along in early evening twilight. Charlotte skipped head of her parents and was just at the street crossing when she fell to the pavement. Helena and Markus were by her side in seconds.

"Oh dear, are you all right? Let me see," Helena said, brushing her daughter's legs with her handkerchief.

"I'm all right, Mama, truly." Charlotte was helped up with a hand from her father. "My legs are just a bit wobbly." For the rest of the way home she held her parent's hands.

At the end of the week, the family visited Kalvarianhof. Everyone was there for a summer lunch of pan-fried fish and three salads, washed down with *Weiss* beer called Radler. The children each had a small glass of half *Weiss* beer and half lemonade, as was the custom.

After lunch, in the back garden, the children ran off to play. Rolf and Ilsa, both now doctors practicing in the village, sat watching the children and chatting the local news. Rolf was the first to notice how Charlotte ran around with her friends.

He sat up and took note of the child's uncoordinated gait.

While Katherina and Levi talked with Otto and Friedl, Rolf nudged Ilsa and said in a low voice "Look at Charlotte." Ilsa picked up on the concern immediately.

"She should be examined right away, don't you think?"

"Yes, right away...and in Munich, by a specialist."

"Will you tell them, or should I?"

"I will," Ilsa said.

She took a deep breath and, gently but firmly and with a slight smile, interrupted the ongoing conversations.

"Helena...Markus. Rolf and I just noticed Charlotte...that is, we noticed how she's running around with the other children."

"Oh yes," Helena said. "Is she bothering you...Charlotte!" she called out.

"No, she's not bothering us at all. We love to see the children play." She hesitated a moment. "It's just that we noticed...Rolf and I, we noticed Charlotte was running in a rather awkward way. Slightly uncoordinated. It's probably nothing, but maybe she should be checked by a doctor." She looked expectantly at the parents.

"Really? What for..." Both parents looked over to their daughter running and kicking a ball back and forth with friends. Everyone at the long table turned to watch the game.

"Is there something wrong?" An edge of concern was in Helena's voice.

"It's just that Charlotte is a bit unsteady...ungainly. It's just something we noted." Everyone was now intensely staring at the child.

Markus spoke up. "*Ja*, Charlotte is at that age, all skinny legs and arms and skinny." He grinned. "Well, you two are doctors, what's your concern?" At that moment, three of the children fell into a pile laughing, got up and chased after the ball.

"See, they're all clumsy at their age." Markus said.

Rolf cut in, "Markus...Helena, it's more than that. We think something...that is, there may be a problem with her coordination and she should be checked.

"*Ja*, well, you're here. Why don't you check her? I'll call her over." Markus half-stood to do it.

"Wait!" Rolf said forcefully. "She needs to be seen by a specialist, it's not our area of expertise. I can recommend a doctor in Munich."

"In Munich? Really?" Several days later, in a hospital in Munich, the examination was complete. The white-robed specialist sat down with Markus and Helena, both very apprehensive. Ilsa and Rolf looked on, hoping and fearing what the diagnosis might be. The doctor wasted no time in delivering the harsh news.

"I'm sorry to inform you that your daughter Charlotte, is showing symptoms of the early stages of polio meningitis. The disease progressively paralyzes the limbs, typically the legs to start, and in severe cases it progresses to the entire body. Fortunately Charlotte is in the early stages of what seems to be a slower form of the disease. We gave her something for her slight fever, but... I'm afraid she must remain in hospital for the foreseeable future."

Helena burst into tears. "It's my fault...I never should have left the ranch. Charlotte wouldn't have gotten sick if we had stayed in Africa!" She mumbled to no one in particular. She slumped into Anji's arms as Wolfgang held her hand.

"Now, now sister, she's a strong little girl," he said. "Let's say a prayer for her."

Markus asked the doctor. "What can we do? There must be something. How about medicines?"

"I'm afraid not, other than the fever medication. There is no cure for polio; we can only make them comfortable while we see how well the patient resists the disease." He looked at the distraught parents. *They are so like many other parents I've seen, even if I change their names, they all look tragically the same* he thought. "It's important that we keep your daughter under constant observation. Sometimes there are complications. We'll give her the very best possible care. I'm sorry to leave you with this news, but I must get back to my other patients."

Markus looked up from "Thank you doctor, but...can we talk in the hall?" They stepped away. "My wife is eight months pregnant. I'm very concerned about her and the child given this terrible situation. I wanted you to know she's to start seeing my friend's sister, a doctor, in her professional capacity."

"Good. It's best to keep a very close eye on your wife given the present situation. Her doctor will know what's best." As Markus returned to his wife, Anji and Rolf joined the doctor in the hall.

The doctor nodded to them both. "You know we will do what we can, however little that is. It really is up to Charlotte's body to fight the disease. Thanks for bringing her; we'll do what we can if she declines."

Katherina's brothers, Moses and Benjamin, came down from Potsdam for a week in support of their friends in the Mathais family, and stayed a few nights at Kalvarianhof renewing their contact with the Levis.

"We're sorry Mama and Papa couldn't come with us. They're both not too well and the trip would have been too much. They send their greetings, prayers, and best wishes for Charlotte, and also said they're hoping for another grandchild."

CHAPTER LX

The Pendulum Swings: September-October 1922

Everyone in the family including close friends like the Levis, kept up a constant visiting schedule with Charlotte and Helena as the weeks passed. "She can still move her legs a bit, so it appears she is not in decline as we see in too many other patients." The hospital doctor was giving his periodic update to Markus and Helena and their two doctor companions, Ilsa and Rolf. "It's a good sign. We'll see over the next few weeks how Charlotte's condition develops."

"Did you hear that, Helena darling, the doctor says it's a good sign. Helena?" Lines under Helena's eyes and the conditions of pregnancy showed a tired woman coping with two major burdens. She sat quietly, one hand's fingers turning over and over the gold cross hanging from her neck. A rosary hung out of the pocket of her stretched skirt. Her listlessness became a concern for everyone.

"I can prescribe something stronger than what she's taking, but we can only go so far because of her pregnancy." Ilsa said to Markus.

"*Ja*, if there is something that can relieve her low mood, that would be most helpful, thanks."

Several days later, Markus returned from work at the wireless research laboratory at the old airport in the village. To his delight, that day he'd been promoted to director of a research team of young electrical engineers. Back at his mother's apartment with the good news, he was met at the door by his wife, and to his wonderful surprise, she was alert and cheerful.

"Darling, the doctor just called. Charlotte's condition is starting to improve! Isn't it wonderful!" Helena hugged her husband, kissed him, and then burst into an animated description of her daily prayers for Charlotte's deliverance and for her own ongoing pregnancy and imminent delivery. "Every day that you're at work, I've gone to a different church to ask their patron saint to intercede on our behalf. God will not let our little Charlotte suffer any longer...I'm sure of it."

"That's such good news!" Markus exclaimed as he whirled his wife around in a circle. She gasped as he set her down. "Oh darling, I'm sorry. I must be more careful with you."

"I'm fine, it's just my back, and it's a chore to walk around much. I'm feeling much better from hearing the doctor's news."

"Did he say anything else?"

"He said that if all goes well, then Charlotte could be released from the hospital as early as next week. He said there're a series of exercises we must do with her when she comes home." She beamed at her husband, then added, "And you with a promotion. I'm so proud of you dearest."

"Thank you, thank you!" He bowed low in an exaggerated gesture, with a big grin on his face. "And, they want me to fly again. I'll be taking the new wireless equipment up to see how it handles changes in the weather and that sort of thing."

"I thought you'd had enough of flying after that dreadful war!"

"All shall be well, my dearest. Nobody's shooting at me anymore."

The following week saw a happy child walk on her own through her grandmama's apartment door, with only the slightest limp to show her brush with tragedy. At the same time, Helena was sure it was near time for her to deliver her third baby.

"I've invited Katherina and Levi to visit for a few nights. It's always a pleasure to have them." Helena said.

"Are you sure that's a good idea? After all..."

"It's fine. They're no trouble, and Kathi offered to help the way she always does. We'll be grateful for her once this baby arrives."

The following evening, after a light supper, the two women sat in the front parlor chatting about their families.

Kathi said "So you're going to have your third child, and in Germany, how wonderful! Now, with Charlotte almost completely well again, we all have so much for which to be grateful."

"*Ja*, I talked with Ilsa and Rolf and they agreed it's ill advised to travel back to South West Africa in my ninth month, and doubly so with the October storms. My husband's pleased, though, he'll finally have a child born in his homeland. I'm happy enough just to meet Mary. Oh, that's her name if she's a girl!" She giggled like she was sharing some secret.

"*Ja*, we can't be too careful with our health now, can we." Helena leaned in to the tea pot. "A bit more for you?"

Helena gracefully accepted the cup. "Everyone has been so supportive since Markus and I arrived. And we've been here...how many months has it been...six, eight, nine? I can't imagine it's been that long, but it has."

While the women enjoyed their conversation, the men sat at the kitchen table, two steins of beer in front of them.

"...and the political situation...did you read in the paper today...here, I've got it right here." Markus scooped up the afternoon edition from the bench.

"This reporter made a list of...well, you read it." Markus pushed the newspaper across to Levi. "Here, below the fold," he pointed.

Levi took the paper and gave it a snap, lining up the creases of the newspaper. "This article here, by Myron Jacobs, is that the one?"

"*Ja, Ja*, that's it...quite the long list!"

After a paragraph detailing the political situation in the aftermath of the war was a list of headlines that covered the page:

January 10, 1920: Treaty of Versailles Starts, U.S: "We are still at war with Germany."
January 12, 1920: Amer. Pres. Wilson Reports: 29,000 Jews killed in Ukraine in 1919
January 15, 1920: U.S: $150,000,000 to Poland, Austria, Armenia in War with Russia
January 23, 1920: Allies Demand Kaiser Wilhelm II Extradition, The Dutch Refuse
February 24, 1920: Adolf Hitler Advocates Anti-Semite Policy, Creates NSGW Party
March 17, 1920: Berlin Coup Restoring Royal Prussian Monarchy Fails.
March 20, 1920: Bolshevik Communists Attack Finland, Poland, Parts of Berlin
April 25, 1920: League Of Nations Gives Britain Palestinian Mandate.
April 26, 1920: Palestine: Arabs Attack British Fearing Influx of Jews.
July 18, 1920: Potsdam: Kaiser Wilhelm's Son, Prince Joachim Commits Suicide
July 24, 1920: French Army Attacks Syrian King Feisal, Imposes French Mandate.

September 30, 1920: French Seize German Togo, Mandated By League Of Nations.
November 1, 1920: Turks Massacre 10,000 Armenians.
January 6, 1921: Berlin: 29,000 German Children Suffer Tuberculosis
January 24, 1921: Paris: Allies Demand $56 Billion In German War Reparations
March 22, 1921: Reparations Com. Demands 1 Billion in Gold, Germany Defaults
July 2, 1921: American Pres. Harding Signs German Peace Treaty Ending World War
August 26, 1921: German Finance Minister Erzberger Assassinated By Nationalists
October 20, 1921: Lisbon: Portuguese Premier Granjo Assassinated By Military
November 7, 1921: Mussolini Declares Himself Leader of Fascist Party In Italy
January 2, 1922: German Inflation: 7260 German Marks Buys One American Dollar
June 24, 1922: Foreign Minister Walter Rathenau Assassinated By Nationalists
July 12, 1922: Paris: German War Commission Asks Reparations Deferred to 1924
July 20, 1922: League Of Nations Gives German East Africa to Britain
July 20, 1922: League Of Nations Divides German Cameroon To Britain & France
July 22, 1922: Germany Barred From International Olympics
July 24, 1922: League Of Nations Gives Britain Egyptian Mandate
August 5, 1922: Fearing Assassination, Albert Einstein Flees Germany
August 5, 1922: Italy: Civil War Rages Between Fascists and Communists
October 15, 1922: In Berlin, Thousands Of Communists Riot Against Weimar Government
October 23, 1922: German Chancellor Karl Wirth Declares Financial Crisis
October 23, 1922: Berlin: German Government May Declare National Bankruptcy
October 30, 1922: Italian King Victor Emmanuel: Mussolini Is To Form Government

It took Levi a few moments to digest the impact of the list's potential implications. He shook his head slightly, as Markus had seen him do many times. "So what do you think, Levi? This economic and political instability and anti-Jewish rhetoric and worse? Where is this going?"

Levi looked at his friend and said, "I've heard it before. We've heard it before. Remember, on the way back from China in the fall of 1900? Heiner? That was mild compared to what we Jews are used to. This Hitler fellow, he's real poison, but not just because he's anti-Semitic. There've always been people like that, lots of them. He's poison because he's a gifted speechmaker. He captures the crowd. He had 50,000 people at a rally recently! He preys on their insecurities and fears and hopes. He says he's going to make Germany great again, that sort of thing. And in these times, he has them in the palm of his hand. That's the danger." He laid the paper down and picked up his mug.

Markus leaned in toward Levi, and staring intently asked, "What should you do, then? Can one person do anything about all this chaos?"

"Support the Weimar Republic." Levi said. "It's duly elected, it's democratic, it's trying to deal with insurmountable problems as best it can. But those winners of the Great War are killing us with their reparation demands, especially France." He took a long draft of his beer. "They really hate us, that's for sure. Too many defeats for them. First the Franco-Prussian war of 1870 where they got crushed for invading Prussia. Then this past war, so much of it fought on their soil...if the Americans hadn't come in, there could have been a completely different outcome. Remember, there was mutiny in the French trenches."

The two men sat quietly, draining their mugs and thinking their separate thoughts.

CHAPTER LXI

Christmas Markets And Winter Winds: November-December 1922

"There you are," Katherina said gaily as she and Helena entered the room. Both women walked together, with Katherina supporting the pregnant Helena. Markus had just put more wood into the large porcelain heating stove to ward off the chill.

"You two look like you're brooding over your beers. We're here to cheer you up! Is that not right, Helena?" The two wives laughed as they gently slipped into kitchen chairs at the table.

"We were just thinking...the two of us, that we should all go into Munich and visit the winter markets. They're so lovely with all the food and gift stalls, and the music and decorations...it'll be fun!" She hesitated a moment, then added, "And we should attend the symphony...Handel's Messiah is to be performed. Helena tells me he composed it in just three weeks and for Easter, but most people think of it as Christmas music. It's so beautiful. It's fine for Hanukkah too, don't you think! How do you fine gentlemen feel about our most romantic idea?"

Broad smiles were on the wives, surprised looks on their husbands. Levi asked, "Really, are you sure you ladies are up to that, given..."

Markus joined in. "Didn't Ilsa and Rolf suggest you take care these last few weeks before..."

He was in turn cut off by Helena. "We'll take them along! Two doctors should be enough, don't you think?" She laughed cheerily. "Wolfgang has already agreed to watch the children. Besides, you gentlemen can arrange for us to be dropped off right in front of the cathedral. That's where the winter market stalls are, so we won't have to walk far in the cold, and you can select an aisle seat in the pews for me, too!"

It was obvious to Markus and Levi that a musical evening out was firmly planned.

"*Ja*, your wish is our command," Levi smiled.

"Ask and it shall be given unto you." Markus added, bowing his head in exaggerated reverence.

"Don't you mock the Bible, husband. God hears every word you say."

"Of course, of course, my love. I'll purchase tickets for tomorrow." He glanced at Levi, slightly rolling his eyes.

Even though they were all bundled up, it was a long, cold drive into Munich, but the four of them, along with Ilsa and Rolf, laughed gaily as they wiped the fog off the car windows to see out.

"Look at the lights, they're everywhere!" Helena exclaimed. "And the Christmas decorations...did I tell you Markus is getting a Christmas tree for the apartment? The children will be so happy."

"Yes, I will, with a little help from my friend here." Markus said. "Levi, do you think we can find a Christmas tree in your forest?"

Levi jokingly said, "Yes, no problem, but they're all Jewish trees! Is that a problem?"

Helena cut in smiling. "That would be fine, Levi. Jesus was Jewish as we all know, as were his followers, so a Jewish Christmas tree seems quite appropriate."

"Well, then, it's decided." Levi said. "This week we all go to Kalvarianhof for tree hunting and a nice warm holiday dinner...and, you can see our menorah, all polished for Hanukkah!" He paused a moment, thinking, then said, "Markus, I've told you this before, but Helena, do you know much about the Jewish traditions of Hanukkah?" Without waiting for an answer he launched into his explanation.

"Hanukkah is an eight day celebration of the victory of the Jewish Maccabees over the Greek-Syrians, and the rebuilding of our temple in Jerusalem. We light candles on our menorah, a kind of candelabra, one candle a night for eight nights. And Mama bakes challah bread. It's our tradition, like your Christmas!" He looked around at everyone staring at him in expectation. "That's the story!" he said.

"Thank you for the history lesson, Levi. It's all very interesting, and your menorah really is beautiful," Markus said.

Katherina spoke up. "*Ja*, so first the Christmas markets and a night of music, then a holiday dinner here with Mama's challah bread!"

The next afternoon, the three couples strolled the food stalls with their hot pretzels and sausages, hot winter wine, and the gift booths with all manner of handcrafted toys, knitted scarfs, Tyrolian clocks, and religious sculptures. Helena stopped at a woodcarver's stall.

"Oh Markus, look here, the patron saint of Munich. The Virgin Mary, all in white and blue, with infant Jesus, and she's standing on a sliver of crescent moon. See, isn't it beautiful? What a wonderful carving. We should have an image of the Mother in our home. I would like that, and the children will too." She stroked the painted wooden edifice. It would be good for them to see the mother of Jesus," she said, almost to herself. Rolf and Anji heard her comments and took note. They looked at each other and smiled as they both pulled their collars up against the cold winter wind.

"Let's go to the Ratskeller, warm up, and have supper before the symphony, shall we?" someone offered. And so the enchanting evening hours passed.

Later, back in the Mathais apartment with the children sound asleep, Katherina thanked Wolfgang for watching them. Helena, coughing from the cold, sipped hot tea. "Your rooms are made up for you, sleep well," she said between coughs.

Soon in bed, the two curled up close for warmth as Levi said, "It was a beautiful evening, wasn't it." Kathi nuzzled her husband as she kissed him good night. "It was a wonderful day, I'm exhausted."

It was a little after three in the morning when low voices in the hall outside their bedroom woke him up. Levi sat up and listened. Katherina, half-awake, said, "What?"

"Something's the matter. I'll go see."

Katherina also sat up. "What is it?" Levi pulled a blanket around his shoulders and stepped into the hall.

Markus was talking to Wolfgang. When he heard the door open, he turned and said to Levi apprehensively, "Helena is bleeding...the coughing must have caused it. I think we should take her to the hospital."

"Yes, yes, of course. I'll get dressed and go start the car."

"Leave the car to me, Levi, you get Kathi up." Wolfgang said. By this time Katherina was peeking out the door.

"I heard. I'll go see Helena." She took the blanket off of Levi's shoulders, wrapped it around herself and went down the hall with Markus following. "Helena dear, how is it? When did it start?" Kathi asked.

"I've been coughing on and off, not badly, I noticed the blood about an hour ago."

"How bad...how much?"

"It won't stop. I need a doctor."

"Yes, of course, darling." Markus said. "We'll take you to the hospital right away, your brother is getting the car...let me help you."

"Let's get you up and dressed," Katherina said.

"Should we call an ambulance?" Levi asked from just outside the room. "I can call one."

"No, no, I'm sorry for all the trouble, just take me to the hospital in your car, I'll be all right." She paused..."It's just my baby..."

The hospital was a five minute drive away this time of night. Hospital personnel assisted her into the emergency ward. After a quick exam the doctor said, "We're taking her directly to surgery. Frau Mathais has lost a lot of blood. She may need a Caesarian. We've started a blood transfusion," the white coated doctor continued, "Going through natural labor may be too much for her given her condition."

"And the baby?" Katherina asked.

"Yes, let's make sure the baby is delivered as soon as possible. We can fully focus on stopping the hemorrhaging then."

Markus, Katherina, Levi, Anji and Johan, and Ilsa and Rolf all waited into the next morning for word from the doctor. Finally about six am, the doctor came out through the frosted glass doors into the waiting room. He looked exhausted but got right to the point.

"You've got a fine little baby girl, Herr Mathais. She's healthy and with her mother who says the baby's name is Mary." The room erupted in cheers, smiles and laughter.

"Thank God, we were so concerned." Katherina exclaimed.

Ilsa and Rolf did not join in the merriment, instead choosing to watch the doctor closely. They were both physicians and knew when there was bad news on the way. "Markus, you can go in to see your wife in just a moment. First, I must tell you your wife is very weak. We stopped the hemorrhaging but Helena is, as I said, quite weak. We are concerned she may be suffering from pre-eclampsia."

The room became absolutely still. Wide tense eyes stared at the doctor. Markus interrupted "What? Herr doctor, what is pre- pre...whatever you said she might have?"

"Pre-eclampsia." The doctor pronounced clearly. "It's a condition that causes high blood pressure and distresses the heart and other organs in the body. It sometimes occurs in women at child birth and it is...or rather, can be, quite serious." He was looking at Markus, and now spoke more gently. "You can see your wife. And your Mary, of course. Just don't excite Frau Helena. She must have quiet and rest. We, of course, are doing everything to treat her symptoms."

Over the next several hours they all waited anxiously. Markus remained with Helena while everyone else sat or paced in the waiting room.

Ilsa and Rolf volunteered to get everyone coffee from the hospital café. While retrieving the drinks, Rolf and Ilsa talked.

"This is serious. You saw how much blood she lost. And now with pre-eclampsia..."

"Yes. Helena's a healthy women, but that condition can close off her organs, and with the high blood pressure...I fear for her, Rolf."

"Yes, me too. We just have to wait and see."

CHAPTER LXII

Dreams of Africa: December 1922

Two days later, in the private room of the maternity ward where Helena had been moved to, Markus half sat, half laid next to his ill wife. His sister, Anji, rested in a far corner chair. Markus had just brought another blanket and was spreading it over the two blankets already draping his wife.

"It's so cold here, Markus, the winter... so cold..." Helena whispered. "I...I want."

"Yes, my love, what is it?"

"I want to go home...to Africa. Promise me, husband....promise me."

"Yes, of course, my dearest. We will all go home to the ranch...soon."

"My baby...see?" Little Mary made not a sound as she slept nestled close in to her mother.

In the shallowest of breaths, Helena whispered, "God has blessed us, hasn't he, Markus...hasn't he?"

"Yes, yes, we are blessed, we have a beautiful little baby, my dearest...now rest a while, just rest." Anji got up from the chair, "Why don't you to go back to the apartment and get some rest. I'll stay awhile and Wolfgang is coming later."

Wolfgang arrived just after the patient dinner trays were distributed. He sat by the untouched tray, near his sleeping sister. He was reading a letter just received from Helena's sister Christina and her husband Richard, congratulating her and Markus on the birth of their third child. The long letter was full of news of the ranch and local happenings in Windhoek, and how everyone looked to their speedy return.

"It's quite a letter," he said, "You'll have to read it yourself. Helena? Helena? Nurse!" he shouted.

The hospital room was crowded. Markus, sobbing, buried his face in the pillow next to his dead wife, still lying where he left her several hours ago. Wolfgang sat slumped in the chair next to the bed wiping his eyes. Anji, Johan and Katherina stood nearby. Sobs, sniffles, and muffled words hung in the air like a bad dream that could not be shut out of one's mind.

Levi, off in the shadows of the hospital room, thought:

No, no, no! My God, this is not happening. This is beyond tragic. How could this be! Not Helena! Not Markus' Helena. He could not stop shaking his head back and forth, in denial of the tragic scene before him.

Ilsa gave her brother Markus a heavy sedative, and one for Wolfgang, before Wolfgang, Levi and his wife took Markus home to the apartment and put him to bed. Rupert and Charlotte were perplexed by the sober mood of the adults, but were reassured that they would see their new little sister Mary, tomorrow.

Later, in bed, Levi said to Katherina:

"How will we...he, tell the kids? And Markus...he's a strong, tough man when it comes to himself. I mean he can survive almost anything if it's only himself to be concerned with. But Helena, his precious Helena gone! I just can't believe it...and I don't know how he will cope with this...this loss, this catastrophe!"

Levi shifted around under the heavy covers then continued his thoughts.

"I saw him cry only three times, ever, but never from battle or injury, just in losing a woman he truly loved."

Katherina: "Tell me."

"*Ja*, the first time was way back in late summer of 1900 on board our ship leaving China after the Boxer Rebellion we both fought in. I remember him, leaning on the railing of that ship, sobbing, as we saw the coast of China slip away. He truly loved Li Ling...that was his girlfriend. He looked out across the water of the South China Sea to the mainland, as we sailed away, and she was gone forever."

"And the second time?"

"*Ja*. The second time I saw him like this, truly completely broken, was when I gave him that letter from my sister Ilsa. He read it and wept. She had just left him at the train station to go north and out of his life. Not until then, after he had me read Ilsa's letter, did I realize how much they loved each other. But it just wasn't possible then...a Jew and a Catholic together and all that. It was tragic for both of them."

Levi shook his head, as if trying to shake an unseen vision out of his mind.

"And..." Kathi said.

"*Ja*, and now this...this, the sadist most tragic of all...Helena, lovely Helena, the love of his life, the mother of his children, Rupert, Charlotte, and little Mary...gone. I just can't believe it...I don't want to believe it." He paused a moment as Katherina hugged her husband gently.

"Helena, snatched away from them...from life. Why? There were so many tragedies in their lives back in South West Africa, and now this, and here...this cruel final blow."

He paused again, as Katherina wiped a tear from her cheek, and said, "I remember hearing Helena say so often, 'Why is God punishing me'. Truly...why *is* God punishing them all? Helena had such faith, such belief. If there is a heaven she must be there, and somehow, I hope, she's relieved of the pain of her tragic life."

Levi pulled the feather bed coverlet up tight around his ears as Katherina snuggled closer against a cold, cruel winter.

CHAPTER LXIII

Darkness Descends: December 1922

The long telegram from Wolfgang arrived at the Conrad ranch in South West Africa on December 22, 1922. Sambolo had picked up the mail in town and brought it, unopened, to the table in the parlor of the ranch house. He left it there and went back to work in the barn.

The shriek from the house brought him running back into the parlor in time to see Heidi slumping to the floor, crying uncontrollably, clutching the telegram. Petre came running from the kitchen.

"What is it, Heidi? What is it?" He asked in an obviously stressed voice. She couldn't speak. She could hardly catch her breath. Petre gently took the telegram from her hand and read it. Tears ran from his eyes, as Sambolo looked on fearfully. He too took the message and read it.

"No, no, no...not Frau Helena, noooo!" Petre took Heidi in his arms, as the three of them formed a tearful clutch on the floor.

Michael's heavy boots crunched as he approached the house. Petre stood to hand him the tragic message.

"Bad news, Michael, very bad news. I am so very sorry."

Through tears and a breaking voice, Michael called Richard so he could be with Christina when he called. Richard hurried home from his office in time to hear the telephone ringing. He reached his wife in time for her to collapse into his arms. No one outside their house heard her plaintive, silent cries.

The last of the tragically fated Conrad clan still in Africa, Christina and Richard, Michael and Heidi, and also Petre and Sambolo, the six of them, sat in the middle parlor grieving, trying to comprehend this latest and greatest of all the bad, indeed terrible events of the past years. Christina held the telegram in her still trembling hand and, in a hoarse voice, said, "Markus and Wolfgang are bringing her home...and with Charlotte, Rupert, and baby Mary. We must make arrangements." The telegram slipped from her hand and fluttered to the floor like a dead leaf. She turned, as if in a stupor; Richard rose to take her arm. With slumped shoulders they walked down the hall to her old bedroom.

Meanwhile, in Munich, a memorial service was being held at the little St. Johan's Catholic Church, the same church where Frau Mathais services were held. Among others, the group of mourners consisted of Otto and Friedl Levi, Katherina, Levi and daughter Rebecca, Levi's sister Ilsa and husband Rolf Kepler, and Willi and Hilda, the cook from Kalvarianhof. Also attending were Colonel Koln and several colleagues from Markus' job, and Anji, Johann, and their daughter Hannah. All crowded the front pews, as Markus and his children Rupert, Charlotte, and baby Mary in Anji's arms, sat nearest the open coffin.

Unannounced, Charlotte got up and quickly walked to the open coffin and gently dropped in a small folded slip of paper. She hurried back to her seat, all eyes on her. She turned to her father and whispered, "Me and Rupert wrote Mama a poem."

All those in attendance, on entering the church, passed by a golden sculpture of Death in the form of a skeleton with his scythe, hanging off the vestibule wall, in the fashion of the Rococo style of the church. A blaze of candles lit the pews. An organ played a dirge as four altar boys and the priest prepared to give the funeral mass.

Prayers Helena had heard and recited many times were spoken again in hushed voices. The priest, read in Latin the Roman Catholic ritual absolution incantations. He offered solace to the family and assurances.

"A loving God has already promised the devout Helena a welcoming place in heaven." Near the end of the ceremony and as part of it, the coffin was to be closed. Until now, the children were surprisingly quiet. But as the lid of the polished wooden coffin was lowered, Rupert leaped up crying, "No no, don't close it, don't close it...Mama!"

German South West Africa

CHAPTER LXIV

A Wish Fulfilled: January 23, 1923

The old Studebaker truck from the Conrad ranch sat near the railroad loading dock in Windhoek, South West Africa, it's engine running. They all wore black. What was left of the happy pre-war Conrad clan, so diminished by that conflict, and a multitude of tragedies, gathered in the waiting room, under a beautiful blue sky filled with white puffy clouds tumbling in the upper winds.

Waiting to welcome home Markus, the children and Wolfgang, were Helena's sister and brother, Christina and William. Nearby were Richard and Heidi. Petre and Sambolo stayed at the ranch preparing an early evening meal and assisting baby Mary's newly hired wet nurse with her lodgings.

The coal-burning locomotive whistled and clanged it's bell, well down the tracks, and pulled into the station in clouds of steam. The station master brought out a step and put it in position so that passengers could step down. As the family greeted Markus, Wolfgang and the children, the grating sound of the freight car door opened enough so a dark wooden coffin could be slid onto the platform.

It was on this same platform that Helena met her fatally injured brother Arnold after the war. How ironic that now she, in her coffin, arrived here too. It caused a shudder of reality to those watching. The sounds of anguish were just discernable above the hissing engine.

For a moment, everyone turned away from the box that held Helena's body and focused on the new arrivals.

"Oh, Wolfgang, I'm so happy you're home, so happy to see you again. Dear brother, I've missed you so, so much." Christina said, hugging him. "And Markus, dear Markus...I am so sorry..."

He made a gesture to say, *Yes, I understand, there simply aren't words to say this well.*

She continued to speak quietly. "And baby Mary...Let me take her. Just a month old, aren't you." Mary cooed and Christina nuzzled her cheek. She hesitated a moment, then burst into tears.

"You're all we have left of my dear Helena...you and Markus and the children."

CHAPTER LXV

A Trail Of Falling Flowers: January-April 1923

The family plot at the Conrad ranch was crowded with graves. Tomas Conrad, patriarch of the family (d. 1921), laid next to his wife Gretle, who died much earlier. Christina's brothers' graves lay nearby: Arnold (d. 1916) of war wounds, Humboldt (d. 1918) of influenza, and Norbert (d. 1919) shot accidentally by a South African officer, and now Helena (d. 1922). The family had been decimated. For weeks after the funeral, gloom shrouded the ranch, interspersed with the sniffles and wails of babies. Heidi and Christina both gave birth safely, bringing new life and hope to the family. Slowly life resumed.

Wolfgang seemed happy to be back in the saddle and chasing stray cattle. Heidi, with much help from Petre, oversaw the care of the brood of children with the help of the wet nurse, and tried with limited success to ease Markus out of his profound depression. He slept late, drank too much and wandered the ranch lands aimlessly. Richard invited Markus into town to the telephone and telegraph company for lunch several times a week.

"Have you decided what you want to do...what you could do, here in Windhoek?" he asked.

"Nothing, no. I'm thinking about it."

Several months passed. One Sunday in May, at dinner, with everyone in attendance, Markus said:

"I have an announcement to make." The entire table stopped eating.

"I've decided to return to Germany, to my job at the airfield. I've thought about this for weeks." He looked around the table at his loving family, all eyes on him. "Really, there is nothing for me here...I mean, besides all of you!" he said, with an awkward smile.

"This was my adopted home with Helena here and all of you. But now..." He hesitated. "Now it just isn't the same. I need to work, to raise my children, to earn a living. I just can't do that here. There are simply no jobs for me. Richard..." He looked at his brother in law, "Richard and I have searched and searched."

Christina said hesitantly "But Markus, the children...who's going to raise the children? We can do that, help with the kids...surely you can find something, some employment." She looked around the table for support.

Heidi was first. "Christina is right Markus, we can help with your children, but I do understand, it's just that it will be so different if you're not here. We'll miss you so."

Michael was next: "Much as I want you to stay and be a close part of the family, I can imagine you want to do what you were trained for, what is your great love...flying and electrical engineering, and you really can't pursue that in Windhoek. I understand." Michael looked at his wife with an unspoken expression of 'It's what has to be'.

"I'm sorry for disappointing you...and I know Charlotte, Rupert and Mary would have a good life here, but they will be all right in Munich too. I'll manage."

A great silence fell across the dinner table. Petre was in the hallway and heard the conversation. He turned away slowly and went back to the kitchen, just as another member of the family spoke up.

CHAPTER LXVI
A Decision: May 1923

Wolfgang had been silent through Markus' startling announcement, but now he spoke up. "This is probably the best time for me to tell you my feelings...my plans, too." All heads swiveled around toward the other end of the table.

"Yes, Wolfgang, what is it?" Michael asked.

"I've decided to go back to Germany, too. I've been thinking about..."

He was interrupted by both Christina and Michael.

"What? No! Your place is here, at the ranch with us. Wolfgang, you can't mean that!" Christina said in an anxious voice. Michael practically spoke on top of his sister.

"Brother, whatever prompted that idea? You love the ranch, you're a rancher. We need you, we love you, all of us...the family. Whatever would you do in Germany? Why go there again? You've seen it, you've experienced it, the turmoil and..." Wolfgang interrupted:

"That's just it, I have seen it...the bigger world out there, and I like it. I want to be a part of it, to find a new life for myself. I'm forty- eight years old. I don't want to be chasing cattle around the rest of my life. I'm sure I can find something, a livelihood there. I want to find myself, what I can be, beyond this, this isolated life. I do love you all, you know that, and the ranch...I will miss you and I'll miss the ranch life, some parts of it...but I need to do this. This is my only chance to find..."

"What!" What could there be there that we can't give you here!" Christina emphasized through tears.

"Love," he said in a whisper so quiet only he really heard it. "Companionship...I've never had...what you all have...a true, close friend...a relationship. Even if it ends badly...Oh, I'm sorry Markus, I didn't mean to hurt you...with that remark...I mean dear, dear Helena's passing, I..."

"You didn't, my friend, you didn't. And you do deserve a chance at life, at seeing what's out there. I hope you find it...happiness, friendship, whatever you call it, I hope you find it, like all of us have in varying ways...in varying degrees."

Christina couldn't take it. She burst into tears, got up and left the room.

Heidi wiped a tear from her eye but managed a smile as she turned to Wolfgang. "I'll miss you terribly dear Wolfgang, but I know how you feel." She looked down at the table and slowly continued:

"I was blessed with a second chance at life, from...from my previous situation at Madame Oldendorf's. I was taken in, here, by the Conrad family, and I found a home and...love." She turned, smiling, to look directly at Michael.

"My true love, my savior," she said. "I know the hollowness, the emptiness of having nothing...nobody. If you can, you should try to find it. You are such a fine man, Wolfgang, you deserve happiness...companionship, a woman to share your life with. I know it would be hard to find that here at the ranch, but in Germany..." she didn't continue.

אֲנִי לְדוֹדִי
וְדוֹדִי לִי

"I AM MY BELOVED'S AND MY BELOVED IS MINE."
SONG OF SOLOMON 6:3

CHAPTER LXVII

Flowers In The Wind: May 1923

I t's a two week old paper up from Johannesburg, Markus. Here, did you see this article?" Michael, sitting with his brother-in-law at the ranch, pushed the paper across the parlor couch.

"The French and Belgians sent a hundred thousand troops and cavalry into the Rhine area of Germany to take the coal and steel, and they even confiscated all the automobiles in this one town...forgot the name...because Germany doesn't have the money to pay reparations. It's just beyond belief!"

"*Ja*, I saw for myself the mess things are in back home...veterans sleeping in the streets, even disabled, Iron Cross men...and the inflation, it's a disaster for everybody. It's a good thing I have that South African money, it'll buy anything. I know things will be tough, but Wolfgang and I will..." He stopped a moment and stared at a short article at the bottom of an inner page.

"What?" William asked.

"My God, look here," he snapped the newspaper and brought it up closer to his eyes. "Inflation hit forty thousand marks to the American dollar! German money is worthless! Are you sure you really want to go back to that? I mean, it's not the Germany you knew before the war, or even from last year."

"Please, don't make it harder than it is for me." Markus stiffened. "I'm returning and that's final...and I do have a job, a good one...except it doesn't pay well." The two men sat there for a few seconds then both burst into laughter.

"Well, you're right about that!" Michael choked out laughing.

That night, Markus had a dream. He saw Helena smiling at him, laughing, in a mist, in a long white dress like she wore before the war and the scars and the deaths.

They were up in the grove of trees on the rise behind the ranch house. It was spring and the wild flower blooms covered the ground. She stood there swaying with the light wind blowing through her hair, a small bouquet of flowers in her hand. He couldn't hear her in his dream, but he saw her telling him, 'I love you, I love my life, I love Africa, I'm home.'

He saw the bouquet of flowers tumble from her hand, the wind gently scattering them as they fell. 'It's time for you to go home too,' he heard her say in his dream. In his mind's eye, she seemed to fade into that mist, still smiling at him. He stirred in his bed, half awake, half asleep. He sensed the early light of a new day, of a new life.

"Thank you my love," he whispered in the silence.

END OF BOOK THREE

"Ich Liebe Dich"

"I love you."

A Note From the Author

I hope you enjoyed *An Incident in Africa*. If you haven't already, please read *The Perilous Journey* and *The Storm That Shook the World* for the beginning of Markus and Levi's family saga. Both books are available on Amazon. If you'd like a hardcover copy of *An Incident in Africa*, you can inquire at gossipparkbooks@gmail.com.

Before you close this book, I leave you with three thoughts:

First: The most valuable gift you can give to any writer is to share your thoughts with them. A short review on Amazon is the best way to do that, though a post on social media or emailing the author is enough to make the writing process worthwhile.

Second: For your pleasure, I have included the first seven chapters of book four, *Like A Gathering Storm*.

Third: Remember, a good book is a friend forever!

Walter Soellner

German South West Africa

CHAPTER I

The Mind's Eye: May 1923

The last several weeks of May, 1923, were a busy but melancholy time at the Conrad ranch, north of Windhoek in what had been German South West Africa. With the defeat of Imperial Germany and its African colonies in the Great War, British South Africa occupied the German colony. Turmoil, exploitation and despair confronted the conquered inhabitants. Like others, members of the extended family at the Conrad ranch also sought new opportunities elsewhere.

Wolfgang sorted through the large chest of drawers in his room, deciding what to take, what to leave behind, and what to give to the church in Windhoek for their relief box. He also tried to sort out his feelings over announcing his intent to seek a new life in Germany.

I must do this, I must...but I'm hurting everyone I'm leaving behind here, I know that, I know, especially Christina, dear Christina, how can I ever forgive myself for leaving her...she to take...must take Helena's place...the only women to oversee the ranch...yes, there's Heidi, sweet Heidi, but it's not the same...and, of course, Michael, my dear last brother...God, I can't believe they're all gone, just him and me...except Richard, he's strong, thank God she has him...and Michael...they'll have to hire to keep the ranch going...he and Heidi and Christina can't do it alone...they could sell some of the animals but the income loss...Petre and Sam...thank God they're with us. Solid as two rocks those two, really solid, they can do pretty much anything...but I have to go...everything over there...it's wonderful, I have to go...I'll find something, someone maybe...I want that...but they mustn't know...I don't want them to know...ever.

His announcement preyed on the minds of others as the days counted down to the date when Markus, his children and Wolfgang were to depart. Christina, on her back in bed in the middle of the day, stared at the ceiling while tears wetted her pillow.

He's really going, leaving us. For how long? Will he ever be back? My brother, my dear brother how could you? What can I say, what can I do to stop you? Change your mind? Wolfgang please don't do this to us...to me...to me. I love you so. What will I do without you? Nobody can stop him, not even me.

Michael was in the barn, brushing down his favorite horse while turning his thoughts over and over.

If he just hadn't gone with them to Germany, he'd stay with us, stay here. Now with Markus and Levi and everybody over there...how could he not be attracted to all of it, the cities and the people. He never saw so many...really sophisticated, not just farmers and ranchers like here. I don't blame him. It's going to be hard with him gone, damn we're losing everybody. Just Christina and me left...if it weren't for Heidi I'd probably leave too. No, no, I wouldn't do that, this is my land. Papa's land. Maybe he'll come back, it's possible. No, probably not, I don't even want to think about it.

Heidi, Michael's wife was in the kitchen with Petre, slicing apples for strudel. *I don't blame Christina for being so upset, I am too. She's angry, feeling abandoned. Thank God she's got Richard. I remember when Mama died and Papa...killed himself...I was so lost and hurt...she's lost so much of her family, more than I had to lose...Wolfie deserves to go...find himself a wife...I've never been anywhere...Windhoek is all I know. That's O.K, but I'd like to travel sometime though. I've never seen Wolfie pay much attention to women, he's handsome enough, but getting on.*

Richard, Christina's husband sat alone in his office at the Windhoek Telephone & Telegraph Company, looking out his window at the rebuilt power station while daydreaming. *If I could have found Markus a job here, Wolfgang wouldn't be leaving. Damn. There's nothing...we South Africans took all the jobs...It's a tremendous strain on Christina. Nothing I can do...give her a lot of attention? She's tough, but...I can't blame him for going. Hard life, ranching, but he loves it, that's true. Still, riding the range, dirty, dangerous...I wouldn't do it. He loves it...giving it up though...maybe he'll come back? Nah. People say they will but they never do...life gets busy. He'll find women, plenty of them in Munich, widows his age maybe. He'll be O.K...it's Christina, Michael, and Heidi who I'll have to help.*

"So he's going back to his people and taking Wolfgang with him...you think he'll be back, Petre?" Sambolo, the stable boy, asked. He and the

Conrad's cook and houseman, Petre, were in their cottage out behind the ranch house.

"Be back? Maybe, I don't know. You've seen the pictures in those German magazines, very pretty country, so green, and the big cities and big houses and castles."

Petre looked over to Sam on his bunk, smiled, thought a bit, then asked, "Are you courting that girl I see you with in town? Is she from your people?"

"I'm...that is, we're going to marry someday soon. I don't want to wait." He looked over to his longtime companion.

"Michael saw me in town with her. He said Christina and he will give me some ranch land and the cabin up in the hills if I do marry her. It was so nice; I was surprised. Then again, the Conrads've always been good to me."

"That's good of them, *ja*, they've been good to both of us. We're better off than most people." They laid there in the stillness of late evening, the low-watt lamp on the table glowed a golden light.

"Petre, you ever have a girl?" Petre rolled onto his side, facing Sam.

"A long time ago. She was from my village. My village...we were driven off by the first Germans. Her family and mine, we ran into the Kalahari. That desert...awful country! We got separated. I never saw her or my family again. Tomas found me half-dead out there, brought me to the ranch and I've been here ever since." He hesitated. "It's all right. The bad times ended a long time ago. Best to forget that pain. We're settled in just fine where we are, you and me."

CHAPTER II

British Occupied German South West Africa: May 1923

The ship to Germany, scheduled to leave May 27, 1923, was booked solid with other Germans who had sold their farms or ranches to victorious British South Africans, or lost their jobs like Markus, or simply didn't want to live under the new South African government.

"But Papa, I want to take my pony! Why can't I take him?" Rupert tried one last time the often repeated question.

His father patiently explained, "You can have a fine pony at Kalvarianhof, my friend Levi's beautiful farm. He promised. Now, up the gangway with your sisters. The ship is leaving soon."

Everyone from the ranch, including Petre and Sambolo, accompanied Markus, Wolfgang, and Markus' children Rupert, Charlotte, and baby Mary, to Wales Bay port on South West Africa's Atlantic coast.

Their steamer trunks were already in their staterooms, and Markus carried in a money belt on his hip six thousand South African Pounds, the inheritance bequeathed to Helena, his so recently deceased wife. Wolfgang, Helena's brother, refused his share, saying, "The Conrad ranch will always be my home. Besides, I'll return every so often to round up stray cattle, just like old times!" He laughed heartily and his merriment was so infectious that everyone joined in, lifting their spirits at an otherwise melancholy departure.

Christina, holding Markus' baby, said, "When will I see you again Mary darling? Will you remember your auntie? You must have your papa bring you back here many times!"

Markus heard Christina and added: "And you must visit us in Munich

211

soon!"

"Soon." Wolfgang agreed.

Moments later, Wolfgang leaned on the portside railing of the *HMS Sheffield*, holding Mary in his arms, while Markus oversaw Charlotte and Rupert's playful waving and shouting to everyone on the dock below.

"You should have good sailing, the cirrus clouds are riding high."

"What's that, Michael?"

"When they're that high up, it usually means there's good weather ahead."

"Oh," Markus said distractedly, "you ranchers sure know how to read the sky." He smiled. "Take care, you and Heidi, and Christina and Richard. Good times are on the way for all of us, you'll see."

With that, Michael hurried down the gangplank and joined the family on the dock. The sound of the great ropes securing the ship smacking the water as they were hauled onboard brought home the finality of the departure and the breaking up of the Conrad family. The *HMS Sheffield* churned the waters into a disquieting boil, adding a final gloom as the remaining Conrads returned to their uncertain lives in Windhoek and the ranch.

CHAPTER III

Turmoil and Grace: June-November 1923

Two weeks later, after sailing into London harbor, taking a cross-channel ferry and then an express train to Munich, the exhausted travelers arrived into the arms and hugs of Markus' sister, Anji, with her husband Johann holding little Hannah. "It's been too long...I'm so happy you're back, brother," she whispered. "And the children, look at you, how you've grown!" She tussled Rupert's hair, cooed at Mary, and admired Charlotte's dress. "How pretty you look in blue and white, Charlotte, just like our Bavarian flag."

Solomon Levi, Markus's childhood friend, was there, too, with his wife Katherina. They pressed in close, offering hugs and greetings. "See Markus, I knew you would come back to Bavaria. Welcome home," Levi said with a smile.

"Thanks Anji, Levi," Markus said. "It's good to be home, so good. What's going on in Munich? From the train we saw trucks full of armed men in the streets! Don't tell me there's still fighting about who should run the government. It's like the war's still going! Who're the troublemakers here in Munich?"

Johann spoke up, and in a serious tone, said, "They're the Brown Shirts, and, yes, it's the same characters as before fighting each other and the government."

Levi family estate of Kalvarianhof

Markus, Wolfgang and the children settled into the Munich apartment once owned by Markus's mother. Despite the turmoil sweeping the streets, Markus resumed his work at the airfield, while Wolfgang, like so many others, looked for work.

In late fall, they were invited out to Kalvarianhof for the day. Wolfgang and Markus spent time with Levi. Ten year old Rupert and Rebecca, Levi's seventeen year old daughter, played with their younger siblings Karl, Charlotte, and Mary, in the meadow near the barn.

Sitting on a crude log bench watching the children, Wolfgang asked, "Levi, what do you make of this Weimar government of yours? I mean, can it get back control of the country, stop the fighting?" He looked intent as he continued. "Back home in Africa, after the war, after the British South Africans took over our country, they at least made a point of running it efficiently. It's that British meritocracy. But here..." he paused, whistling through his teeth. "There's fighting somewhere most every day, and when the Bolsheviks and the fascists aren't fighting the government, they're fighting each other. It's crazy!"

"*Ja*, it seems like anarchy, or near enough, but the Weimar government is still in control of the country, most of it anyway. We hope for the best and they do what they can." He glanced at Markus and held the stare. It did not go unnoticed by his longtime friend.

Markus spoke up. "Levi's right. The Weimar Republic is on track, but it's weakened because of all this far right, far left friction and the money situation." He gave a slight smile: "Frankly, I'm still a monarchist. We had a good life under the Kaiser, remember, 'til the war. If the king had been more temperate, not so impulsive and belligerent... *Ja*, well, that's ancient history now."

"Right." Levi replied dismissively.

After a sumptuous dinner of Rouladen and cabbage salad with apple cake for dessert, most of the family retired to the overstuffed chairs in the most beautiful room at Kalvarianhof. The walls, tables and shelves were filled with wondrous and exotic artifacts from Levi's travels to China, the South Seas, the Ottoman Empire and Africa. Tribal masks from the Massai tribes of the Serengeti, silk rugs from Constantinople, carved wooden deities from German New Guinea, and Ming paintings and porcelains from China created a veritable museum in the Levi farmhouse.

"*Ja*, these are very hard and perilous times for most," Otto reflected, sipping *Jagermeister* from a cut crystal glass. "Here at Kalvarianhof, isolated as we are, in this museum my son created, it's easy to forget what's going on in the cities and across the country." He looked at Markus and Wolfgang. "I've been collecting newspapers for over a year now—not everything, just the odd front page and editorial. Here, take the stack, taken together it makes quite a picture." He reached down beside the sofa and scooped up the torn pages. "Stay the night and take a look, *ja*? I'll tell Freidl," he said, not waiting for an answer.

Later that evening, with the children snug in bed, Katherina, Otto, and Friedl said their good nights as Markus and Wolfgang spread out front pages cut from the Munchener Post on the alcove kitchen table. Levi looked on, nursing his beer.

"So much chaos in Europe." Wolfgang said. "Look at these headlines."

March 10, 1922: Weimar Government Bans All Public Monarchical Images
March 14, 1922: Mussolini's Fascists & Socialists Clash In Rome
March 15, 1922: France Seizes German Raw Materials For Reparation Payment
May 3, 1922: Weimar Government Requests U.S. Army Remain On Rhine
May 15, 1922: Weimar Cedes Upper Silesia To Poland
May 22, 1922: Bulgarian King Boris Abdicates To Communists
June 24, 1922: Walter Rathenau, Jewish German Foreign Minister Assassinated
July 20, 1922: League Of Nations: British Given German East Africa, Cameroon
July 24, 1922: League Of Nations: British Given Palestine And

Egypt

July 26, 1922: League Of Nations: France Given Syria, German Togo

August 5, 1922: Noble Winner Albert Einstein Flees Germany Escaping Assassin

August 30, 1922: South Russia In Revolt Against Bolsheviks

September 15, 1922: German Chancellor Josef Wirth: Bread First, Then Reparations

October 30, 1922: Mussolini's Fascists Again March On Rome Demand Power

November 21, 1922: French Clemenceau: Stop Rebirth Of Militarism Under Hitler

November 30, 1922: 50,000 Gather At Nazi Socialist Demonstration For Hitler Speech

December 16, 1922: Polish President Narutowicz Assassinated

January 25, 1923: 100,000 French Troops Occupy German Ruhr Seeking Reparations

April 3, 1923: Catholic Vicar General in Russia Executed For Soviet Opposition

April 4, 1923: German Unions Protest French Occupation

May 1, 1923: Nazi Paramilitary Forces Seize Military Barracks Near Munich

July 12, 1923: British PM Lloyd George Demands French Leave German Territory "Before New War Breaks Out"

August 6, 1923: Bread Riots Break Out In Northern Germany

August 7, 1923: German Mark Reaches 3.3 Million To The U.S. Dollar

August 10, 1923: German Leftists Seek German Soviet Republic

September 2, 1923: Hitler In Fierce Speech Attacks Weimar Republic

September 13, 1923: King Alphonso XIII Of Spain Supports Spanish Military Coup

October 20, 1923: Bavarian Government Breaks Relations with Weimar Berlin

October 21, 1923: German Rhineland Declares A Socialist/Communist Republic

October 27, 1923: Kahr Declared Bavarian Dictator, Weimar Declares Marital Law

October 27, 1923: Kahr, Fearing Violence, Bans Hitler Beer Hall Meetings

The next morning at breakfast, Katherina and Friedl were feeding the children when always inquisitive Charlotte said, "We're not having antelope? We had antelope at Mama's in Africa all the time." That didn't stop her from gobbling down her boiled egg and ham.

Friedl answered her. "Child, we don't have antelope in Germany, but we do have venison."

Rupert and Charlotte both shouted out, "What's venison?" and then laughed at their simultaneous question.

"Now, now, quiet down, your father is still sleeping. Venison is deer. Deer meat. We have lots of deer in the forest surrounding Kalvarianhof. I'm sure, if you are very quiet, you'll see some when you walk in the woods."

Wolfgang walked into the kitchen. "Good morning, everyone." He stood there scratching the back of his head. "Do I smell coffee?"

"Here you are Wolfie, come sit down. Where's Markus?" Kathi asked.

"He's up...be down in a minute."

"Up down, up down, Papa's up and down, up and down! Ha ha ha!"

"You kids are pretty lively this morning." Wolfgang said, reaching over to tickle Charlotte.

"Oh, the Wolfie's got me, got me!" she laughed.

Katherina slid a basket of fresh baked rolls in front of Wolfgang and a bowl of butter. "Marmalade?"

"*Ja*, thank you."

"Friedl and I prepared several baskets of food for you and Markus to take home. What with the inflation, the mark is worth nothing, nothing at all. One egg in Munich costs...I don't even know what it costs anymore." She paused. "There're eggs, four loaves of bread, a ham and sausages and the last of the vegetables from the garden." Again, she paused. "It's a wonder there're any vegetables left at all. They get stolen all the time. City people suffer so in hard times, and just like during the war they're selling everything for food. They come out and..."

Markus interrupted Katherina with his own arrival. "Good morning, good morning!"

"Papa's up! Up down, up down! Ha, ha!"

Otto came in right behind Markus and shared his greetings. "I assume you had quite a reading of our newspapers last night."

"Thanks for saving them, Otto. Things are a real mess right now."

Entering the kitchen, Levi commented, "The situation has to improve soon or there'll really be a revolution." He thought a moment, "Actually, that's what we've got now."

Katherine, stood by Levi and gently pushed her husband. "Come, eat your breakfast. You can't do anything about it on an empty stomach!" There was silence for a moment; then, all the adults burst into laughter.

"*Ja*, Levi will solve everything...right after breakfast!" More laughter.

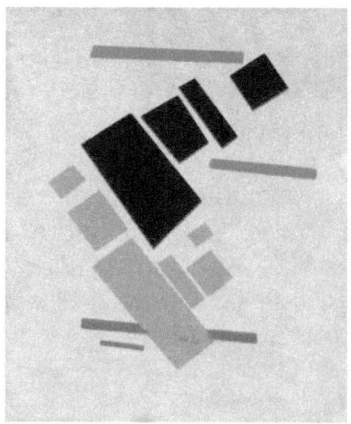

Spirit of Flight, Kazimir Malevich

CHAPTER IV

Flight and Melancholia: November 1923

They enjoyed their coffee and hot rolls and honey and the lovely late fall morning sun coming through the kitchen windows. Returning to the previous conversation, Levi said, "As a matter of fact, all is not doom and gloom. There're lots of interesting things, good things, going on all across the country."

"Really, what?" Wolfgang asked.

"Yes Papa, do tell." Rebecca said.

"*Ja*, so to begin with, Markus and I survived the war and we have a democratic government. Yes, I know it has problems but I feel...I hope the chaos in the streets ends soon. And we have this new jazz music from America that Wolfie loves so much."

Everyone looked at Wolfgang who had a mouthful of buttered bun. He shrugged and smiled sheepishly and everyone laughed.

"And we had Herr Albert Einstein who won the Nobel prize in physics for his work on photoelectric theory. He's exploring something about light and time and speed and matter...I have no idea what is significant about that. Ask Markus!"

"*Ja*, neither do we!" Freidl exclaimed.

Levi warmed to his little exposé. "We have that new design school, the Bauhaus, in Weimar...very modern, very sleek and practical...and that beautiful post office in the Bauhaus style."

"*Ja*, quite!" Rebecca exclaimed. "I saw a photo in the newspapers."

"Oh, you know about these things?"

"Yes I do!" She began, "The new painting style is called Expressionism. It's kind of like Impressionism except it has more feelings and more emotions in the colors. And they distort things like a house that bends with the wind." She sat up straight while talking, just the way she was taught in school.

"Thank you, daughter, for that art lesson. Kalvarianhof doesn't bend in the wind, but when it does blow, the curtains move in every room!" Katherina said, smiling broadly as she patted Rebecca's shoulder.

Wolfgang, who had listened quietly until now, broke in. "Did you know Markus bought a painting in Munich? It's in one of those new styles, just squares and shapes and colors. I don't see anything in it but he likes it." Everyone turned to face Markus.

Levi smirked. "So you're joining the culture crowd and buying paintings now?"

"*Ja*, well, while I was looking for work, I visited my old friend, Gustoff, in Munich. I walked by an art gallery several times. One day I walked in and saw a painting by this Russian painter, Kazimir Malevich. It was the name that caught my attention, 'Spirit of Flight'. I just stared at it, for a long time, trying to figure out what it had to do with flying." By now everyone, children included, watched Markus intensely. He looked around sheepishly.

"I went back several times, and it was still there. Eventually I figured out what I liked about that painting. It reminds me of what it's like when I'm flying. There are no words that describe how wonderful it feels when I'm in the sky...it's limitless, pure freedom. No realistic picture could ever capture that feeling, but somehow that painting does it. So I bought it."

There was silence for a moment until Kathi said, "We'll see your painting the next time we're in town. I'd like to see how it feels to fly."

Markus got up, excused himself, saying, "I'll be right back." He returned with a package the size of a large book wrapped in brown paper.

"Levi, my friend, I know how much you love art and particularly Albrecht Dürer's prints. I found this on my excursions in Munich. I hope you like it." All eyes were on him as he handed the package to Levi.

"What is this, Markus? I can't wait to see!" He tore the wrapping, and held up for all to see, an etching of *Melancholia* by Albrecht Dürer. "*Ja, mein Gott*, this is beautiful." He held it up close to his face examining the delicate, fine etched lines that made up the image.

"Thank you so much Markus, I'll have it join my other Dürers, *Rhinoceros* and *Knight, Death, and the Devil*. What a wonderful gift!"

"*Ja*, it's an interesting subject. The gallery director told me Dürer had some unusual subjects, like your rhinoceros. Dürer never saw a real rhino, so his image is a bit off. And I'm sure he never saw a knight or the devil!"

Everyone burst out laughing at the comment.

Levi passed the framed etching around for all to see and said, "I know a little about this piece. *Melancholia* is full of a variety of objects that only he knew the meaning of, and even today scholars can't decide on what it all means. That's what is so intriguing about the piece."

Melancholia by Albrecht Dürer

"I know you'll enjoy adding it to the collection Otto is so proud of. It's the least I can do for all you've done for me, for us, over the years...in China and since then!" Again a round of laughs.

Levi followed up. "Speaking of beauty, Markus have you seen the new Mercedes-Benz models? The best autos in the world! Papa, you should trade in your old Benz and get one!" Otto rubbed his thumb and index finger together. Everyone understood his gesture.

Levi took a quick drink of his coffee and returned to listing the good things happening in Germany. "Ah, the moving pictures are great fun, but some of the films are pretty scary. I saw an advertisement in the newspaper for *The Cabinet of Dr. Caligari*. We should all go to the Munich theater and..."

"No, who needs to see such things?" Otto said. "The war was scary enough."

"Of course Papa, it's just entertainment." Levi said quickly. He continued, "Katherina, you were telling me earlier about a conversation you had with Herr Dr. Professor Adelmann...?"

Katherina's eyes lit up. "Oh, yes! The Ishtar Gate from the city of Babylon! The pieces are in Portugal, but there are plans to bring them to Berlin, and reconstruct the whole thing. I've seen photographs from the dig, it's a treasure!"

Rebecca said excitedly, "Mama, maybe someday you'll discover a treasure, too!"

"Why darling, you are my treasure," Katherina said with a smile.

CHAPTER V

A Shot In The Ceiling: November 8, 1923

Wolfgang hurried through the streets of Munich near the train station. He didn't want to be late to hear Bavarian statesman Gustav von Kahr, and others, speak at a government rally in the vast *Buergerbraukeller* beer hall. The man was expected to explain how the government planned to resolve the conflicts that plagued it.

Weaving through the crowded sidewalk, he noted many people wearing brown shirt uniforms of the National Socialists. Wolfgang ignored them and slipped into the noisy meeting place.

"*Fraulein, eine beer, bitte*!" he shouted to a buxom waitress carrying six beer steins. He settled in, off to the side but near up front to better hear the speeches.

So this is how it's done, big speeches to big crowds...but will anything come of it? As he sat there, half listening, half thinking, he was startled by a commotion at the back of the hall. Suddenly loud shouts, pushing and scuffling occurred with one of the long pine tables overturning sending a dozen beer mugs flying.

From out of the melee a thin man of average height, wearing a brown shirt uniform, leaped up onto a table, raised a pistol into the air as he fired a shot into the ceiling. Adolf Hitler, accompanied by his armed stormtroopers in the hall and with dozens more outside, advanced to the podium. Pushing away the speaker, he declared: "The national revolution has begun!"

For the next several hours, he harangued his captive audience, while his machinegun-armed stormtroopers guarded the doors. The Bavarian leaders, now held hostage and forced to listen to his rambling rhetoric, finally agreed to support Hitler's coup. Wolfgang sat transfixed, listening to the man with the pistol demand the local politicians join his march on Berlin to overthrow the Weimar government.

Hitler brought his supporter, General Erich von Ludendorff, a hero of the *Weltkrieg*, the World War, to the podium to reinforce his demands. Because Ludendorff was a hero of the Great War, Adolf was convinced that the people would join him. Noticing several men slipping out the doors, Wolfgang made his way to the back of the beer hall and was gone into the night.

Wait 'til Markus hears about this. He won't believe I sat through a coup right here in Munich.

Finally the doors opened, the crowd poured out, and Hitler and his gang retired to Munich's military headquarters, seized by Adolf's friend Ernst Roehm and his brown shirts in advance of Hitler's arrival. The next morning, after the local government fled to the city of Regensburg, Hitler and Ludendorff and a band of stormtroopers attempted to march through Munich. Shots rang out as Weimar forces and city police stopped the advancing troops. Chaos erupted, the brown shirts fled, along with their leader, and the coup failed.

"You should have been there Markus!" Wolfgang and Markus sat in their shared apartment overlooking the park the next evening. Wolfgang had purchased several newspapers and the two men sat with the children, finishing a dinner of potato dumplings in a pork broth with boiled spinach and rolls. "Look at these headlines, you have to read this article." Wolfgang pushed the paper across the table to Markus. The November 10th, 1923 headline read:

Adolf Hitler Leads National Socialists In Failed Coup

Markus pointed half way down the page. "I see Herr Hitler fled. He's in hiding somewhere. He'll turn up; they'll catch him. He's such a danger with those Fascist ideas borrowed from his friend Mussolini, and his anti-Semitic tirades. But a lot of people listen to him. I've heard him; he's got this way of speaking. He's good, really good with the crowds."

"*Ja,*" Wolfgang agreed. "You can imagine how the Levi's feel with a character like that on the loose."

Invited out to Kalvarianhof the following weekend, Markus and Wolfgang sat with the Levi's in the middle parlor with a massive heap of glowing coals in the fireplace. The children stretched out in front of the hearth, reading books.

"This feels so good on a cold day like…" Markus was interrupted by the jingling of the postman's bicycle bell.

"Here are the newspapers and mail," Otto said, getting up. He subscribed to two papers, eagerly shared by everyone.

"Ah, they caught him, they caught Hitler. I knew they would." Otto said.

Katherina, reading the other paper commented, "Here it says he was hiding in a villa forty some miles from here. Some American owns the place."

"Thank God they found him," Friedl said, "that vile man and his evil ideas...I hope they lock him up!"

"I'm sure they will, dear. Probably for years." Otto said.

Over Friedrichshafen

CHAPTER VI

The **Amerikaschiff** *and Tuxedos: December 1923*

Late one evening, Wolfgang arrived at their Munich apartment bursting to tell Markus his good news. "I believe I've found a job!" he began enthusiastically. "I told you about that cabaret jazz club I've visited. Well, I got to talking with this Franz fellow who's in charge. We had a few drinks before now, but never talked about anything in particular. Tonight I mentioned I was looking for a job and he said he was looking for someone...big, like me." Wolfgang chuckled a moment before continuing. "And handsome enough, he said, but not too handsome, and old enough, but not too old. I'll just be there to help guests and for if things get rowdy. When a patron gets too drunk, I'll help him out of the place." He paused, "And along with my pay I get free dinner and a few drinks!"

Markus had been lying on the couch but sat up at the last part of Wolfgang's story. "Wolfie, that sounds great! You've been looking for a job for months, so if you're sure it's what you want...Congratulations! But I'll bet you have to work long hours, 'til two or three in the morning."

"*Ja, ja*, I know. That's all right with me...but I have to ask a favor Markus."

"Yes?"

"I need to buy a tuxedo, it's the new look for men in the cabarets, but I don't have any money. Could you...?"

"Of course, Wolfie, that's no problem. You can probably get a good suit, a very good suit if you pay with some of the South African money I brought home. By the way, I should get one too!" They both had a good laugh. He got up and said, "Let's have a drink, a toast to our futures. I have some good news of my own." Markus poured two short glasses of St. Remy French Brandy. "I know it's French and they're all bastards, but I love this stuff. It's left over from before the war...it was my mother's, would you believe!" They both laughed.

"*Ja*, so what's your good news? Meet a beautiful woman?"

Markus winced, "No, no, nothing like that. I've been asked...or maybe assigned... Well, pushed really, into assisting with the wireless equipment on a new zeppelin, the LZ 126. It's called the *Amerikaschiff*, the American ship. The Weimar government is building it for the Americans. Their President Wilson ordered it as part of our reparations payment to them. It's one of the biggest zeppelins ever built and with the latest of wireless equipment." The men clinked their glasses together, took a long drink, and clinked again.

"That sounds wonderful! Are they building it out at the village airfield near Kalvarianhof?"

"No, there aren't facilities for such a big project there. I'll have to go to Friedrichshafen, that's where *Luftschiffbau Zeppelin*, 'The Zeppelin Company', is located. I'll be staying there for some time...Don't know how long. It's a real opportunity for me, that's for sure." Markus was feeling the brandy now. "And guess what? I'll be on the flight crew as wireless officer when we deliver it to the Americans at Lakehurst, New Jersey, later this year! I'm flying to America!" he said with a strong emphasis on "flying". He paused a moment. "I'm just a bit concerned about the hydrogen, the Americans won't sell us helium." He looked at Wolfgang, brightened and promised, "But it'll be the safest ship ever built!" He let out a roar, and Wolfie joined in.

Wolfgang hadn't seen Markus so happy in months. They danced around the apartment laughing, and finished the bottle of brandy. Finally the two half-drunk men plopped down on the couch exhausted. After a while Markus said, "I need to find help for Rupert, Charlotte and Mary. You can't take care of them Wolfie, not with your new job." He contemplated a moment. "I'll call Levi, he always has good ideas. Kathi too."

Kalvarianhof 1924

CHAPTER VII
The Governess, December 1923

A week later, Markus and his children visited Kalvarianhof at the invitation of Levi's sister Ilsa. Markus's sister, Anji was also there. Rupert and Charlotte played in the hayloft of the barn while their father held Mary and sat in the kitchen alcove with Levi, the sisters and Katherina.

"We have just the governess for you, Markus." Anji said with Ilsa looking on. "One who will be delighted to care for your children while you're away working on that airship...that is, if you approve of her." The women looked at each other with identical grins.

"Thank you, ladies. I look forward to meeting her...*ja*, so who is this woman, and what are her recommendations?" He looked at Anji and Ilsa, and then at Katherina and Levi, whose grins widened.

"What?" he said.

"We could bring her around to your apartment. She lives in Munich."

"Yes, and?"

"She's Lotti von Hohenzollern." Anji and Ilsa said in unison.

"Who?" Markus said, sitting up.

Anji took up the conversation. "Lotti von Hohenzollern... *Ja*, well, you know, there're a number of princesses in Europe. She's from an old aristocratic family, from Romania. She's a widow and very involved in the new social assistance movement for veterans in the city. Lotti loves children, though her own child was taken by influenza. Lotti's husband died in the war." She hesitated a moment, looking at her brother. "And she has lots of free time. So what do you think?"

Markus answered with an amused grin. "And how exactly do you know this Princess Lotti?"

The two women reveled in the mystery. "You'd be surprised just how many things and people we know that you don't!"

"I am, I am. *Ja*, so when will I meet Frau Hohenzollern?"

"Tuesday evening at your apartment. The arrangements are already made."

"Well, that's...wonderful," he said, shaking his head.

That Tuesday, at the Mathais apartment in Munich, Markus recognized the signs of good breeding within moments of Frau Lotti Hohenzollern passing through the front doorway. Anji and Ilsa escorted the tall, slender woman into the parlor where the three children were playing with Wolfgang. Rupert and Charlotte ran to Anji and Ilsa, clasping their hands in greeting.

"Now, now, children, I want you to meet a dear friend of mine," Anji said.

When introductions finished, the three women turned their attention to Markus. "Please, come in Frau Hohenzollern, my sister and Ilsa have prepared coffee," he said.

"Do call me Lotti. All my friends do, including your sister and Ilsa."

"Well then, Lotti, I'm Markus." They looked at each other with shared interest. "These are my children. Rupert is eleven, Charlotte is three, and Mary is just a year old."

Lotti, smiling, bent over and spoke directly to the children. "Good evening Charlotte. How do you like your new home here in Munich? And you Rupert, how about you?"

Rupert replied for them both. "We're Africans. We lived on a big ranch 'til Mama died. We had cattle and we hunted antelope. Have you ever had antelope?" Lotti laughed and said no, she never had, but she imagined it tasted much like venison. Then Charlotte asked a question and soon the entire family was laughing in the kitchen.

When the children were put to bed, the adults returned to the kitchen and poured more coffee. Lotti offered, "I hear you're to fly to America in a zeppelin. I've been there. I could tell you all about it, if you'd like to hear." Wolfgang, sitting quietly off to the side, thought, *This could be interesting... very interesting.*

Lotti

I hope you enjoyed the first chapters of *Like A Gathering Storm*, the fourth in my five book historic fiction series. For updates and more information, please visit www.waltersoellner.com or find me on Facebook as Walter Soellner.

List of Historic and Fictional Characters

Historic Characters

Asam brothers: sponsors of the Asam Baroque Church in Munich

Benito Mussolini: Italian Fascist revolutionary, later dictator

Count Ferdinand von Zeppelin: aircraft inventor

Count Harry Kessler: German diplomat, secret agent, arts patron

Crown Prince August Wilhelm: son of Kaiser Wilhelm

General Paul von Lettow-Vorbeck: Prussian commander in German East Africa, only German commander to successfully invade British territory

Hitler: German Fascist revolutionary, later dictator

Joaquim Augusto Mouzinho de Albuquerque: Portuguese military hero and administrator. Allegedly committed suicide in 1902

Kaiser Wilhelm II of Germany & King of Prussia: Reigned 1888 to 1918

King Ludwig III of Bavaria: Reigned 1913 to 1918

King Victor Emmanuel of Italy: 1900 to 1946

Pope Benedict XV: Pope from 1914 to 1922

Saint Rita: patron saint of long-suffering women

President Woodrow Wilson, U.S. president from 1913 to 1921

Queen Victoria of Great Britain and Empress of India

Fictional Characters

Anji (Mathais) Frank: sister of Markus, wife of Johann Frank

Arnold Conrad: son of Tomas

Captain Llewellyn: British South African officer billeted at the Conrad Ranch

Captain Roger Perkins: British South African artillery officer in Windhoek

Carlos de Mouzinho de Albuquerque: son of Senhora Angelina

Charlotte: daughter of Markus

Christina Conrad: sister of Helena, daughter of Tomas
Commander Northrop: British South African military commander in Windhoek
Dr. Rungi: Levi family doctor, lives near Kalvarianhof
Father Bernard: Catholic priest at St. Johann's church in Munich
Father Lorraine: Catholic priest at St. Joseph's church in Windhoek
Frau Fanny Mathais: mother of Markus and Anji
Hannah Frank: daughter of Anji and Johann
Heidi Roth: young woman living in Windhoek
Heiner: old soldier friend of Levi and Markus
Helena (Conrad) Mathais: Wife of Markus, daughter of Tomas Conrad
Henderson: foreman at the power station in Windhoek
Herr Gustoff Liebermann: owner of architecture company in Munich
Herr Leopold: owner of a German trading company operating in Portuguese East Africa & Lisbon
Humboldt Conrad: brother of Helena, son of Tomas
Ilsa (Levi) Kepler: medical doctor, sister of Levi, wife of Rolf Kepler
Johann Frank: husband of Anji
Karl Levi: son of Solomon Levi
Katherina (Obermaier) Levi: archeological professor at the University of Munich, wife of Solomon Levi
Li Ling: early girlfriend of Markus
Madam Wilhelmina Oldendorf: owner of a whorehouse in Windhoek
Markus Mathais: Catholic German WWI veteran living in German S. W. Africa, wireless expert and aviator. Friend of Levi
Mary: youngest daughter of Markus
Michael Conrad: brother of Helena, son of Tomas
Moses and Benjamin Obermaier: brothers of Katherina Levi
Norbert Conrad: Brother of Helena, son of Tomas
Otto and Friedl Levi: owners of the Kalvarianhof estate near Munich. Parents of Levi and Ilsa
Petre: cook and houseman at Conrad ranch
Rebecca Levi: daughter of Levi
Richard Thomas: Director of Windhoek Telephone and Telegraph Company
Rolf Kepler: husband of Ilsa, medical doctor in Munich
Rosita: cook, housekeeper for Senhora Angelina in Lisbon
Rupert Mathais: son of Markus
Sambolo: called Sam, stable boy at Conrad ranch
Senhora Angelina de Mouzinho de Albuquerque: daughter of General Albuquerque

Sofia Kepler: daughter of Ilsa and Rolf
Solomon Levi: called Levi, Jewish WWI veteran living at Kalvarianhof, architect. Friend of Markus.
The night rider: anonymous Windhoek vigilante
Tomas Conrad: Conrad clan patriarch in German South West Africa
Willie: teenage farm hand at Kalvarianhof
Wolfgang Conrad: brother of Helena, eldest son of Tomas

German South West Africa

Bibliography

Anderson, R. (2004). *The Forgotten Front: The East African Campaign 1914-1918*. Gloucestershire, England: Tempus Publishing

Barraclough, G. (1982). *Concise Atlas of World History*. New Jersey: Hammond Inc.

Benton, Benton & Wood, (2003), *Art Deco 1910-1939*. London, England: V & A Publisher

Christopher, John, (2010). *The Zeppelin Story*. Gloucestershire, England: The History Press

Craig, G. A. (1982). *The Germans*. N.Y.C.: G. P. Putnam's Sons.

Critchler, S. (2008). *The Book of Dead Philosophers*. N.Y.C.: Random House

Daniel, C. E. (1995). *Chronicle of the 20th Century*. N.Y.C.: Dorling Kindersley

Daniels, Jonathan (1966). *The Time Between the Wars*. Garden City, New York: Doubleday & Company

Decaire, Camela, (1996). *Visual Timeline of the 20th Century*. N.Y.C.: DK Publishing

Deighton, Len, (1978). *Airship Wreck*. N.Y.C.: Holt Rinehart and Winston

Diamond, J. (2005). *Africa*. Washington, D.C.: National Geographic Magazine

Gilbertert, M. (1970). *Atlas of the First World War*. N.Y.C.: Oxford University

Gliddon, G. (2005). *The Sideshows*. Gloucestershire, England: Sutton Publishing

Grun, Bernard. (1979). *The Timetables Of History*. N.Y.C.: Simon and Schuster

Hadenberger, W. (1915). *Deutfchlands Croberung Der Luft*. Berlin: Berlag Hermann Montanus

Herald, Jacqueline. (1997). *Fashions of A Decade, The 1920s*. NYC: Facts

234

On File, Inc.

Inman & Macdonald, E. (2000). *Jerusalem & The Holy Land*. N.Y.C.: Dorling Kinderseley

Joll, J. and Martel, G. (2003). *The Origins of the First World War*. Essex, England: Person Edu. Limited

Kessler, Harry, (1971). *Berlin in Lights, The Diaries of Kessler 1918-1937*. NYC: Grove Press

Klemperer, Victor, (1999). *I Will Bear Witness, 1933-1941*. NYC: Modern Library

Krebs, C. B. (2011). *A Most Dangerous Book, Tactitus's Germania*. N.Y.C.: W. W. Norton & Co.

Laffin, J. (1965). *Jackboot, Hist. of the German Soldier 1713-1945*. N.Y.C.: Barnes & Noble

Lobsenz, N. (1960). *Africa*. N.Y.C.: Golden Press

Lyford, G. &. (2005). *Germany*. N.Y.C.: Dorling Kindersley

Marhoefer, Laurie (2015). *Sex and the Weimar Republic*. Toronto, Canada: University of Toronto Press

Marshall, S. (1964). *American Heritage Hist. Of World War One*. N.Y.C.: American Heritage Publishing

Muller, K. &. (2009). *German Colonial Troops 1889-1918*. Vienna, Austria: Verlag Militaria Pub.

Nicolson, Juliet, (1988). *The Great Silence, 1918-1920*. London, England: John Murray Pub.

Persico, J. (2004). *Eleventh Month, Eleventh Day, Eleventh Hour*. N.Y.C.: Random House

Reimer, Dietrich. *Kriegskarte von Deutsch-Sudwestafrika 1904*

Reynolds, E. &. (2000). *Kingdom of the Soul*. N.Y.C.: Prestel

Robinson, J. &. (2009). *Handbook of Imperial Germany*. Bloomington, IN.: Author House

Sibley, J. R. (1971). *Tanganyikan Guerrilla, E. Africa Campaign 1914-18*. N.Y.C.: Ballantine

Sleicher, John A. (1918). *Leslie's Illustrated Weekly Newspaper, August 17th, 1918 edition*, Entire issue

Strachen, H. (2004). *The First World War in Africa*. N.Y.C.: Oxford Univ. Press.

Wallis, Frank, (1988). Ribbons *of Time, World History By Year*. NYC: Weidenfeld & Nicolson

Wasserstein, Bernard, (2012). *On The Eve, Jews of Europe Before WW2*. NYC: Simon & Schuster

Weitz, Eric D. (2009). *Weimar Germany, Promise and Tragedy*. Princeton,

N.J.: Princeton University Press

White, W. E. (1967). *By-Line: Ernest Hemingway*. N.Y.C.: Charles Scribners Sons

Williamson, G. (1994). *The Iron Cross*. Denison, Texas: Reddick

Willmott, H. (2003). *World War One*. N.Y.C.: Dorling Kindersley

Woolley, C. (2009). *Uniforms of the German Colonial Troops*. Atglen, PA.: Schiffer Military History

LEVI FAMILY TREE

ABRAHAM LEVI
Birth: 1815, Augsburg, Bavaria, Germany
Death: 1895, Kalvarianhof, Bavaria, Germany

OTTO LEVI
Birth: 1860, Kalvarianhof, Bavaria, Germany

FRIEDL LEVI (TENNENBAUM)
Birth: 1862, Lustheim, Bavaria, Germany

SOLOMON LEVI
Birth: 1880, Kalvarianhof, Bavaria, Germany

KATHERINA LEVI (OBERMAIER)
Birth: 1881, Uruguay

ROLF KEPPLER
Birth: 1879, Munich, Germany

ILSA KEPPLER (LEVI)
Birth: 1884, Kalvarianhof, Bavaria, Germany

RACHEL LEVI
Birth: 1904, Kalvarianhof, Bavaria, Germany
Death: 1904, Kalvarianhof, Bavaria, Germany

REBECCA LEVI
Birth: 1909, Kalvarianhof, Bavaria, Germany

KARL LEVI
Birth: 1920, Kalvarianhof, Bavaria, Germany

HANNAH KEPPLER
Birth: 1920, Munich, Germany

OBERMAIER FAMILY TREE

MALICHI OBERMAIER
Birth: Stetin, Pomerania

MIRIAM OBERMAIER (SVETIN)
Birth: Stetin, Pomerania

KARL OBERMAIER
Birth: 1862, Stettin, Pomerania

BRITTA LOUISA OBERMAIER (SCHOENFELD)
Birth: 1866, Stettin, Pomerania

SOLOMON LEVI
Birth: 1880, Kalvarianhof, Bavaria

KATHERINA LEVI (OBERMAIER)
Birth: 1882, Yekatererinburg, Russia

MOSES OBERMAIER
Birth: 1886, Uruguay

BENJAMIN OBERMAIER
Birth: 1888, Uruguay

RACHEL LEVI
Birth: 1904, Kalvarianhof, Baveria
Death: 1904, Kalvarianhof, Bavaria

REBECCA LEVI
Birth: 1909, Kalvarianhof, Bavaria

MATHAIS FAMILY TREE

BARNHARD MATHAIS
Birth: Bavaria, Germany

CAPTAIN GEORG MATHIAS
Birth: 1850, Munich, Bavaria
Death: 1899, Munich, Bavaria

FANI MATHAIS (HILABRUNN)
Birth: 1856, Ismaling,
            Bavaria
Death: 1922, Kalvarianhof,
            Bavaria Germany

MARCUS MATHAIS
Birth: 1881, Munich, Germany

HELENA MATHAIS (CONRAD)
Birth: 1887, Windhoek,
            German SW Africa

JOHANN FRANK
Birth: Munich, Germany

ANJI FRANK (MATHAIS)
Birth: 1888, Munich, Bavaria

RUPERT MATHAIS
Birth: 1913, Windhoek,
           German SW Africa

HANNAH FRANK
Birth: 1920, Bavaria,
           Germany

238

CONRAD FAMILY TREE

WOLFGANG CONRAD
Birth: 1883, Windhoek,
         German S.W. Africa

ARNOLD CONRAD
Birth: 1884, Windhoek,
         German S.W. Africa
Death: 1919, Windhoek,
         German S.W. Africa

TOMAS CONRAD
Birth: 1858, Windhoek,
         German S W Africa
Death: 1923, Conrad Ranch,
         Windhoek, German
         SW Africa

HUMBOLDT CONRAD
Birth: 1885, Windhoek,
         German S.W. Africa

MARCUS MATHAIS
Birth: 1881, Munich, Bavaria
         Germany

RUPERT MATHAIS
Birth: 1913, Windhoek,
         German S.W. Africa

**GRETA HELENA CONRAD
(GRUENWALD)**
Birth: 1869
Death: 1907

HELENA MATHAIS (CONRAD)
Birth: 1887, Windhoek,
         German S.W. Africa

MICHAEL CONRAD
Birth: 1890, Windhoek,
         German S W Africa

NORBERT CONRAD
Birth: 1890, Windhoek,
         German S W Africa

CHRISTINA M CONRAD
Birth: 1891, Windhoek,
         German S.W. Africa

239

About the Author

Walter Soellner was born in Los Angeles and grew up in Detroit. With BS, MA and MFA degrees in Art and Design, he taught at the University of North Carolina at Charlotte for four years before accepting a teaching position at Evergreen Valley College in San Jose. Walter took three Art and Culture sabbaticals, during which he taught a semester at Hust University of Science & Technology in Wuhan, China, studied Polynesian cultures in Hawaii, and studied Mesoamerican cultures in Mexico City.

Events in these novels were influenced by personal and family history, including that of the author's parents, and the experiences of his German relatives in the first half of the 20th century. The Soellner estate, called Kalvarianhof in the novel, remains in the family to this day.

Walter began his serious writing career on a train from Munich to Berlin in 2007. Eight years later, after research trips to all the countries in Europe, as well as Egypt, Israel, Russia, Greece, Turkey, Kenya, Tanzania and China.

Kalvarianhof: The Perilous Journey released in 2015, followed by *The Storm That Shook the World* in 2016, and *An Incident in Africa* in 2017.

The fourth novel, *Like A Gathering Storm*, is expected in fall of 2018.

Walter at White Dragon Temple, Yangtze River, China

Egypt

www.ingramcontent.com/pod-product-compliance
Lightning Source LLC
Chambersburg PA
CBHW021959170626
46808CB00001B/213